I SHOULD BE
SO LUCKY

I SHOULD BE SO LUCKY

JUDY ASTLEY

LARGE PRINT

Oxford

First published in Great Britain 2012
by
Bantam Press
An imprint of Transworld Publishers

Published in Large Print 2012 by ISIS Publishing Ltd.,
7 Centremead, Osney Mead, Oxford OX2 0ES
by arrangement with
Transworld Publishers
A member of The Random House Group Ltd.

All rights reserved

The moral right of the author has been asserted

British Library Cataloguing in Publication Data
Astley, Judy.
    I should be so lucky.
    1. Large type books.
    I. Title
    823.9'2–dc23

ISBN 978–0–7531–9082–1 (hb)
ISBN 978–0–7531–9083–8 (pb)

Printed and bound in Great Britain by
T. J. International Ltd., Padstow, Cornwall

Acknowledgements

I don't want to have a "Thanks-To" list that sounds like an Oscar speech but there are several people who have, in their various ways, helped me to get this book written.

So, my thanks to:

Elizabeth Garrett for the most wonderful writing retreat week at Cliff Cottage, and to Katie Fforde and Catherine (Captain) Jones for being such fabulously fun retreat mates. We even managed to get lots of work done somewhere between the gin and the dolphin-watching.

To Chris Chesney and to Danny Relph for giving me a tour of Danny's premises at Palmbrokers Ltd and essential information about the kind of film/TV/advertising-industry plant-hire that is the green stuff, not massive machinery.

To Susie Bould for permission to include her First-Date-Hell experience. May she for ever have boyfriends of utter delight.

To Sam Eades for letting me use the truly horrible Incident of The Bag. Top tip from this: if you ever get your handbag nicked and you then get it back, give it a good sniff before you use it again.

And as always, thanks to my fab agent, Caroline Sheldon, and to Linda Evans and Alison Barrow at Transworld, without whom, etc.

CHAPTER ONE

Viola knew it was time to go home when the many shades of pink in Charlotte's sitting room made her think of the messier surgical events in *Casualty*. At the point where the claret-coloured sofa seemed to be morphing into a giant haemorrhaging liver, she stuffed that week's book-group choice (*Sense and Sensibility*) into her bag with a firmness that Jane Austen, even at her most waspish, really didn't deserve. The others were talking holidays and handbags now anyway, two subjects on which Viola didn't have a lot to say, having bought neither that were worthy of discussion for a couple of years. The book had long since been dealt with, swiftly and without mercy; the Austen aspect having descended into a discussion about the fat-hiding quality of Empire-line frocks and whether sprigged muslin would ever again be an on-trend style statement.

Party's over, Viola decided. With difficulty, she hauled her whirling brain back to reality and queasily tried not to picture Slit-Wrist Scarlet (contrast-feature wall, over fireplace) listed on Farrow & Ball's paint chart as a bloody trickle instead of a neat rectangle, sandwiched between Picture Gallery Red and Dead

1

Salmon. Charlotte must have been in a state of severe iron deficiency the day she chose the decor for this room.

"Sorry, everyone, lovely evening but I have to go now. Curfew." She wobbled a bit as she got up. The massed perfumes of the seven assembled women in an overheated room were surely dangerously potent: what with that and the collective hair products they'd all go up in a whopping fireball if anyone lit a match. And of course once *that* thought had crossed her mind Viola immediately looked round nervously to make sure Lisa wasn't casually lighting up a B&H and about to blast them all to pieces. That instant tension was what you got when you had the kind of life where the default setting was for everything to go as wrong as it possibly could. But Lisa was halfway out of her chair, taking Viola's departure as a break opportunity, and nodding apologetically gardenwards, ciggies and lighter safely unlit in her hand.

"Oh, Vee! What do you mean, *curfew*?" Charlotte's smile was a mocking one. "Come on, stay a bit longer; it's only just gone ten. You're nearly fort— I mean over *thirty*, not thirteen!"

Sometimes, I don't like you an awful lot, Charlotte, Viola thought suddenly. Wouldn't it be great to be able to say that out loud? But you didn't do that, not to a woman from whom you've accepted an evening's worth of hospitality and more than your share of luscious lemon drizzle cake. She stayed patient and polite but determined. "Can't stay any longer, I'm afraid. I promised Mum I wouldn't be late back."

2

"*Your mother?* Darling, it gets worse — you're not *still* camping out at the old family homestead, are you?" Charlotte was openly jeering now. The others (apart from sweet Amanda) smirked a bit but looked awkward. Jessica blew Viola a cheery goodbye kiss. Lisa waved through the back-garden window but the choices hung in the room's hot air: humour your hostess or support her victim? Viola vaguely pondered this tricky social dilemma on their collective behalf. Then she caught Amanda firing a warning glare across to Charlotte, who looked instantly alarmed and clapped her hand to her mouth. She'd remembered. This happened a lot.

In the sixteen months since Rhys had died Viola had learned that she carried her youthful widowhood around like a big ugly disfigurement: something not to be mentioned but impossible to overlook. From the beginning it had made even those she was closest to overcareful of her, wary of saying the wrong thing in case they accidentally pushed Viola into shattering emotional meltdown. In fact, Charlotte's unthinking teasing was a welcome change from being treated with velvety care. All the same, it didn't make Charlotte any easier to love.

In the hallway, as Viola pulled her jacket from the heap draped over the banisters, she had a flashback to being *actually* thirteen, when getting ready for games in the school gym's changing room meant exposing the awful truth — that her mother insisted she wear a vest under her uniform shirt to ward off chills, even in May, and even though she was also wearing a bra (albeit with not much in it). It was always the girls like Charlotte who had thought it fun to tease, to round up the others to point and laugh, knowing that they'd got plenty of backup in case you felt brave enough to retaliate. You'd ring a helpline for less than that these days, she thought as she put her jacket on quickly and called a brief goodbye through the sitting room door to the rest of the group.

"My mother is keeping an eye on Rachel for me, Charlotte," Viola said as Charlotte opened the front door. "I don't want to push my luck there." She hesitated, more than half expecting Charlotte to point out that, at close to fifteen, the last thing Rachel would want or need was to be "kept an eye on", which would then lead to explanations about the creaky, creepy, dark house, the unreliable door locks and rusting window catches. But Charlotte was glancing back into the room where the others had gone into shrieky-laughter mode, and she was eager to be in on the joke.

"OK, sweetie." Charlotte air-kissed her briefly. "I know it must be difficult for you. We're always here if you need us, you know, Vee. Don't forget. Call any time. And I mean *any* time, for *anything*. And, you know, I'm so glad you came out tonight. Shows you're getting back to normal, which you so *need*. After all, make the most of it. Any of us could be run over by a bus tomorrow." Charlotte then squeezed her hand, giving her a deep, between-the-eyes sincerity look, but had shut the door firmly by the time Viola was down the steps.

4

People often said that "any time" thing when there'd been a death. Viola had noticed that, since Rhys. It was kind and well meant but not particularly realistic. For what would happen if, in the middle of the night, she called Charlotte and said she had a raging migraine and would she mind coming round at seven in the morning to make sure that sleep-addicted Rachel got up and left for school in time, and that she'd got her violin, gym kit and lunch money with her? Exactly. It was the true awkwardness of asking friends for that kind of help that had sent Viola back to relying on the shelter of her family when things went wrong. And how horribly often they did . . . As for being run over by a bus, if Charlotte (breathtakingly tactless) had left that door open a few minutes longer, Viola would have been able to tell her that she'd already had a near-disastrous encounter of that kind, thank you very much: with a big red number 33, at the age of eleven, while cycling all dreamily careless across the road to the ice-cream van.

Naomi tiptoed across the parquet-floored hallway to lean her ear against the door that connected to the apartment at the side of the house where Viola and Rachel were currently living. Not a sound came from beyond the heavy oak door, which wasn't good. Rachel was a teenager — surely there would be noisy music? Or the TV on at an unsociable volume? Or maybe she'd got those little white bud things clamped in her ears to listen to music, the way everyone on the streets did. If she'd got a boy in there with her, Naomi hadn't seen him arrive. She rather wished she *had* seen one. If she had caught Rachel sneaking a boyfriend in for an evening of dangerous underage consorting, Naomi could have bustled into the flat quite legitimately, pretending she was just being good-manners sociable rather than guarding her granddaughter's virtue. She wasn't actually against teenage sexual activity: heaven only knew, the hormones kicked in with magnificent fury in those years, just as nature intended, but safe-ish sixteen was a good year away yet and she didn't want Rachel being exploited by some crass young twerp with no clue what he was doing.

If Rachel wasn't alone, she could take them some of the fairy cakes (she refused to call them cupcakes, as they now seemed to be known) that she kept a handy supply of, safe from marauding mice in a Queen's Jubilee tin in the old spidery larder. She would have sat on the smaller of the two crackled leather sofas in there, across from the thwarted couple, grilling the poor boy about his school exams and listening to his accent to make sure he wasn't the kind who said "innit" every five seconds. Or worse, was one who sniffed. She detested sniffers. If she was close behind one in the Waitrose checkout queue he always got the sharp spike of her shopping trolley. On your own premises it was possibly acceptable to offer a box of tissues. Certainly, if Rachel had her mother's luck in picking male friends, he'd be sure to be both an "innit" boy and an incurable sniffer.

She thought about trying the door and just walking in. The company of Rachel would be welcome: television on Tuesdays wasn't inspiring; she'd finished all her library books and there wasn't an unread murder mystery left in the house. Or she could knock on the door. She *should* knock, of course. Just walking in would be wrong, even if it were a lot more fun. But it was part of the agreed deal of Viola and Rachel being on the premises — that they would keep separate households, have their privacy. Of course it was just possible Rachel had simply gone to bed. Didn't she have exams coming up soon? Viola had said something about them, she was fairly sure.

Naomi — with reluctance — moved away from the connecting door, crossed the hall (neatly avoiding the loose bits of parquet) and went into the kitchen to make a mug of tea. She should put the light on, but it was such a waste. "Good lighting is essential. It's safer." Viola, Kate and Miles, in a rare moment of sibling solidarity, had all given her the lecture when the electrics were being rejigged. In spite of daily yoga and being able to horrify the grandchildren by still being able to contort her feet to behind her ears, Naomi was finding that her knees weren't quite what they were, and in the past year she'd had a few adrenalin-surge moments on the stairs when it had felt as if her joints were locking up like a rusting engine and that putting a foot down in the right place on the next step wasn't going to happen. Running twelve light bulbs at once in one room, however, could only be an outrageous expense, whatever they claimed about low voltage and green options. When she was a young thing of eighteen and first escaped from Burnley to a grim but thrilling Bayswater bedsit, the household managed well enough with one bulb per room and a torch on string for the lav. No one had died of dark.

She would take her tea into the sitting room and watch the news on TV, she decided. That way, she would be in the right place to see Viola's headlights swinging into the driveway when she got home. Perhaps she'd come in and join her for a shot of bedtime Scotch. After all, in spite of this being-separate thing when it came to living arrangements, what was the point of having your own family as your neighbours if you didn't at least pass the time of day with them?

"It's OK, Dad, she's gone!" Rachel let her long-held breath go in one whooshing sigh and bounced back to the sofa where her father — on a "just passing" visit — sat as still as a spooked cat, a mug of tea halfway to his mouth.

"Does she do a lot of that? The checking-up thing?" Marco flipped one long leg across the other, tweaking at his jeans and taking a peek at the sharp, shiny toes of his cowboy boots. Rachel gave him a look and teased, "They're just shoes, you know, Dad. You are *such* a girl!"

Marco fondly stroked the surface of the inky snake-skin. "Boots, to be exact. But they're new, Rache! You know what it's like when you've found the *exact thing* you didn't even know you were looking for. I *heart* them, fell desperately in love the moment I saw them in the window at R. Soles. But tell me about your grandmama. Doesn't it creep you out when she breathes through the wood like that? Does she do it when your mother's here?"

"No — when Mum's around and Gran wants something she makes a big thing of knocking on the door and saying she's sorry to disturb us. It's fine . . . but you know, really, it was only supposed to be for a little while after Rhys died and Mum was so upset cos all those loony people kept writing on our fence and shoving vile notes through the door, but it's been, like, more than a *year*? I want to go back home. I think we should. I love Gran and all, but this place spooks me."

"It would spook anyone." Marco looked at the purple chenille curtains that moved gently in the draught from French doors that were closed but not airproof. "This place is all noise and movement, like there's always someone else in here, rustling about."

"Eek! Don't say things like that, it's too scary."

"Sorry. Anyway, it's probably mice and lack of double glazing. Hey, look, I'd better go. Your gran might go for a round-two raid and burst in here to see if she can catch you snogging some poor spotty geezer on the sofa, and we both know how thrilled she'd be to see me."

"Spotty? As if. I do have *some* taste," Rachel scoffed. "But it's been really good to see you. And to meet your new boots."

"And it's always a delight to see you, girl." Marco pulled back the chenille curtain and peered out. "OK, looks clear enough. I should be able to skirt round the shrubbery to the gates without Nana Naomi catching sight."

9

"Be careful you don't get mud on your snakeskin." Rachel giggled.

"Shudder! I'd rather take them off and carry them through the nettles in just my socks."

"Oh, Dad!" Rachel laughed as Marco stepped out through the doors into the darkness. "You are just so . . ."

"Gay? Yes, darling, I know. Everyone knows." He kissed the top of her head and hugged her. "Goodnight, princess, and come and hang out at mine if you're mizzy here. We're always thrilled to have you around."

"I will. Soon. And thanks for coming over. It was fun; better than maths homework, anyway."

"Oh, thanks! Glad to have been so very useful. Now I must rush, James will be wondering where I am. Do send my love to your gorgeous mum and tell her I'll give her a call soon. It's time we had one of our lunches. Right, stay by the window and watch me do my *Great Escape* number."

He peered into the night, looking around like someone badly acting a spy routine, scuttled over to the dense shrubbery that ran from the side of the house to the front gate and vanished into the bushes. Rachel closed and locked the doors and stood watching the trail of trembling foliage marking the progress of her father. If Naomi were looking out of the front windows she'd imagine there was a bear weaving its way through the hydrangeas. Then he waved briefly from the pavement side of the gates and vanished. Moments later Rachel heard the revving of a Mini Cooper and her father was off, back to his light, bright apartment in

Notting Hill where his light, bright partner James would be waiting for him.

The traffic was slow and heavy for a late mid-week evening, as if — Viola idly thought, as she and her Polo crawled along the dual carriageway — while she and the book group had been wolfing cake and sympathizing with Marianne Dashwood regarding her knack for picking the fit but feckless option when it came to men, there had been a dire national emergency announced on TV and Twitter, and half the population had taken to the roads to bolt for rural safety. A small earthquake in Earls Court, perhaps. Or the Thames filling up with weird water-borne radiation that was causing the capital's kettles to glow scarlet as the water heated. As she came to yet another red traffic light she looked into the nearby cars, half expecting to see hastily piled-up bedding, cat baskets, children in pyjamas, sleeping. But no — mostly it was . . . couples. It was always couples. Lately when she'd looked at the loved-up, the paired-off, she'd felt a sad stab of envy.

Back at Charlotte's, the others would by now have been asking each other if Viola was seeing anybody yet. She'd bet the question had come up the moment the front door had shut behind her — she'd ask Amanda about it at work tomorrow. Amanda, bless her, would tentatively have suggested maybe it was a bit soon; Charlotte would have said no, it was high time to get back on the dating circuit, Viola wasn't getting any younger. What none of them would have come out with (because you just didn't, ever, not even if you were as gormlessly tactless as Charlotte) was that Rhys had been a selfish, cheating bastard and giving him even sixteen days' grieving grace was possibly more than he deserved, let alone sixteen months. Soon, people would sidle round to the *whyever did you marry him* question. They probably had already in private, though not yet to her face — but any day now they would. Especially her sister Kate, who'd managed to look as if she predicted doom even on the wedding day, taking her aside from other guests before the ceremony to ask her about five times *if she was sure*. At the time she'd just giggled and told Kate she was being like the kind of fussy mother who keeps asking a small child if they need a wee. But maybe Kate had second-guessed disaster: Rhys had turned out to be a complete sod with a complete absence of the fidelity gene, but his sudden death had been a huge shock, even though she'd spent most of the funeral service wondering which of the many assembled women in the congregation had been the mistress he'd sped off to leave her for on that fatally icy February night.

Ahead of her were more red lights, but also a blue flashing one. So that was the hold-up: an accident. Traffic was down to one lane and police were directing alternate lines of cars past the scene. Viola felt her heart beating faster. Reminded of Rhys's demolished Porsche, she really didn't want to see cars crunched up like sweet wrappers, maybe someone still trapped and frantic; really didn't want to imagine scenes of desperate rescue inside the parked ambulance that she could now see on the verge. One that wasn't going anywhere was always a bad sign, wasn't it? Because if there was hope, it would surely be speeding with full siren-blast to the nearest A & E.

Quickly, she turned up the nearest side road. The diversion she had in mind would be the long way round and would take her past Bell Cottage (now rented out), shared during those tempestuous months with Rhys, but needs must. She stopped at the roadside to call Rachel, tell her she would be home in fifteen minutes, and then sped on her way, pleased to be free of snarled-up traffic and wondering why so few others had opted for a detour. Who were those people who slowed down to look at crash sites? How could anyone want to do more than get past as fast as was safe and not have their minds scarred by the sight of someone else's catastrophe?

Later, she wondered if her doomy thoughts had had some karmic influence on what happened next. As she slowed down for a big shrub-shrouded roundabout before rejoining the dual carriageway, something went clunk at the back of the Polo and Viola felt a sudden lack of give in the steering wheel. In a heart-pounding panic, trying to remember what the Stig always told the celebrity guest drivers on *Top Gear* about how to steer into skids, she tried to brake, but the car had developed its own sense of direction and lurched sideways, almost bouncing across the raised kerb and on to the roundabout before coming to a thudding halt in the middle of a large bush. For several moments she sat silent, trying to calm her thumping heart and feeling desperately thankful that all of her seemed to be in one functioning piece and that she hadn't been punched in the face by an airbag. Can't have been that bad then, she thought, still shaking as she pushed the door open as far as she could.

"Oh, brilliant," she sighed, as her hand was immediately attacked by spikes and thorns. The bush was one of the nasty stabby kind. Every little twig on it seemed keen to dig into her to remind her that she was invading its space. Considering this was only a suburban roundabout, she appeared to have landed in the middle of a small forest. And just when she needed them, there seemed to be no cars around. Not that they could have seen her. The black Polo was so engulfed in foliage it was as if the stuff had grown around it, like the forest of thorns round Sleeping Beauty's castle. Viola just hoped she'd be off the traffic island in under a hundred years. Tentatively she stepped out, trying to push down as much of the undergrowth as she could.

"Hey, are you all right? What happened there?" A man appeared next to her, taking her hand and treading the branches out of her way and leading her to a clearing, further into the centre of the island. He was dressed all in black, a fair bit too old to be wearing a hoodie, and the fleeting idea that he was a good old-fashioned cat burglar, diverted between local break-ins by her careering Polo, came into her head. Where had he come from? He must have sprinted across the road.

"I think so," she said, pulling leaves from her hair. "My car, though . . . I think there must have been a puncture or something, it went all . . ."

14

"It's OK. It looks rescuable. Are you with the AA?"

"Yes, thank goodness. I'll give them a call . . ." She stepped back towards the car door.

"No, wait, you'll get covered in scratches. Mahonia are spiky bastards; it'll rip your coat to shreds. Let me help; I'm guessing your bag is on the passenger seat?"

She hesitated. How safe was this? Not remotely safe, would be her guess. If she'd been right to come up with the burglary-career option, then he could be halfway down the street with her credit cards and cash before she'd got free of the last of the twigs. All the same, she waited where she was as he crunched easily over the branches to the far side of the car. In the weak shine from the Polo's sidelights his teeth gleamed as he looked back and smiled at her: a wolfish sideways grin that didn't quite reassure her — it brought to mind the way that people who say a toothy Alsatian dog "just wants to play" make you immediately want to get behind the nearest high wall. In contrast to the bright teeth, his face looked streakily muddy and his hands were covered in earth. As her eyes adjusted to the gloom she could also make out that beyond him, further into the clearing, there was a small green Land Rover, against which was propped a spade. So that was where he'd sprung from so swiftly.

What, she asked herself, would anyone be doing in the middle of a woody traffic island late at night with a spade? Only one thing, one horribly gruesome thing came to mind, along with an image of a shallow grave and every lurid police drama she'd ever seen. Her mother, it occurred to her, would have been thrilled. As

15

an avid reader of murder mysteries Naomi would have been right there, congratulating Viola's rescuer on picking the perfect spot for a bit of late-night body-burying.

"Oh dear Lord," she breathed, catching sight of a deep and recently dug hole. What the hell was this guy *doing*?

"Here's your bag." Her rescuer returned and handed it over. "I hope your phone didn't drop out of it in all the lurching about. The battery's given out on mine."

"Um . . . thanks." She fumbled around inside the bag, completely incapable of getting her trembling hands to find what she was looking for.

"Look, you're really shaken up, aren't you?" he said. "Why don't I just give you a ride to wherever you were going and you can sort it out in the morning from somewhere a bit warmer and easier than this? Your car's not in anyone's way, after all."

"Actually, maybe I should just ring for a cab. I mean . . ." She indicated the spade and the mound of freshly dug earth. "You're, er . . . busy. I'll just go and leave you to whatever it is you're doing."

Oh God, whyever had she said that? She should have pretended not to notice anything at all. Now he'd have to kill her too. A desperately sad image came to mind of Rachel packing her possessions and trailing off to Notting Hill to live with Marco and James. Others followed swiftly: Naomi getting her magpie-feathered funeral hat out and weeping into a triple gin. Her sister and brother on their way to identify her corpse, agreeing that she'd always been the jinxed one and now look.

"No, really, it's no trouble at all — so long as you're not heading for Scotland or something!" he insisted cheerily, flashing some more of the slightly crazed smile. "Just climb into the Land Rover and give me a minute to finish off here. All I ask is that you don't tell anyone you saw me here tonight."

"Oh, absolutely!" Viola almost shouted the words. "I absolutely promise I'll never tell anyone, ever, not in my whole life. Trust me. Please."

He looked puzzled. "Well, it's not that big a deal, but thanks."

"It *isn't*?"

He picked up the spade and grinned at her again. "No. Because I don't know what you think I'm up to here, but I'm only planting a tree. A quince tree, to be precise."

Oh. Planting a tree. A quince tree. Yes, of course he was.

CHAPTER
TWO

"Eh, lass, that's just the sort of thing that *would* happen to you," Naomi chuckled at Viola the next morning after Rachel had left for school. "But that man who brought you home, he could have been anyone. You can't be too careful, especially with your luck. What I told you when you were little still applies, you know: *never* get into a car with a stranger. You could have been strangled in a ditch with your pants gone."

Viola said nothing, but counted silently to ten as she filled the kettle in her mother's kitchen. The kettle was a heavy old thing and the plug felt a bit wobbly, as if it were about to fall to pieces, like so much of this rapidly crumbling house. Naomi might still be able to whizz around like someone twenty years younger than her age, but surely at some point soon she really would need to be living somewhere easier and safer than this great mouldering Edwardian pile, especially once Viola and Rachel moved back to their own home. And that would have to be soon, she'd decided overnight. Very soon. It wasn't only Charlotte twitting her about "camping at the homestead" that had done it, though that had made her think about how long she'd been avoiding getting back to real life. No — it was the backlit vision on the doorstep that had finally made up her mind for her.

Arriving home at close to midnight, Viola had slithered awkwardly down from the Land Rover's passenger seat and the front door of the house had been immediately flung open, sending a shaft of brilliant light across the gravel, effectively floodlighting the car. There, framed by the doorway, was Naomi in her long, shocking-pink kimono, her arms outstretched like an angel about to take off and the bright green dragon pattern on the silk breathing furious orange fire. She had purple sheepskin slippers on her feet and was shouting in a high piercing voice that would wake the comatose, "Vee, Vee, is that you? Where the 'eck have you *been*?" For the second time that evening she'd felt like a nagged teenager, mortified and seethingly rebellious in equal measure.

"Oo-er — looks like you'll be grounded for weeks for this!" her rescuer had teased. Viola hadn't seen the funny side. You don't, she'd thought grimly, at thirty-five.

"If she had her way, I would be. Probably for life," she'd groaned, glaring at Naomi, mentally j*ust daring* her to stride up to the car and demand of the tree-planter precisely what he thought he was doing, bringing her daughter home *at this time.* For a woman who'd spent her long-ago teenage years hanging out in the smoky all-night jazz clubs of Soho, Naomi worried an awful lot about after-dark danger.

"Will you give me a call tomorrow, just so I know you got your car back OK?" he'd said, grinning with either sympathy or suppressed hilarity — it was hard to tell in the dark. He leaned over and handed her a card through the open window.

"I will, and thanks for the lift and everything. I must go, sorry . . ."

"Yes, you must! I'm guessing you'll be packed straight off to bed with a big telling-off!"

She'd heared him laugh as he swung the car round on the gravel and drove out through the gate, which she took plenty of time to close after him so as to gain a few moments to calm her fury at her mother, otherwise there would have been serious danger of her calling the tree man back to dig another deep hole, this time to plant a human. She'd then gone into the house, giving Naomi the most minimal explanation, feigned tiredness and raced into the flat, shutting the door firmly after her. Rachel, the only one who had any real claim to be worried, had been fast asleep.

"Mum, burst tyres happen to everyone," Viola said now as she dealt with the boiling kettle.

"But coming home with an unknown man doesn't," Naomi lobbed back, determined to have the conversation she'd been denied the night before. She wasn't being jocular, as she had been earlier. "Now he knows where you live, anything could happen."

"Oh God, Mum, I'm not *twelve*!" Viola laughed off the implied threat but it was a brittle kind of sound, covering rising annoyance. "It wasn't what you'd call a Big Risk."

She felt mildly dishonest here — after all, she'd been the one who'd suspected her rescuer of secretly burying a corpse. She hadn't mentioned the tree-planting aspect to Naomi. No such details were required, she'd decided, otherwise she'd never hear the end of it. "What does anyone want to go gardening at night for?" would be the first question, and, to be honest, that was something any half-sane person might ask.

"And risk or not, he was very kind, as people mostly are," Viola insisted. "Thanks to him, I got home fast and safely and the car is now at the garage having its tyre sorted. I can pick it up later this morning before I go into work. I've only got one afternoon session today. A *Wuthering Heights* intensive with four boarding-school chuck-outs, though this close to the exams it's a bit late for them to . . ."

"You didn't tell him *who you are*, did you?" Naomi interrupted, not looking at Viola. She expertly prised the lid off the old biscuit tin and scrabbled about among the contents to find a chocolate digestive.

Viola had known that question was coming, because it too often did after Rhys had died and she'd moved in here. Waiting for it made her feel tense, that and the effort of not snapping about being treated like some silly adolescent.

"I'm not anyone, Mum," she replied wearily, it being far from the first time they'd had this discussion.

"You know what I mean. You know what folk are like."

"It's been over a year now. I think I'm a long time off the tabloid-interest radar, don't you? I bet there's hardly anyone out there who even remembers who Rhys was." She felt an unexpected ripple of pity for him, faithless bastard though he'd been. He'd so adored both his fame (which he was supremely confident would escalate any day soon from the level of soap star to superstar) and his infamy, but the waters of interest swiftly close over those out of the public eye, especially those permanently out of it.

Rhys had been a music-biz one-hit non-wonder with a mediocre boy band, but had had the kind of lucky looks that rescued him, as he hit his thirties, from the usual road to has-been obscurity by qualifying him for the serial-shagger role in a twice-weekly medical drama called *Doctors and Nurses*. He'd played a randy, rather cack-handed surgeon who couldn't keep his own anatomy under control, let alone fix other people's. Off set, he'd become less and less keen to leave the character behind at the studio and specialized in gambling, casual women, speeding fines and the odd drunken bar brawl: if the tabloid press were having a slack day scavenging for celebrity gossip, Rhys could usually be relied on to provide some kind of handy little nugget for page four. Worse, since he'd once told an interviewer that he liked women with curves, he'd acquired a small adoring posse of female admirers who gave up going to slimming clubs and took up the avid pursuit of Rhys instead.

The posse ran a Facebook fan page, sent birthday cards, would knock on the front door of Bell Cottage and claim they happened to be passing or a car had broken down. There were only about twelve of these admirers, but what they lacked in numbers they certainly made up for in brazen persistence. Was it one of them he'd run off to be with, Viola would wonder in the middle of the night. He'd always claimed he could barely tell any of them apart . . . but maybe that wasn't entirely true. There'd definitely been someone hugely special. Rhys was like a cat — once he'd settled into a good, comfortable home, it would take an earthquake to shift him, but, at the end, shifted he had been.

Viola had hated his tabloid coverage: "Where exactly is the show-biz glamour in a pub fight, and all on the front page of the *Daily Grot*?" she would challenge on the days there were photographers hanging around the gate in the mornings and Rachel had to push her way past them on her way to school. Rhys would just shrug and come up with his ever-ready answer: "What does it matter? You and me and Rachel, we know it was no more than me standing on a bloke's foot, saying 'sorry, mate' and buying him a beer. They exaggerate for a living." But then he'd do his delighted-with-himself laugh. "And hey, who cares if they make it all up? It's another sprinkle of glitter on the old image!"

Under threat of his role being killed off in *Doctors and Nurses*, Rhys had been actively putting a more positive shine on his bad-boy image when Viola had met him, and was having a phase of being keen to be seen doing good works instead of bad deeds. Her sister Kate had booked him to be the guest auctioneer at a charity fund-raiser event she'd helped organize and Viola had gone along as a guest. Kate, smiling animatedly, had been showing off her celebrity catch, and had introduced him rather excitedly to her sister. Kate had then been inexplicably miffed when Viola had accepted a lift home with her pet star in his bile-green Porsche. "You were only supposed to *chat politely* to him," she'd hissed down the phone the next day. "Not bloody get off with him!"

"But I sort of thought that's what you wanted!" Viola had been puzzled. "You practically threw us together! And you and Miles are always saying you'd like to see me settled again, which is a weird term — makes me feel like a badly rooted tree." I can't get it right, she'd thought, sighing at the fickleness of families. Kate was stolidly long-term married. She, on the other hand, had been long-term single since the divorce from Marco, and was beginning to wonder if anyone — anyone *ever* — would ask her out again. But Rhys *did* ask — and he didn't have to do it twice. He was all charm and fun, seemed to adore her on sight and she, slightly needy and not believing her luck, fell like a stone for him.

"Because it's just . . . just bloody *typical* of you," Kate had fumed the day after the charity gala. "You just march in and take what you want like a spoiled . . . Oh, never mind. It'll all come to nothing anyway." Except it hadn't. Not then, anyway.

But it wasn't press intrusion that had driven Viola and Rachel to leave their home and take refuge in Naomi's flat after Rhys's death. The photographers hanging around on the pavement lost interest immediately after the funeral. That same little coterie of Rhys's few but lunatic-level fans, however, had turned up to watch the funeral party leave the house and then seemed to hang on and around for ages after ("What are they here for? In case he comes back as,

24

like, a *ghost*?" Rachel had asked), appearing regularly to decorate the magnolia tree by the gate with fronds of fabric that quickly became damply filthy in the suburban winter rain. They made a shrine, pinning photos of him to the fence, tied flowers to the gate and, when Viola slid out and removed their tributes after a couple of days' grace, they turned nasty, posting spiteful, hurtful, anonymous notes through the letter box telling Viola his death was all her fault: if he was out driving too fast in the icy early hours, he must have been desperate to get away from home, and from her. The "B" of Bell Cottage had been changed to an "H".

Neither she nor Rachel could cope with this kind of persecution, so she'd packed up and stored their possessions, put her much-loved home up for rent and moved into Naomi's flat. But last night . . . the Land Rover had taken her past the house. No lights were on; there was no sign of life from the tenant and her lovely little house looked lonely and abandoned. She fancied that maybe it missed her and Rachel — they'd had the place a long time, since way before Rhys, from back when she and Marco were first together. Also, although the car flashed past quickly and the only illumination was the pale orangey light from the street lamp, there didn't seem to be any tacky Rhys memorabilia anywhere obviously in sight, not so much as a faded rose crumbling to desiccation on the fence. Either his admirers had gone off to get themselves a life (at last), or they were honing their shrine-making skills at the home of some other luckless dead celebrity. The tenant's lease would be up soon. It was, Viola felt in her bones, time to go home. It was just going to be a matter of finding the right moment to tell Naomi.

The working hours were good and pretty flexible and the pupils were a lively and ever-surprising bunch, even if the pay wasn't great. Viola told herself this every time she drove in through the ornate iron gates of the tall Georgian house that was the Medworth and Gibson Tutorial College (*never* to be called a crammer, according to Sandra Partridge, the principal, so of course it always was). Thanks to the tenant's rent, she could just about afford for this work to be part-time, which had mattered a lot over these last long months since Rhys's death, when she'd felt dismal and low and overwhelmed by so much time-consuming admin that had needed to be sorted. At Med and Gib, as it was known, she worked haphazard hours teaching English Lit to a client base made up of the rich and spoilt, but mostly rather sweet and needy, teenage dispossessed, trying to stuff their heads with enough exam-technique information to make up for the fact they'd been expelled from school, dozed away time on drugs and drink or generally spent months skiving.

Viola parked her Polo in the staff spaces behind the building and stepped out into the dusty sunshine, deliberately avoiding looking across to the area by the kitchen bins from where the sound of male teenage giggling could be heard. She took a quick glance at the car's new tyre, admiring how clean and smart it looked compared with the others, like someone with scuffed trainers trying on a lovely new shoe. One front wing of the car was a bit thorn-scraped, but nothing that needed expensive attention. She had her rescuer's card in her jacket pocket and she took it out and read it. *The Fabian Nursery*, it said, then his name: Gregory Fabian; an email address, phone number. What kind of nursery? Plants, presumably, if the night-time digging wasn't just a weird hobby. Wouldn't it have made good business sense to say on the card whether it was flowers or babies?

"I spy smoke rings coming from the podgy pink face of Benedict Peabody." Amanda, emerging from her own car on the far side of Viola's, nodded her head in the direction of the bins and the laughter.

"No, don't tell me! I don't want to know. If we go and investigate it'll turn out to be a spliff and then we'll have to report it. And then he'll deny it and the fallout'll go on for ever."

"You're right," Amanda agreed. "Anyway he's leaving in a few weeks, travelling the poor long-suffering beaches of Indonesia for a few months, I imagine, like they all do, then straight into daddy's bank."

"As an intern?"

"Yes. But it's only a gesture. Give him a couple of fast-track years and papa will get him on to the board, or whatever it is banks have."

"Ye gods!" Viola laughed. "Don't you just kind of *despair*?" The two of them crossed the dusty tarmac that served as a break-time loitering area for the pupils.

A few were dotted around on benches in the sun, texting furiously, but none of them actually chatting to each other.

"Charlotte was talking about you after you left last night."

"I thought she would," Viola said as they went into the college's cool, pale grey panelled hallway. "I bet she asked if I was seeing anyone."

"Pretty much." Amanda laughed. "She's decided it's your friends' responsibility to help you find a new man, and that he should be somebody one of us knows and can give a kind of reference for. She said Internet dating wouldn't be any good because you'd be sure to pick the weirdo. And that getting married to first a gay bloke and then a certified love rat disqualifies you from being trusted to find someone for yourself."

"Wow, thanks for that, Char," Viola murmured, though privately conceding there was some sense in Charlotte's reasoning.

"So she said we each have to find you one person we actually know and get you to meet him under supervision and see how you get on."

"I can't think of anything worse. I don't want another man. I want to tick over in peace and quiet on my own. Well, just me and Rachel. And anyway, how would it work? Would there be three of us on each date, like in Princess Di's marriage?"

"Didn't get down to the details. She just muttered something about 'informal little suppers'."

"Eugh. No, thanks. I can see it now: it would be like a job interview — Charlotte at the end of the table, telling us how much we have in common. I've never gone for that 'having things in common' thing, like both of you being crazy about mountain-walking or opera. I prefer someone with their own interests."

"Ah, but you see . . ." Amanda stopped, turning to Viola just as they reached the staffroom door.

Viola looked at Amanda and they both burst into giggles. "Yes, I know, don't tell me," Viola said when she'd recovered a bit. "That's *exactly* where I've been getting it so very, very wrong."

Wuthering Heights. A-level exams were now only a couple of weeks away, so it was all a bit late to get this quartet of students to understand the appeal of Heathcliff as a romantic hero, of Yorkshire as a venue for passion and to learn that pathetic fallacy didn't actually mean "feeble lie", but Viola had been doing her best. It was a hot day too — the sun blazed in through the windows, sending the long shadows of the glazing bars across the floor and surely making all of them think of a prison. After an intense ninety minutes the two girls were sleepy and bored and Benedict Peabody was flushed, reeked of cigarette smoke and kept breaking out into giggles for no apparent reason. Funny, that.

"I still get, like, *soooo* confused?" one girl wailed. "Why do most of the boy names in this book have to begin with *aitch*?"

"My mum's got the box set from when it was on telly," Benedict told her. "You can come round to mine

and watch it. Tonight would be good. No one's home."
He gave a deep, dirty chuckle.

"Er, like, thanks but *nooo*?" The girl's face was
twisted to an expression of near nausea. Benedict made
kissy noises at her.

"Why don't all four of you watch it together?" Viola
suggested. "There isn't any more we can discuss about
the book itself at this stage — you've pretty much done
all you can, but it'll be a useful last-minute reminder of
how it all fits together."

"Yah, a helicopter view," Benedict said, flicking his
blond-streaked fringe back and looking pleased with
himself. It crossed Viola's mind that in a few months he
would be using such corporate jargon on an everyday
basis, at what was literally the Bank of Dad. She made
a mental note that any unexpected spare cash she ever
came into must be invested only in a sock under her
mattress. It had to be the safest option.

"So, sure, at mine tonight — it'll be well deep. I'll
chill the fizz." Benedict smirked. "And make some
calls . . ." He pulled out his iPhone and started tapping
into it. The tutorial, it seemed, was now over.

Now what have I done, Viola thought later as she
climbed back into the Polo. How thrilled would the
Peabody seniors be, coming home later to find four (or
by then, possibly forty) teens boozing their way through
the family wine vault and claiming it was all their
tutor's idea? And if they were watching anything on the
Peabodys' home cinema set-up, she'd be willing to bet
her newly fixed car that it wouldn't be *Wuthering
Heights*. Still, too late now. And they were all over

eighteen — officially, at least, grown-ups. If their evening went horribly wrong, it would be *their* responsibility. Absolutely not hers.

CHAPTER
THREE

After work, Viola took a detour before going back to the
flat. Having planned to take a closer look at her own
rented-out house to make absolutely sure it was clear of
Rhys ribbons and such, out of curiosity she first drove
along the road where last night's roundabout was sited.
It didn't look anything like so sinister in daylight, and
the shrubbery wasn't quite as alarmingly dense as it
had appeared the night before. There wasn't much
traffic, so she parked on a side road and quickly crossed
to the island, looking for the patch of ground where
Gregory Fabian had been planting his tree. At least in
daylight she could avoid that spiky plant . . . What was
it? Oh yes — mahonia: entirely made of thorns and
malice, it had seemed at the time.

She picked her way carefully across to the centre and
there, in a small clearing and on a damp, clean patch of
fresh earth, was the young quince tree. It was all twigs
and gawky stems, like a young adolescent, and its leaves
looked too big for it, but still, it was surprisingly tall.
He must have carried it here strapped to the Land
Rover's roof. And he must have brought a big container
of water as well, as the earth was darkly damp and
smelled of rich, fresh compost. It seemed a lot of effort

to go to in order to plant a tree in a public yet rather anonymous spot.

She gently touched the tree's soft young leaves and out loud wished it happy growing and a long life, feeling slightly foolish as she did so, wondering if the Prince of Wales felt the same, chatting to his crops. Not that his were planted in the middle of traffic islands. In fact, why was this one? Who in their right mind would put a fruit tree anywhere but in their own garden? Back in the Polo, she took her phone out and called the number on Greg's card.

"Hello, Fabian Nursery, how may I help you today?" a breathy young female voice answered. A nursery assistant? Viola pictured a plump young girl with a toddler on her lap and the sweet, persistent scent of baby lotion and formula milk.

"Er . . . may I speak to Gregory Fabian, please?"

"Oh sure, I'll find him. You might have to wait a few minutes, he's out the back with a compost delivery."

So — not babies then.

"Hello, Greg here!" He sounded very chipper, she thought, which was good.

"Greg? Hi, it's . . ."

"Ah, the distressed damsel! So Mummy let you use the phone then. I thought all your toys would have been confiscated and you'd be banished to the naughty step for a fortnight."

"Oh, very funny! She's a Lancashire mother — they don't hold back when they've got something to say."

"I gathered. How is the car? Did you get it back OK?"

"I did, and it's fine. I just wanted to say a massive thank you — you were so kind last night. It was so lucky for me that you were there, even if you . . ."

". . . Even if you thought I was burying a body." He chuckled.

"How did you know I thought that? Not that I did, of course . . ."

"Oh, yes, you did! The look on your face . . ." He laughed, deep and annoyingly triumphant. "It was *such* a giveaway. You half didn't believe what you were imagining; I could tell you were trying not to think it, but it was written all over you — *he's a serial killer.*"

"I'm glad you found it so funny." Viola could hear herself sounding prim.

"Oh, I did!" He had a warm laugh, teasing, but kindly, not in Charlotte's barbed way.

"But you must admit, planting a tree wasn't going to be anyone's first guess, now was it? And anyway, *why* were you?"

"Ah. I thought you might ask that. How can I put this? I was releasing it into the wild."

"*What* wild? It's on a West London roundabout, not running about in a meadow with its mane flowing!"

"True," he conceded. "But then I'd worry a lot if it were running about at all, frankly. Fruit trees only do that for people who've been taking weird substances, I'm told. Tell you what, why don't you come and buy me a thank-you drink sometime soon and I'll tell you all about it. Or would that be tricky?"

Viola hesitated. It was a useful phrase, "would that be tricky?" It quite possibly covered the two basic options of "Do you find me disgustingly repulsive?" and "Do you have a husband?"

"By which I mean — will your mother ever let you out again?" He laughed again, but this time sounded slightly nervous. There was a short silence while each of them considered the fact that he'd effectively just asked her out.

"Or you could just come and have a look at the nursery if you like, and I can show you the trees that are still in captivity." So now he was backtracking. She couldn't work out whether this was disappointing or not. Not, would be the sensible answer.

"Actually, I'd love to see the nursery, if that's OK. I've lived here ages but have never heard of it before. Ooh, sorry — that doesn't sound good, does it?"

"Hey, no worries. It's a bit specialized, so most people haven't. At the weekend? Next week? Just send me a text when you want to come over and I'll make sure I'm not out doing a delivery or something. It's only a couple of miles from you, close to the river. Hard to spot from the road but there's a sign up."

She was glad it wouldn't be a pub, she decided. That would feel like a date and she didn't want that, not yet, not with anyone, whatever Amanda and Charlotte and the book-group coven thought. But in case she ever did, it would have to wait till she was back in Bell Cottage. There had to be absolutely *no* chance of a repeat of the night before. If Viola wasn't to spend the rest of her life as a single woman, fiercely protected by her nightwear-clad mother from louche admirers and the sin of the post-midnight hours, then she and Rachel had to be out of that flat.

Her phone rang just as she was setting off again to take a look at Bell Cottage. "Did you know your tenant's moving out?" As ever, her straight-to-the-point sister Kate didn't bother with a hello or how are you. Viola wondered if this was because of their age gap — ten years, Viola being very much the afterthought baby of the family. From infancy she was used to being told things, rather than being asked about them. Miles and Kate, near-adolescents by the time she came along, had sometimes seemed like extra parents.

"Hello, Kate, and no, I didn't. I'm on my way there now, actually. How do you know?"

"I didn't know you were going there. How could I?" She sounded defensive.

"I don't mean that. I meant how did you know about the tenant? She's got more than another month on the lease — I was just about to give her notice that it wouldn't be renewed, actually."

"Really? Oh well, I'm sure you'll get another renter easily enough. I'm there now, outside the house. There's a removals van. I hope you're not far away because I've got places to be."

Viola had only intended to drive past slowly, like a burglar casing the joint, checking for Rhys photos and that his name wasn't freshly spray-painted on the gate. She hadn't wanted to stop and spy through the fence, but just remind herself that the place was actually *hers*. So what was Kate doing there? She lived out near Esher. Viola's little white house — up a long quiet avenue between a church and the park — wasn't likely to be on her way to anywhere.

Kate's Range Rover was parked a discreet fifty metres or so behind a removal truck. The double iron gates to the garden of Bell Cottage were wide open and a big blue sofa was being carried out and loaded. As Viola drove up, she could see boxes in the garden, ready for their turn in the van. So it seemed Kate was right.

"See? I told you. Didn't she tell you she was going?" Kate opened the Polo door and sat down heavily beside Viola. She was looking plumper, Viola noticed; her hair was showing a new flecking of grey at the roots and she was a bit out of breath.

"No. But the rent is paid up to date so I suppose she can do what she likes. It's great, as it happens, really works out well."

Kate turned to look at her, bright blue eyes sparkly with suspicion. "Why were you giving her notice? What's she done? Mad parties? Upset the neighbours? She hasn't trashed the place, has she? It would be just your luck to end up with the tenant from hell. You should have let me or Miles check her over before you took her on."

"No, no, nothing like that." Viola squashed down her irritation at Kate's assumption that she couldn't get anything right. "Rachel and I, we're . . . um . . ." She hesitated. Once the words were out there would be no retracting them. She gave herself a moment to reflect whether moving back here was what she really wanted. From the car she could see the open and empty garage where Rhys had kept his adored green Porsche. As he'd backed it out in such a rush on that last fatal night, he'd smacked it hard into the magnolia tree before revving hard and racing off along the avenue. Would the scar in the bark always be there, or would it heal up? It would be a horrible downer if there was going to be a daily visible reminder of that night. Her dreams were bad enough without small tweaking clues forever in view. She climbed out of the car and hesitantly walked in through the gates, passing a pair of men struggling with a box felt-tip-marked "Kitchen". Kate was just behind her. Viola stroked the old tree, feeling for damage. It seemed OK. Bark trauma all healed up. Lucky tree.

"Come on, Vee, you and Rachel are *what*? Selling the place? Great idea, actually. Best thing you could do. Leave all that past behind and start again." Kate took hold of Viola's arm and pulled her away from the tree, back towards the road.

"No, Kate, I hadn't even thought of that. I don't want to sell it — Rachel and I are going to move back in. It's time."

"Are you MAD?" Kate shrieked at her. "You mean you want to come back *here* with all the bad memories?"

"Only the very last bit was bad, Kate. And don't forget I lived here long before I even met Rhys, so this place is far more about me and Rachel — and Marco too, of course — than about me and Rhys. I loved it here, this was the home *I* made. Rhys, well — you know what he was like. Sometimes I thought I'd see more of some anonymous lodger than I did of him. Moving out was only ever going to be temporary, I said that right from the start, just till those dippy women went away. I can't stay in Mum's old flat for ever — it's been a great refuge from all the . . . well, the *stuff,* but you know, it's not home, not *our* home."

Kate was curling a strand of her hair through her fingers. She always did that, Viola remembered, when she was thinking hard and fast.

"And what about Mum? You can't just leave her on her own. She's getting older — how will she cope?"

Viola looked at her, puzzled. "You want Rachel and me to stay there *for ever* with her? In that flat? But that was never the plan. Mum's been cool with that all along. Why aren't you?"

"Well, someone's got to be her carer. I know she's in incredible nick right now, but she'll be seventy-six next year. Miles and I thought that you could . . ."

"You and Miles have been discussing me? Deciding where I should live?"

"Not *deciding,* exactly. No — just, well, going over possibilities. Thinking about what's best, all round."

"Who for?"

"Well . . . Mum of course. Who else?"

Viola wanted to say "Me and Rachel?" but decided against it in case it sounded horribly selfish. Kate was certainly capable of twisting it so that she would *feel* selfish — it was another much-older-sister trick. Viola's needs, preferences and feelings clearly didn't count here. Kate liked to be firmly in charge.

"I've been thinking about Mum too," she said instead. "And I know the house is way too big and starting to need a lot of work. On her own, it's soon going to be too much for her and she'll need to be somewhere that's easier to run. So, I had this thought in the middle of last night: you know her friend Monica who lives in that new sheltered housing place up on the hill, all those swanky apartments with the lovely gardens? Don't you think Mum might like it there? I was going to suggest it to her. Carefully, of course." She laughed. "You know what she's like — if you don't somehow make it sound as if it's actually *her* idea, she'll dig her heels right in."

Kate frowned. "And how is she going to fund that? Can you imagine the annual maintenance charges? Those places cost a fortune to live in."

"Oh, that's a no-brainer, surely?" Viola said. "She could sell the house."

"Oh, Vee — don't be ridiculous! It's been the family home for over thirty years! Absolutely *not*!"

CHAPTER
FOUR

Nobody has love letters any more, Naomi thought to herself rather sadly as she sat out on the sunny terrace with a Liberty flower-print folder in front of her on the old iron garden table. She could only feel sorry for the current generation with their disposable emails, swiftly deleted texts and nothing by which to recall some of their most romantic moments. What would they have left to touch, read and remember, many, many years after all the great loves of their lives? At best, there might be a few birthday cards kept for their loving messages, but other than that it would be printed-out emails, impersonal and businesslike, but nothing handwritten, no character, no clue to the deep-down bones of the person.

She opened the folder. Inside was a small heap of cream and pale blue envelopes, maybe twenty or so of them. She took the top one out and sniffed at it, inhaling the dusty scent of old dry paper and a hint of her own scent from many years ago: Elizabeth Arden's White Linen, her perfume of choice that winter of 1976 when she'd been a thirty-nine-year-old hectic full-time mother of two and corporate-entertaining wife, with a feeling creeping up on her in the nights that not too far ahead was only a greying middle age and the falling-away of looks, promise and opportunities.

Sometimes, back then, having rushed to get Miles and Kate to bed, she then had to cook and serve up a full-scale dinner-party menu to clients of her husband, being smiling and charming to people she'd never met before. At times like that, she'd find herself thinking of long-past Friday nights at bar-room folk clubs, listening to heartfelt protest songs and really believing that the world would become a gentler, less greedy place. Instead she was permanently exhausted and felt her life sliding by with little purpose outside raising the children, while she just felt older by the day.

It wasn't like that for wives these days, she knew. With everyone claiming that sixty was the new forty, women who *were* forty still looked, acted and probably felt like they were barely older than teenagers. Lucky old them, she thought now, approving their joyously extended youth. Her friends back then, even the few who, like her, had had those free-thinking bohemian years, had already taken to wearing skirts of sensible length and had taken up good works, fancy cooking and bridge. But not Naomi. Fifteen years into a marriage where her chief love rival was her husband's ever-increasing capacity for whisky, Naomi had taken up passion.

Naomi opened the first blue envelope. The edge of it was holed and torn, like frayed fabric that had had too much wear, but the blue-black ink was unfaded. "Darling Mimi" the letter began. Nobody else in her life had ever called her Mimi, only Oliver. When they'd met, they'd been out on a balcony for a firework display at a party, seeing in the new year with cold champagne. She was watching Miles and Kate running around with other guests' children in the garden below, overexcited at midnight with sparklers. She'd left her gloves inside the house and Oliver, an artist friend of the host, had noticed her shivering, taken her hand in his and slid it into the pocket of his sheepskin jacket. "Poor little frozen hand," he'd said, squeezing it gently. "Just like Mimi's in *La Bohème*."

He'd never once called her Naomi. "That's what your husband calls you," he told her weeks later when they were in bed together for the first time. "For me you'll always be Mimi."

When Viola got back to the house she realized she was still no wiser as to the reason Kate had been at Bell Cottage earlier. She'd never know now — Kate would, if asked, literally wave her away, flapping her elegant little fingers, and completely dismiss the visit, telling Viola she was making something of nothing. All the same, it had looked odd, as if she were snooping around. She'd been a great one for dropping in without calling when Viola and Rhys had lived there.

"She'll be demanding a bloody key next," Viola had grumbled to Rhys out in the kitchen when she'd come home, exhausted and laden with bags from taking Rachel school-uniform shopping on a sweltering Saturday, and found Kate sprawled on the sitting room sofa with her shoes off and a big glass of wine in her hand. She'd been taken aback when Rhys had immediately stuck up for Kate, claiming that it was good to have some company, seeing as Viola was off out enjoying herself on one of his few free days. "Few?" she'd queried, wondering how the twelve days' filming out of the previous month counted as full-time work. Not the most tactful thing to say to an actor: he'd stormed out at that point, insisting on Kate — on the far side of that glass of wine — leaving her car at the cottage, and driving her home. She vividly remembered how, hugging Kate an apologetic, brief goodbye, she'd smelled sweet, delicate jasmine scent on her sister and had been quite happy to see the back of the pair of them so she could soak away the hot dust and sweat of the crowded high street in the bath.

Of course, there was always the chance that maybe Kate had just been passing — she could have been on her way back from the park at the far end of the avenue and could claim she'd been walking her poodle in there. Except, Viola thought, she was pretty damn sure she'd been dogless at the time. It was a hot, sunny day — once Kate had stopped the car she would have put Beano on his lead and let him straight out into the fresh air. Still half wondering about it, she went into her mother's kitchen and sorted a pot of tea and some ginger cake, then took it out on a tray into the garden, where Naomi was looking through a floral folder of papers.

"Tea for you, Mum. That's a pretty folder," she commented. Naomi closed the file as Viola approached. "Just old letters, nothing important," she said. "Kate phoned just now and said she thinks a family Sunday lunch over at hers this weekend would be a lovely idea. She's phoned Miles and he's coming too."

"Ah, does she? Right . . . This Sunday?" Viola put the tray on the table and Naomi moved the folder out of the range of any possible spillage, tucking it carefully between her thigh and the arm of the chair.

"You and Rachel will be around, won't you?" Naomi asked. "Or had you made some other plans?"

"No, no plans for Sunday." Well, not firm ones anyway. Not yet. A letter from Viola's tenant had been waiting for her on the hall table as she'd walked in, explaining that an unmissable job in New York had suddenly come up, that she had to leave immediately and the keys would be with the agent. Sunday would have been good for starting to reorganize the house, thinking about repainting, making a list of any repairs and updating that were needed. If she was going to do that, though, it would mean saying no to the lunch and telling Naomi right this minute about moving back home, before she'd run the idea past Rachel, although obviously she'd have to tell both of them before Sunday, anyway. It was just that some things need a bit of leading up to.

"Well . . . I'll be here, at least. Rachel might want to go over and see Marco. She loves it over there in Notting Hill, but more on Saturdays than Sundays, when Portobello Market is busier. I'll ask her, but I'm sure it'll be all right."

Viola wasn't remotely surprised about the lunch. It was typical of bossy big sister Kate to rally the troops like this and she must have done it in a double-quick hurry the moment Viola had driven off, probably sitting in her car outside Bell Cottage, calling Miles and just about *ordering* him to turn up for an urgent family conflab. She would be banking on the certainty that, faced with opposition from herself and their brother, Viola would cave in and do as she was told like a good baby sister, promise to stay in the flat for the rest of Naomi's lifetime and put her own house on the market first thing on Monday morning. But she wasn't going to be bullied, she resolved. As soon as she'd spoken to Rachel about moving back home, she'd raise the subject of future care with Naomi. She was only grateful that Kate hadn't rushed in first to tell their mother. Even she must have worked out that the subject needed delicacy.

Rachel, after a slow school afternoon, knelt on the floor of her aunt Gemma's sitting room in her flat overlooking Kensington Church Street, surrounded by bin bags full of mostly well-worn old cardigans. On the glass coffee table in front of her were boxes of fancy buttons and beads, rolls of ribbon, sequinned and embroidered motifs and polythene bags full of brightly coloured feathers. The window was wide open, letting in dusty air and the sounds of traffic, and the feathers fluffed and fluttered in the breeze.

"Marco and James had a look at the stall last week and suggested we try selling some for men as well, so I picked up a few real grandad gems at the Chiswick car-boot sale on Sunday," Gemma said, lighting a joss stick beside a statue of Buddha in the fireplace. "Trust those two to see the gap in the market, bless them. But it could go either way — they'll either walk off the stall or they'll be a dead loss." She put her hand into one of the bags and hauled out a tobacco-coloured cardigan with dark brown leather buttons and elbow patches.

"Hey, look at this, Rachel. Cashmere. Real treasure!"

"It's hideous." Rachel giggled. "Who'd wear that?"

"I don't think it's been worn at all yet, this one," Gemma said, inspecting it closely. "There's no pilling or bobbling and it's got definite crease marks as if it's been kept folded in a drawer for best, and maybe a best didn't happen. It's a generation thing. I bet your gran has things hanging in her wardrobe that she's only worn maybe once, on the grounds that they're 'too good'. You can't help thinking about the back story with old clothes, can you?" She leaned back against the couch, which was draped with tattered patchwork velvet. "Maybe he was an old childless widower, and the nephews and nieces came to clear out his clothes. He'd always been careful with money so, with the quality things, they didn't want to just hurl them into a charity shop but decided to do a nice cheery car-boot sale and raise enough to sponsor a rescue greyhound or something."

"Or just buy . . . stuff?" Rachel suggested, feeling she probably had a more realistic grasp on the workings of young minds than her dad's idealistically hippy sister.

"No — I'm not having that!" Gemma laughed and shook her head, her beaded dreadlocks dancing about. Rachel had always thought they looked like half-cooked pasta that someone had dropped into a bucket of hay.

"I've decided he was fond of an evening's dog-racing, out with his ancient mates for a night of beer and betting — so greyhounds it is." She opened a box of buttons. "What do you think? A mixture? Big, bold ones? Metallic? We'll have to leave the elbow patches on, so we don't want it too bright. Pheasant feathers would go well too, do you think?"

Rachel reached for the scissors, took the cardigan from Gemma and started snipping carefully at the thread beneath the leather buttons. "These buttons might look good on something pink, or maybe pale green?" she suggested. "A girly cute cardigan that you wouldn't expect to see big leather things on. Like the opposite of Doc Martens that have got ribbon instead of laces."

"Great idea," Gemma told her, laying out a selection of buttons. "You're getting a really good eye. If I give you a few of these to take home and gussy up, will you be able to get them back to me in time for next Friday's market? You can come along and help if you like. What's the school situation? I don't want to get you into trouble, so don't just skip classes if they're essential ones."

Rachel thought for a moment. If she and her classmates had to pick a favourite day on which to bunk off, almost any of them except the geeks would choose Friday. The girls almost had an unspoken rota, because there were only so many of them who could claim to be off to the dentist or begging early leave for long trips to visit the distantly located half of their divorced parents. Ah — but last night her mother had told her they were moving out of the flat and back home (Yes! At last!). Maybe she could pretend she had to do something like . . . oh, go and look at a house? The school didn't have to know yet that "We're moving house" meant going home to their old place that was actually closer to school, rather than further away.

"Yes — I think I can do Friday. I can get the bus from outside school and be there about eleven." That would mean missing quite a lot of the morning as well, she realized, feeling a bit guilty. But it was a one-off. And by then it would only be a couple of weeks till the school holidays. Not *that* big a deal. And really, if you thought about it, working on a stall on Portobello Road should actually count as work experience.

Later, she strolled up the last few yards of Kensington Church Street and headed for Notting Hill Gate tube station to get the train home, hauling her school bag plus a bin liner with six cardigans from Gemma's collection in it, along with a selection of trimmings to stitch on to them. She loved it that Gemma trusted her to revamp them, using her own ideas and taste. *I'm a designer.* She tried the words on for size. Not quite fifteen and her own efforts were going to be up for sale on Portobello Market. Yes! Lost in her thoughts, she had to dodge sideways to avoid a chihuahua on a pink lead at the top of the station steps and she crashed into a boy who was running up them. The bin bag fell and the staircase was strewn with knitwear and buttons.

"Sorry!" she called to him as she raced down the steps to scoop up the garments before grubby-footed commuters could trample them into the London grime.

"'S all right," he drawled, picking up the tobacco-coloured cardigan. "Eugh, this yours?" He held it up and pulled a face, then handed it to her and she stuffed it into its bag, feeling flustered and hoping she hadn't lost any essential buttons. "You don't *look* like a vagrant," he said, staring at the whole length of her, rather rudely. He was smirking at her, the expression on his face thoroughly supercilious.

"No, well, I wouldn't," she snapped. "You don't see a lot of those in a school uniform, do you?"

"Oh yah — funny!" He was now walking down the last of the steps with her. "Which school?"

"Not round here, miles away, near Richmond," she said, making her way down the steps. He wasn't bad-looking. Not that she was staring at him. Why had he now changed direction to come down to the station with her? They'd reached the barrier and she swiped her Oyster to open the entry gates.

"So what are you doing over here, with your bag of old clothes?"

"Why do you want to know?" She was thrilled by his curiosity. That was the thing with girls' schools, you felt so ludicrously pleased if a boy who didn't look totally bleugh so much as glanced at you. She really *was* staring at him now, taking in his soft, round face, perfect teeth, blue-grey eyes, blond surfer-streaky hair that was too long, but in a good way, not in the old Justin Bieber wraparound way. It was private-school

50

hair, she decided; it was falling into his eyes so he had to keep flicking, and only posh boys flick. She should just wave goodbye right now and go down the last steps to the platform, but here were the two of them, going nowhere, one each side of the entry barrier as other travellers rushed through.

"I just like to know who's hangin' down ma endz." He shrugged and grinned at her. "Catch you round?"

And then he was gone. Hadn't even asked her name. Getting her number tagged in his phone would have been something to tell at school. She felt deflated, disappointed, even though he had that yah yah voice that she and her friends always found so funny, especially when he was trying to talk rapper. If her best friend Emmy was with her, they'd be giggling, "Eugh, he's like *soo* Jack Wills," and pulling faces the second he was out of sight.

But all the same, he'd said this was his "endz". Notting Hill was also Rachel's endz because it was her father's and she was often there. Maybe the boy was right; she might see him around. She really hoped so, anyway.

CHAPTER
FIVE

It was Friday evening before Viola got a chance to talk to Naomi about moving back home. Naomi had been out with her friends Monica and Elspeth in the afternoon to see a horror film and had come bouncing back home glowing with the thrill of having watched something truly, disgustingly macabre. "Only a nice *Midsomer Murders* repeat will settle me now," she said with deep satisfaction, leaving Viola wondering what kind of woman finds a crime drama with at least three gruesome murders "calming". Viola made a jug of Pimm's and they sat out on the terrace in the warm evening sun.

"I feel a bit bad about leaving you here alone," Viola said, once she'd managed to tell Naomi her plans to move back to her own home. "Are you sure it's all right? Kate thinks I'm being selfish."

"Of course it's all right! I've been living here on my own for years. I'm not going to start mithering about the lack of company now. It's not about that business the other night, is it? Because moving out for that would be just plain daft."

"No, no, it's nothing to do with that." Viola briefly crossed her fingers against what wasn't far off a lie. "I'd been thinking about moving back and now the tenant's given notice and is going a bit early it seems like a sort of sign."

Naomi, superstitious to the point of crossing the busiest road to meet a black cat, looked satisfied enough with that. "I know you feel you and Rachel need to get on with your own lives in your own home, and I'm glad you knew you had this place to run to when you needed it. But don't think you've got to rush at it, just because your house is empty. If you need more time here, you can stay as long as you like. Because you're the one that needs looking after, aren't you? Not me. So when you do go, promise me you won't do anything silly."

There was a pause while Viola mentally filled in the words: "Like hook up with yet another complete no-hoper of a man."

"No going up ladders," Naomi warned after some long seconds, her forefinger up, threatening to wag.

"Mum, that was nearly twenty years ago!" Viola laughed.

"Seems like yesterday to me. You wait till Rachel's the one sneaking out nights and then trying to climb back in way after midnight like you did. Even now I worry when you're out that you've lost your key again, and you'll do something daft and break your neck trying to get in. You were lucky it was only your ankle that time."

Viola briefly thought back to her teenage years and how she and her friends had only really felt like "themselves" when they were out. How else, other than by some dangerous climbing, were you supposed to get back into the house when you'd lost your key down the loo in the pub and were sliding home at 2a.m., hoping you could sneak into bed without your mum noticing you were way past curfew time? It had only been as her foot had gone through the rotten tread on the ladder that it crossed her mind there'd been a good reason why it had been left to fall apart beside the log pile rather than been tidied away in the shed.

"Well, I wouldn't break any bones climbing in here, would I? The flat's on the ground floor and the lock on the French doors would probably give way with a sharp tug. In fact, before Rachel and I go back to Bell Cottage, I'm going to make a list of things that need mending here. We must get someone in to fix them for you. Or . . . I was just wondering about that place where Monica lives. Have you ever thought of . . ."

"No, I haven't thought," Naomi interrupted abruptly. "I'm staying here and I don't want any fuss." She was starting to get huffy. "*And* I don't want folks in here, poking around. The fixtures and fittings have stayed in one piece this long, I reckon they'll see me out." She got out of her chair, moving as nimbly as a twenty-something, the tiny mirrors on her old Moroccan hippy skirt twinkling in the sunlight. "Right," she said, with a sudden sunny smile, "I think a nice piece of ham, an egg and some fried potatoes would be the thing. Then *Midsomer*."

There were some occasions for which you were very grateful for a bit of backup, Viola thought, as she sat

54

squashed beside Rachel in the back of Marco's Mini watching Oxshott woods roll past. One more person on her side in the face of Kate and Miles's opposition to her moving out of their mother's house was very welcome. Rachel was quiet, absorbed in stitching a row of silver sequins round the neckline of a fluffy lime angora cardigan. Naomi was in the front beside Marco, for once having very little to say other than questioning the accuracy of the satnav and asking him to switch off the voice on the grounds that they knew perfectly well how to get there and that it "sounds bossy".

"Pot and kettle," Viola heard him murmur, catching his eye in the rear-view mirror and sharing a humour moment. She was so glad he'd called on Saturday morning to ask her out for one of their regular lunches. "I'll be all alone," he'd told her. "Poor darling James has been forced to go to an *utterly* dull team-building thingy in the Midlands. What paintballing your workmates has to do with banking is beyond me. It probably explains a lot about the state of the global economy." She could almost feel him shudder down the phone, and he'd been delighted to be asked along to Kate and Rob's with her today instead. Kate didn't mind at all about the extra guest — she and Marco had always got on well. She'd even made lusciously opulent velvet cushion covers for the flat where he and James lived.

"It'll be fun to see Kate again," Marco had enthused. "I hope she's doing her roast pork. I shall wear pink. It always makes Rob feel so chuffed that I'm being a screaming stereotype. It's something to tell his golfing chums."

Rob and Kate lived in the middle of a golf course in a house with toughened glass windows. Viola wondered how they could feel safe there in summer, when if they were out in the garden a mishit golf ball could (and did at least daily) come hurtling over the fence at any moment.

"You can see all the way from the fourteenth tee to the water hazard from our top windows," Rob would tell visitors, as proudly as if this was right up there with a view of the Sydney Harbour Bridge.

"You couldn't risk a greenhouse," was Naomi's opinion. "I met a woman once whose greenhouse window was broken by a golf ball and when she made a salad months later she found glass *inside a tomato*."

"I don't know why *he* had to come with us." Naomi had got Viola to herself in the kitchen while Kate was down the garden showing Marco and Rachel the frogs in her pond. "It's supposed to be a family day."

"Marco *is* family, Mum. He'll always be Rachel's dad, and besides, you know I love him to bits — we're still absolutely best mates. You have to get over this; it's been years."

"Oh, you know I adore him really, but he should never have married you. Not if he were going to change his mind and start preferring men. I mean, a husband who suddenly decides he's *on the other bus*; what does that say?"

Viola picked up Kate's Cath Kidston floral oven glove, took the lid off a pan and prodded a fork into a

56

piece of boiling carrot. It was the safer alternative to prodding it into her mother, who was on one of her favourite longterm topics: that Marco turning out to be gay after marrying her daughter was a slur on Viola and by extension a slur on herself and her entire family, possibly going back several generations and set to afflict many a one to come.

"He was only young. We both were. We hardly knew what we were — apart from me being a bit pregnant." Viola added teasingly, "And anyway, it could just as easily have been me. I could have discovered I was a lesbian and run off to live with a girl."

"Now you're just being daft," Naomi said. "You're only saying that to provoke and it's water off a duck's. I just hope the next man you take up with isn't as much of a disaster area as the first two have been."

Viola drained the carrots into a colander and considered possible interpretations of the term "justifiable homicide".

"Don't worry about that," she said, feeling a bit deflated. "There won't be a next one."

"Yes, well, you say that now. But you're still young — just — so think on," Naomi told her, leaving Viola thoroughly warned that romance was absolutely a three-strikes-and-you're-out game, and she was about to run out of chances. And also years. "Just"? That was new.

In the interests of golf-ball avoidance Kate and Rob had compromised on the possibility of a sunny outdoor lunch in the garden and had slid back their heavy patio doors as far as they'd go, "to let the outside in", as Rob put it. The sweet scent of pinks wafted in but was quickly defeated by the clammy aroma of Kate's famous roast pork and steamy vegetables. Kate liked a fully dressed table and it was draped with double cloths, heavy damask napkins, and (as Marco whispered to Viola) enough cutlery, glasses and plates to furnish an embassy banquet. With that, the swagged and tied-back floral curtains (made by Kate, along with every cushion cover, bedspread and padded headboard in the house) and all the wall space crammed with Kate and Rob's family photos, Viola felt smothered and claustrophobic and wished they were outside in the fresh air having a casual barbecue. It would make breathing easier when the inevitable telling-off happened. And she knew it would — she'd already caught Miles and Kate exchanging looks. Building up to the strike, getting the timing right, she'd guess. Miles was looking flushed and twitchy. He kept touching the side of his head as if to check his hair was still there. Not much of it was, these days, but as if to compensate there was quite a lot more stomach.

"I see you've put Aidan's degree certificate up along with yours and Rob's," Naomi commented, pointing to a newly framed addition to the wall: a photo of Kate and Rob's elder son, an embarrassed-looking young man in a mortar board, clutching said certificate in its just-presented rolled-up form. Close by were Kate's and Rob's own graduation photographs. In hers, Kate had a blonde bubble perm, and the now-balding Rob sported a wispy gingery mullet in his.

"You look so goody-goody in this, Kate," Viola remarked. "But I remember being so impressed that you had a really punky kilt thing on under the academic gown, all safety pins and rips. Everyone else was all tidy in knee-length skirts and white blouses. I thought you were the coolest sister."

"A long, long time ago," Kate said, looking dreamy, as if she'd been a different person. She might well have been, Viola thought, considering Kate's journey from all-out punk to such formal tableware preferences. "And on that wall," Kate went on, handing round the potatoes, "I've just enough space for Henry's, then we're done, all finished." Viola saw her shoot a glance at Rob and was surprised to see a look of near-hatred on her face. Rob, benign and jovial, was oblivious, and carried on telling Miles about his chances of becoming golf-club captain.

"Never was one to hide her light, that one," Naomi murmured to Rachel. "Give me paintings on a wall any day. A craggy landscape with some proper stormy weather in it, like my Oliver Stonebridge ones in the hall. Or they could put up a great big Rothko print or two. Family photos belong in albums, for private viewing, not up and out for showing off."

Viola, still a bit shocked by the look that should have felled Rob, also thought the "we're done" statement sounded strange, as if Kate's family life would be somehow "cooked" by then, and would need no more nurturing. Of all their clan, she wouldn't have had Kate down as being anything less than forever family-minded, one hundred per cent domestic goddess (in

59

spite, as Miles pointed out as they ate, of being foolhardy enough to opt for pork when there wasn't an R in the month) and a potential nightmare for any future daughters-in-law. Irons, to Kate's household men, were things that lived in golf bags and had little knitted Aran hats. She used to tell Viola off for never ironing bedlinen, having once caught her doing a perfunctory fluff-and-fold and piling everything straight into the airing cupboard.

It wasn't till the pudding (a chocolate tart, with strawberries, raspberries and clotted cream) was served that the real subject of the gathering at last surfaced for discussion. Viola had been wondering whether Miles or Kate would raise it first. They'd been waiting for their moment. She guessed Naomi felt the same and smiled at her across the table. Naomi winked back.

Miles always made Viola feel like a pupil who has disappointed a concerned teacher. So far, he'd contributed little to the lunch conversation other than to tell them that his wife Serena was away on a weekend watercolour course and was sorry to miss them all.

"I bet," Kate whispered to Viola. "Last time it was a bridge cruise. Never home, lucky cow."

"Now, Viola. I hear you're moving out of Mum's flat," Miles began, the moment everyone had picked up their spoons, adding with a slow, sad smile, "and leaving her on her own."

"Yea, 'tis true — we're going home!" Rachel said.

Miles, formal in a cream linen suit that somehow didn't dare crease, and striped tie, turned to her. "You needn't sound so delighted." Rachel flinched.

60

"Why not?" Marco defended her. "She'll get her own room back and all her stuff out of storage, she can have friends round. What's *not* to like?"

"Well, it does rather leave a problem, don't you think?" Miles leaned forward towards him across the table. The tie threatened to dangle in his pudding. Viola watched it, fascinated, hoping it would. That would challenge her so-older brother's air of supreme authority.

Marco put his head on one side and made an exaggerated thinking face. "Um . . . does it?"

"When you pull that face you look like a budgie," Kate snapped at him. He winced. "This is serious," she declared.

"Pudding wine, anyone?" Rob waved a bottle of Vin Santo.

"Not now, Rob." Kate now turned on him. "We're talking." She paused, then smiled at Viola.

"Now, Viola, darling," she began. "Have you really thought this through? Miles and I are thinking your memories of Bell Cottage can't be happy ones."

"I've already told you, Kate. My memories of living there are more happy than not. We're going back. Mum's fine with it." She thought fleetingly of Rhys. He'd lived there with her and Rachel for less than a year, and hadn't added much more to the place than his toothbrush and a *Top Gear* boxed set. "He's not a settler," his own mother had warned. "Don't think he won't wander." Oh, he'd wandered all right. Why had the fact he'd promised her he'd changed made her believe he actually *had*? What an idiot she'd been.

"You can't be OK with this, Mum?" Kate turned her attention to Naomi. "Who's going to look after you?"

"I'll look after myself," Naomi insisted. "I always have. I didn't need babysitting before Vee and Rachel moved in and I don't now. Nothing's changed in the time they've been with me. While I can still drive, walk and find my way to the bathroom in good time I'll be all right."

"I think Viola's being very selfish," Miles said. "She's had your hospitality for all this time and now you're getting frailer she's bailing out." He paused. "The best thing all round would be for Viola to stay put. Maybe spread out from the flat a bit . . ."

"Or," Marco suggested, "you could sell your house, Naomi. Get something easier to manage, blow the rest on gin and toy boys. I know, you could live in seaside hotels, have room service and put bets on the gee-gees in the afternoons."

"Don't be ridiculous!" Miles snapped at him. "She can't sell the house!"

"Why not?" Viola said. "What's to stop her?"

"It's the *family home*. The base. *Our* base," Kate began, exchanging a glance with Miles across the table.

"That's right." He backed her up. "For over thirty years. You don't just *walk away*."

"But you haven't lived there since you were eighteen, either of you." Viola was puzzled. "And, Miles, *you* were about sixteen when we moved in — so hardly there at all, really. If it's anyone's childhood home, it's surely mine. And *I* don't mind if Mum wants to go somewhere else, somewhere a bit easier to cope with. It's not about bricks and stuff, surely?"

"No, Viola, stop this. They're right. I can't sell it," Naomi said. "And I won't. But will you all *please* stop talking about me as if I'm not here? I'm not a *parcel*, not a *thing* to be passed around and dealt with. Viola must go back to her own home, just as she'd always meant to, and I'll carry on as I did before she came. I haven't suddenly lost my marbles or the use of my limbs over the past year and I don't want to talk about this. Next thing, you'll have me in a home."

Kate and Miles laughed. "Absolutely not!" Miles assured her. "There's no question of a home, but we do feel . . ."

"No, that's enough!" Naomi stopped him. She started getting to her feet, staggering slightly as the voluminous tablecloth tangled itself round her leg. "Marco — please will you take us home now?"

Before they left, Viola went upstairs to the bathroom. Rachel was inside it so she went into Kate and Rob's room to use their en-suite loo. The bedroom was looking showroom neat — no clothes and shoes lying around, no books open on the bedside table. Even Beano the poodle was tidily curled up and dozing in his basket. The double bed, though — Viola saw that it had only one pillow, centrally placed. A pink floral nightdress was poking out from beneath it. You could only conclude that Kate and Rob now occupied separate rooms. Kate's usual collection of framed photos seemed to have gone from all the surfaces too, apart from a few on a table beside the bed. Viola picked up the nearest, surprised that it showed her own wedding, not Rob and Kate's. It was a casual, happy shot of herself and Kate, both laughing, either side of Rhys, who had an arm round each of them. He was looking at Viola, grinning hugely, as if delighted (at least for that day) to have won her. She felt tears pricking at her eyes and put the photo down again quickly. He'd been a rat, for sure, but for a very brief blissful while, until he'd started to break out of the marriage cage, he'd been *her* rat.

CHAPTER
SIX

Viola hadn't had the Rhys dream for a while, but the night of the lunch at Kate's it turned up in the early hours, leaving her wide awake too soon to get up but too late to get back to proper sleep. At first after the crash it had descended on her almost every broken, miserable night, but gradually it had slipped away, coming back only a couple of times in the past few months. Lately, she had almost dared to hope the dream had stopped for good, but obviously no such luck. She should never, she thought to herself as she turned the pillow to the cool side, have looked at that photo in Kate's bedroom.

The dream was pretty much identical each time. Viola was in the green Porsche with Rhys, screaming for him to stop as the car hurtled like a broken fairground ride towards a vast tree, one that seemed to be coming towards them, lurching out of the woods and over the edge of the roadside, deliberately aiming to smash into the speeding car. She could make out the intricate, twisted patterns of its bark; smell mushroomy old wood and feel the chill against her face from cold damp leaves, almost as if she were rolling on the woodland earth. Then instead of the expected impact she would be walking away from the crumpled, smoking car to join a waiting crowd of women, recognizing the faces of every one she'd ever known, from tiny girls at her first school, university mates, her barely remembered grandmother, her sister and mother, her daughter, her friends. And somewhere among this collection would be Rhys, completely unhurt, gloating and triumphant and smiling all around at these women, saying, "See? It was nothing." And they were all delighted and celebratory apart from furious, terrified Viola — the spoilsport, the bad fairy.

In the first confused waking moments, Viola would still feel she was right there on the edge of the group, searching for the one face she didn't know, the one who wasn't there, who he'd been with when he died. And she was a hundred per cent sure he *had* been with someone — in real life, not in the dream. Whoever he was leaving her for, this suddenly discovered absolute unchallengeable love of his life, had been in that car. The police had thought so too. The crash had been on a remote road and the call to the emergency services had been from a distraught woman who wouldn't give her name. If she'd been injured, she hadn't hung about waiting for the ambulance. But it was no longer as if Viola really wanted to know about her — it wouldn't change anything to be confronted with some random woman who had run away from her dead (or far, far worse, dying) lover. What kind of woman did that? A very young one? A terrified one? Someone astoundingly concussed? But it was no use speculating: whoever it was had faded back into whatever life she'd had pre-Rhys, just as Viola was trying to now. If only the dream would — please — leave her alone. She'd fight it off and try her absolute best to will it never to visit her again once she'd moved back home, she resolved as she got out of bed before it was light and went to make a cup of tea.

He'd probably have forgotten all about her by now, Viola thought later as she clicked on Gregory Fabian's number in her phone. She felt ridiculously nervous about calling him, ashamed that she'd left it so long. Good manners should have sent her visiting the Fabian Nursery well before this, to thank him properly for taking care of her and driving her home. She'd have gone on Sunday if it hadn't been for the three-line whip of Kate's lunch, though of course that would surely be any garden centre's busiest day. Then, just before his phone could ring, she quickly switched hers off again, deciding that as she was still, post-shower, wrapped only in a not-quite-big-enough towel, she needed to be dressed in order to talk to him. Mad, she told herself as she rubbed her damp hair dry, he CANNOT see you. You DO NOT need to be fully clothed and with hair done and make-up on, just to fix up some simple visiting arrangement. But then, just as she'd dropped the towel and was about to put on her knickers, the phone rang.

"Hello, you. I saw your number come up on the phone — must have been an iffy signal so I thought I'd call you back. I was beginning to think you'd deleted me!"

Aagh! Gregory Fabian. She sat on the bed, naked, rather pointlessly crossing her legs and clutching the towel to her body.

"No — not at all! Sorry, it's just been a bit busy and stuff. Exams and all that, you know how it is." Oh, ridiculous: how could he possibly know? He had no idea what she did for a living. All he knew about her was that she couldn't drive straight and that she had a barmy mother with daughter-control issues.

"You're a student?" he asked.

"No! I teach — at a cram — I mean a tutorial college."

"Crammer. We're allowed to call it that, aren't we?" he said. "Is it Med and Gib?"

"You know it?"

"Not personally. A friend's son was there a few years ago. They managed to haul him kicking and screaming through his A levels by the skin of his expensively straightened teeth. He's an estate agent now." He laughed. She wasn't sure how to respond, not knowing him well enough to guess whether he'd appreciate sympathy or (her preferred choice) a sardonic response such as "Aha, so there is a God!"

"So . . . um . . ." She stumbled along. "If it's still all right, I was wondering about coming to see the nursery soon? Would that be OK?"

"Yes — please do. Today? Now? Lunch?" He seemed very enthusiastic — perhaps he was hoping she'd buy a whole border's worth of herbaceous perennials.

It was just after 9a.m. and there were no classes that day, although she intended to call in at Med and Gib briefly before lunch to find out the timings for her exam supervision duties. Her students had opted for study leave, which, in most of their cases, was an oxymoron if ever there was one. But this morning she'd arranged to call in on the rental agent and collect the keys to Bell Cottage, then go and have a quick look over the place while Rachel was at school.

Marco had sweetly offered to go with her and she'd accepted, not because the visit risked renewing old unhappiness — she could (at least, she'd thought she could, till the dream wrecked her sleep) deal with that — but because being a designer he had a fine eye for colour. He could be relied on to help with any new paint choices and steer her away from impulsive inclinations towards purple ceilings or an excess of gloomy taupe. Marco had a late-morning meeting in Fulham and couldn't spare a lot of time, so perhaps she could do both — after all, they wouldn't have to do more at the house than just check to see how clean it was and what needed fixing, replacing or painting. How long could that take, even allowing for a drop-in at the college?

"Yes, OK — at about midday? Would that be all right? I just need to . . ."

". . . put some clothes on?" He finished the sentence she'd had no intention of saying out loud.

"*What?* How did you . . .?"

"Oh God, I'm sorry!" He sounded amused but flustered. "Sorry, I was just being flippant. I didn't mean . . . Are you *really* not wearing anything? Aaagh! Sorry!"

"It's fine." She couldn't help giggling. "No worries, I'll see you later."

He coughed and put on a mock-serious voice. "Absolutely. I'll tidy the place up a bit and get the best roses stacked at the front to tempt you in and to grovel for your forgiveness for my untoward remarks. You know how to find us?"

"I do — I Googled you, just quickly for the address."

"Great, see you in a while then. Just come into the office and ask for me if I'm not around, but I will be. Oh and, er . . . drive carefully."

She could almost see his teasing smile. She was grinning broadly herself, she realized, as she clicked the phone off and caught sight of her flushed, beaming face in the bedroom mirror. Lucky nobody really *was* watching her make that call — naked, giggling: a touch of the Slightly Mad, possibly.

It felt strange to Viola to have the keys to Bell Cottage back on her keyring and, added to her others, feeling pleasingly heavy in her hand. It had been so long now since she had had the removal team in, swiftly packed up all but the most basic furniture and banished almost all of her and Rachel's possessions to the Big Yellow storage lock-up. She'd walked away from the house without once looking back, not wanting her last impression of it to be the damaged magnolia tree with its clumsily taped-on photos of Rhys and the badly spelled messages of devotion pinned to the gate alongside rotting flowers sealed inside rain-spattered cellophane. It would all be all right, she told herself

70

now as she turned the car into the avenue and drove past the church; whatever Kate and Miles thought about how and where she should live, it was definitely time to come back. It would all work out. And if it didn't, they'd move.

Viola arrived before Marco, left the car in front of the garage in her old familiar parking spot, then stood on the path facing the central front door, staring at the outside of the building, taking in its familiar features, checking to see what had changed. Apart from a bit of recently flaking paint on the doorframe and the New Dawn rose that had grown so much that it now smothered the little porch roof and looked as if it was trying to force its way in through the bedroom windows, it was all just the same, just as she'd left it months ago.

Marco's Mini whizzed into the driveway and stopped a millimetre short of the Polo's bumper.

"Perfect parking!" he called to her as he climbed out. "How's our lovely old gaff looking? Have you been inside yet?"

"No, I've only just got here. I thought I'd wait for you."

"Yeah — I get it." He put an arm round her and gave her a squeeze. "Hard to face the memories? You could just put it on the market, you know. Come and live in Notting Hill near me and James?"

"Notting Hill? Like I could afford to! No, sweet idea but I'm sure I can deal with the memories, because so very few are bad ones and I'm *not* going to let them crowd out the good stuff. Mostly, I still think of it as

71

when you and I moved in here, which were the best times, the Rachel-as-a-baby times. Rhys made very little impression on it, really. Even when he *was* there I still thought of it as just mine and Rachel's because he brought so little to it, apart from the crazy women knocking on the door and hoping he'd come out to play. I should have known that he wasn't a keeper. Everyone warned me. Why didn't I just live with him for a bit instead of getting married? It was his idea, you know. He seemed absolutely set on doing the family thing, had me totally convinced and yet he was trying to pull a waitress even on our honeymoon. What an idiot I was."

"Well, of course you were convinced — he wasn't a top actor for nothing, was he? And we can all be idiots. Look at me: all those years denying I was gay just because my father thought all poofs should be lined up and shot. But then if I hadn't, we wouldn't have Rachel. Something good often comes out of the tricky stuff. Shall we go in? I'll hold your hand."

Viola opened the front door and stopped for a moment to sniff the air. It didn't smell like her house, not at all.

"Blimey, was she ever keen on vanilla!" Marco wrinkled his nose. "She must have bought up a job lot of air freshener."

"Or candles. She looked like the candle sort," Viola said. "You know, late thirties and single, candles all round the bath, smelly gunk and rose petals in it, a big fat glass of Pino G and a book that isn't too precious to matter if it falls in the water."

"Is that how you're going to be now?" Marco asked.

"*Me?* With candles?" she laughed. "Are you mad? I'd be sure to knock one over, set fire to the bath mat and end up naked on a ladder over some poor fireman's shoulder, with all the neighbours watching."

"Yes, you're probably not wrong there. But I'd pay folding money to see it. Your bum would look hot on YouTube."

Viola left the front door open to waft in fresh air to replace the vanilla scent. Even that could have been worse — it could have been Rhys's usual overdose of Calvin Klein. If that had been so ingrained into the carpet that she couldn't *not* remember him every time she walked up the stairs, it would have been a no-brainer about selling the house.

The decor didn't seem to have suffered since she and Rachel had last lived there. The creamy-yellow walls of the sunny double-aspect sitting room had a few faded patches where pictures could have been but, really, she could get away with not repainting it, although she decided she would, if only to freshen it up with a lighter, brighter version of the same colour. The kitchen looked as if it had hardly been used, and the giant pale pink fridge had been so thoroughly cleaned out that it looked in better condition than when she'd last used it herself.

"Do you think she ever cooked?" Marco asked, opening the door of the immaculate oven.

"I'd say not. But it won't stay like that for long, not with Rachel slamming pizzas in the way she does, straight on to the shelves and then leaving bits of crust behind so the house smells of burnt stuff and the bits never quite come off."

"She does that at ours too — James has bought her a special pizza-base gadget from his beloved Lakeland but she never uses it. Hey, though, your fridge — love the colour. But don't you think this kitchen would look brilliant with *more* pink?"

"Mmm. It would zazz it up a bit. *I* need zazzing, so I'll go for whatever it takes to help. Maybe that wall behind the dresser." She pointed to it. "Shocking pink, or would that be too mad?"

"Absolutely. It'll show wonderfully through the open shelves. I'll sort it for you, no worries. I've got a couple of tame scenery painters that we use on the sets. They're always up for a bit of moonlighting and there's not a lot of work on right now," Marco told her, making a note in his iPhone.

She came over to him and gave him a happy hug. "You are such a star, Marco, thanks so much for all this. You'd make a lovely husband. Well, you did, actually."

"Thank you, Vee. And you made a lovely wife. If it wasn't for the elephant in the house that was wearing a tiara and Judy Garland's ruby slippers, who knows where we'd be now?"

"Well, you wouldn't have James, and that would be a shame. He's lovely too."

"We just need someone perfect for you," Marco said.

"Oh, now please, don't you start! I've already got Charlotte and Amanda on my case, deciding it's time to put my team strip on and get back out on the pitch."

"Well . . . they've got a . . ."

"No — enough! I'm not good at men and that's that. I'll take up embroidery and good works instead."

"Careful", he warned her. "You'll be getting cats next!"

Putting off the moment when she went upstairs and reclaimed her own bedroom, Viola unlocked and opened wide the big French doors at the back, realizing immediately that though the house was in pretty good condition, the same couldn't be said for the garden.

"Ye gods, it looks like the garden's just one wild old meadow!" she called to Marco, who was checking how easily movable the dresser was. "Marco, come out here and look at the state of it!"

The grass desperately needed cutting and was completely, though prettily, overgrown with daisies. The borders each side of the lawn had dandelions and buttercups crowding out the dahlias, lupins, evening primroses and verbena that she and Marco had planted so many years before and which had come up reliably and generously each summer since. Right now, they looked like they were struggling to hang on to their territory against invasion from rampant willowherb and ground elder.

"No way am I coming out there! I'm not padding about in long damp grass in these new boots," Marco replied from the safety of the doorway.

"You big wuss!" She laughed, pushing back the cascade of clematis that tumbled down the fence. "How much damage would it do? Would a real cowboy throw a strop and refuse to get off his horse to lasso a steer because he's *got new boots* and the prairie is a *bit damp?*"

"But I'm an *urban* cowboy!" he protested, venturing only as far as the edge of the paved terrace. Viola went back and joined him and together they checked over the herb patch which was overrun with rosemary, mint and marjoram, crowding everything else out. It would take a lot of effort, but in a week or so it would be the summer holidays. Work would then be only at the level of a couple of tutorials a week for the students whose parents decided that taking a preparatory run at the new school year with a few extra lessons would keep their children safely off the streets. Sorting the garden in a fully hands-on way would be a welcome project: an essential element to making the place *hers* again.

Reluctantly, as time was getting on, Viola closed the French doors, locked them and faced the moment of going upstairs, almost afraid to go into the room that had witnessed the last awful scene between her and Rhys. This was the big test: would she find that, after all, the place was for ever tainted by the memory, to the point where she couldn't see a way to move on and enjoy life here again?

"You OK?" Marco asked, sensing a change of mood as they prepared to go upstairs.

"Yes — I'm fine, thanks. I had a dream about the crash last night and it's made me think about who he was with. What happened to her? Why did she never ever turn up? You'd think she would, one way or another. Maybe she has. I'll never know, will I?"

Marco squeezed her hand. "No, you probably won't, but it wouldn't change anything if she did, would it? Don't let a dream hold you back, Vee, don't let *him* get in the way of the rest of your life."

"I know, I know. And I won't. So . . ." she rallied and smiled brightly, "let's go and look. All of upstairs will need paint, just to colour away, you know — that last day. I can just about run to new carpets too, I think."

"I get it, I completely get it," Marco said, hugging her. "And you don't have to live here at all, remember. Moving to somewhere else wouldn't be that hard — all your stuff is in storage, everything tidied and ready to roll."

"No, I want to give it a go because if I don't move back in and try living here again then I'd never know if it would have worked or not. You and me and Rachel had a great time here, and I love the area. I'd only be looking for something pretty much identical if I *did* move, and then paying pointless thousands that I can't afford in stamp duty. It would be mad. And it would feel like a defeat."

She went into her bedroom and over to the window, facing the door, picturing the last scene with Rhys, trying to work out how she felt now.

"You know it won't last!" she'd shouted as he'd hauled his crammed suitcase off the bed and headed for the stairs. "It's just another in that long line of your sluts." From then it had almost felt like slow motion as he'd stopped, put the case down on the landing and walked back into the room. She'd held her breath, realizing too late what he would do. The slap was quick, vicious, and when she opened her stinging eyes after it, he was halfway down the stairs.

"This one's everything to me. *Everything*," had been the last words she'd heard him say, his voice trailing away as he bumped the case down to the hall.

Well, none of that had been the room's fault. The windows overlooked the bright and sunny back garden, and the walls were painted a subtle grey-blue. She looked around, seeing it as a house-buying stranger would, opened and shut the wardrobes, inspected the little en-suite bathroom with its vivid blue and green Moroccan tiles, and waited to feel something momentous. But it seemed the room had forgiven and forgotten, and she sensed it welcoming her home. Exciting. And a delight actually to feel that way — she'd been so blank for a long time now, it was as if she was coming out of fog.

She turned to Marco and smiled at him. "Palest turquoise?"

She could hear him letting go of a held breath. "Yes — and I know *just* the shade. A touch of Caribbean but light and subtle, better for the British climate. Perfect."

"Brilliant. And I'll see if I can get Kate to make me some new curtains too. And Marco?"

"Yes, darling?"

"Cliché or not, I think I really will get a cat."

CHAPTER
SEVEN

"Apparently," Amanda told Viola, "a party of some of our dear little charges had got a bit out of hand on Thursday night. A couple of the lads, including our very own sweet Benedict Peabody, were arrested after a lot of noise complaints, but there was nothing definite they could hang on them. No real damage, just a lot of broken glass, kicked-about cans in the street, too much racket and the neighbours in those big wedding-cake-type houses having their beauty sleep disturbed."

The college seemed strangely empty after the past weeks of individual last-minute pre-exam tutorials, which were spent in equal measure calming students' nerves and trying to gee up the too laid-back into some sort of work ethic. Viola, rushing from Bell Cottage, found she had time to chat to Amanda, and they were in the college staffroom with tea and biscuits and some gossip mags that another tutor had left. These reminded Viola, yet again, of Rhys. A photo of himself in one of these magazines gave him a buzz for days. He'd been hugely sulky that none of them were keen to give more than half a page to coverage of his and Viola's wedding. "What the fuck else does anyone think I'm doing it for?" she'd caught him saying down the phone to his agent, and she'd almost bailed out on the whole event right then till he apologized, saying he was just piling on the pressure. "Make the idle bastard try a bit harder," he'd soothed her, kissing her neck in the way that always made her shiver.

"Oh Lordy, Thursday! I can't help feeling the party was very much my fault, you know," Viola said, dunking a gingernut into her tea and watching with no surprise at all as the wet half fell to the bottom of the cup. "It was me that day who suggested they all go round to Benedict's to watch *Wuthering Heights* on DVD, for a bit of last-ditch revision. I had a feeling as soon as the words were out that this wasn't going to turn out well. The boy was just a bit *too* enthusiastic. He was texting before the class was over, a look on his face like he was up to something. Letting his thousands of Facemates know, I expect. I bet the photos of the carnage are up there for all their future employers to wince at."

"He's a teenage boy, they're *always* up to something!" Amanda laughed. "You can't take the blame for what they do. He'd have thought up some other reason to get the crowds in if he hadn't already, what with the Peabody seniors being away and him having a free house. And bless him, I overheard him this morning in the corridor, grumbling that he wasn't doing anything, just 'cotchin' wid da bredrin' and then saying the housekeeper had sorted the broken windows. Imagine having a housekeeper; wouldn't that be heaven? You'd never have to plead for half a day off to wait in for the plumber. Anyway, he looked pretty pleased with himself, all bouncy and bumptious and with those two dippy girls hanging off him. His cred rating, or whatever they call it, must be way up."

Viola sighed. "I know I'm not *really* to blame, not deep down," she said. "But it's sort of typical. One day, *one day*, I'll suggest something, or *do* something, and it'll all work out fine. No complications, no hassles, nothing going ludicrously wrong." She felt like curling up on the staffroom sofa with her hands round her knees and her forehead resting on them, like a child who thinks that by making herself smaller and keeping her eyes shut, she'll become both invisible and unreachable. Miles had called her just after she'd spoken to Greg, saying he wanted to meet her for a chat soon, just the two of them. "A matter of importance," he'd told her, trying to sound mysterious, as if, after what had been said at Kate's on Sunday, she wouldn't have the first clue what it was about. It certainly wasn't to discuss his promotion prospects or his wife Serena's fury about her third-year-in-a-row failure to get into the Royal Academy Summer Exhibition. How old did she have to be before life stopped being a series of tellings-off?

"Well, hey — here's something that can't go wrong." Amanda sounded comforting. "My cousin's band is playing at a pub in Chelsea on Friday night, blues covers, that sort of thing — quite good, actually. I thought you might like to come along with Leo and me? I'll drive — so you won't have to worry about ending up in the trees with a flat tyre again. You can have a glass of wine, relax, forget all about these students and their idiocy. What do you think?"

Viola pondered for a moment, feeling mildly suspicious, thinking of Charlotte's plan to get her hooked up with a new man. But Amanda's pretty, wide-eyed face was looking perfectly innocent: not at all sparkly and overkeen as if trying to pretend there wasn't a hidden agenda. All in all, it did sound like a good idea; a social life hadn't exactly been a priority over the past months. She'd fended off quite a lot of invitations because they usually sounded like carefully chosen mercy missions, such as films with absolutely no love interest, as if she needed sensitive handling. It didn't make for comfortable outings, having people look sideways at you any time long marriages or death were mentioned, or noticing someone being nudged hard when there was gossip about other charmless, cheating actors. Music, though — good noisy stuff in a darkened room and no one paying attention to what she was thinking. That could be just what was needed. And hey, if it turned out to be a set-up, she could always plead a headache and do a runner.

"Yes, thanks — actually I'd love to," she decided. "Rachel's going to be staying over with Marco and James that night, so that kind of works out really well."

A night out, good sounds, a couple of glasses of wine. She closed her eyes as the thought breezed past quickly: just like normal people.

It was funny how you could live for years in one area and still have to look at a map to track down undiscovered corners, unexpectedly rural ones, barely twelve miles from the centre of London. Viola had been out and about in these magically wild bits of the district with Kate many times during the past year, Kate calling round on sunny weekends and dragging her out to stop her brooding in the flat, making her walk the poodle for hours with her across fields and woodland completely out of sight of any houses, and with no one around except other dog-walkers and the occasional jogger. It reminded Viola of being a small child again, when Naomi would persuade (and probably pay) the teenage Kate to take her out for hours on Sunday mornings or late summer afternoons, walking the family spaniel and letting Viola pick huge bunches of buttercups that would have lost most of their petals by the time they got them home. The two of them would sit by the river throwing the dog's ball into the water for her to swim out and retrieve, while Kate, for lack of someone else to offload to, would chat on about whichever boy she was pursuing, who was usually one who was inconveniently pursuing some other girl. Even Rob, Viola remembered, had been engaged to someone else when Kate had met him, and had taken his time disentangling himself from the fiancée.

Viola had found the post-Rhys walking as therapeutic as Kate had insisted it would be, being able to let fresh, clean air in to breeze away the gloom and having nothing to think about except where to put her feet so as not to slide over in a muddy puddle. Kate would talk away just as she had as a teenager, not requiring any response, chatting about her clients, such as the woman who had gone all nineties retro and was having festoon blinds everywhere, and about being asked to make bedroom curtains from a toile de Jouy pattern so pornographic she'd had to lock the workroom door against uninvited visitors. If Viola started to try and talk about Rhys's accident, about those unknown details such as who had his new woman, this sudden absolute love of his life, been, Kate would deftly block this direction of conversation, gently steer Viola to safer ground, persuade her, just as Marco had, that going over questions that could never be answered was *not* the way to moving on with the rest of her life. And each time Viola returned to the flat and to Rachel and Naomi, she felt just that little bit better, until the next time she was awake at 4 a.m.

Viola, knowing that with her luck a satnav would almost certainly lead her straight into the Thames, drove with her map book propped between her lap and the steering wheel, hoping it wouldn't tumble down to get stuck under the brake pedal. She was now heading down an unfamiliar tree-lined lane, assuming, as the sign saying Fabian Nursery had pointed her this way, that it would appear as she reached the end. The sign by the main road had been so small, paint-faded and hard to spot that you could have been forgiven for thinking Gregory Fabian really loathed the idea of attracting customers. She'd actually stopped the car at the turning, reached out of the window and pushed a chunk of ivy away from the lettering, feeling like a mother smoothing a child's overgrown fringe out of its eyes. Eventually, after bumping down a rutted, overhung track, she came to a pair of five-bar farm-style gates leading to a long, ancient brick wall beyond which she could just make out a low building with a much-mended roof, the green-stained top windows on an old, ornate glasshouse, and several polytunnels. Fronds of giant bamboo waved in the near distance. A collection of big, muddy rocks was piled up beside the path and a load of old tree trunks leaned against the wall. A fat grey pony looked up from grazing in an orchard of low fruit trees across the path from the gate and eyed her, as if he was speculating on the possibility of a pocketed carrot. For a place that was close to the Heathrow flight path, it could hardly have been a more bucolic scene.

Gregory Fabian emerged from a doorway in the wall and came to open the gate for Viola. His dark blond curly hair looked as if it had been attacked by a thorn bush, he had a streak of mud across his face and a fraying rip over the knee of his jeans. She parked beside his Land Rover, which was crammed with potted daisy trees, some of them with their branches escaping and poking out of the open windows. A flatbed truck and a Transit van, each bearing the Fabian Nursery logo, were alongside, the truck laden with topiaried box trees, reminding her of old-fashioned poodle tails. A girl with Goth make-up was driving a forklift truck piled high with sections of ancient balustrading.

"You don't seem that keen for people to find you," she said as he led her towards the ramshackle building.

"Sorry — the sign needs redoing. I keep meaning to get someone on to it, though I know it'll be me who fixes it in the end. We don't tend to get casual callers," he told her, as they passed an open door to an office containing a mud-stained computer and untidy heaps of paper. "But then this isn't your average garden centre — you wouldn't come here for your petunias."

"I wouldn't go anywhere for petunias," Viola replied. "I don't like them much."

"We have something in common then." He looked at her, nodding rather seriously. "That's always a good start."

As before with the estate-agent comment on the phone, Viola wasn't sure how to react. He seemed quite hard to fathom, not that she needed to try. After all, was she likely to see him again after today? Bizarrely, the thought that she *wouldn't* see him again made her feel a bit odd inside. Maybe it was the rescue on the roundabout the other night — a very minor version of that thing where if someone saves your life, you are bound to them for ever. Ridiculous, she told herself. What he'd saved her was only a little bit of time and effort, though the fact that he'd restored some much-needed faith that people really could be just plain nice for no ulterior reason wasn't to be discounted.

"Come and see some of the stock," Gregory said, leading her past an open-sided shed crammed with gnarled old olive trees, followed by an area devoted to all kinds of ferns. Further on was a steamy polytunnel so densely packed with various palms that the two of them could hardly squeeze in. Display didn't seem to be the Fabian forte. "We can get you pretty much anything you want. A hundred red maple trees, topiaried box, ivy by the ton, on or off the trellis."

She reached out to stroke some ivy fronds that were hanging from a doorway, then pulled her hand back, startled. "Ugh, it's not real!"

"No, well, quite a lot here isn't." He faced her, smiling, amused by her confusion.

"So if it's not a garden centre, what is it? A cover for secret experiments with GM crops?"

He laughed. "No, nothing so random. It's all for hire, rather than buying."

"Renting? Who'd rent *plants*?"

"Film companies, TV, advertising people, events, parties. I can rent you a marquee-load of big fat Kentia palms for your wedding, if you like, or a whole grove of olive trees for a holiday ad that'll be made in an Acton shed because these days no advertising budgets will stretch to a location trip to Greece." They were now walking through the beautifully ornate Victorian greenhouse she'd glimpsed from the track, built along the ancient brick wall. It was stocked with more ferns, palms and banana trees. Bird of paradise plants, hibiscus and bougainvillea took up the far end.

"Are these real?" She stroked a gorgeous strelitzia.

"Yes, those are real. A bit of an indulgence, because I like them and among this world of fake old tat it's good to have something genuine and exquisite. But the bougainvillea isn't. You can order it by the metre."

"I'm getting the feeling I had when I went to Disneyland," she told him. "I was so confused by what was real and what was fake that I didn't trust the ducks on the lake to be anything but remote-controlled."

"Tricks of this duplicitous trade, I'm afraid. It's all about make-believe, isn't it? A shabby old business in a way, when you think of it. All a con, but it pays the bills."

"Amazing. The things you don't know . . . I'll never look at a TV ad with woodland and plants in it again the same way. So how many of you work on this?"

"Mostly just me and Mickey — we set it up years ago and we run it together — for the moment, anyway. Plus there's Beth out there on the forklift, a fat bloke called Jez who lives entirely on crisps, and then several casuals who come in when there's a big order on. Er . . . are you hungry? Is it too early for a bit of lunch?"

"Lunch? Is there somewhere local?" she asked.

"Very local." He turned and grinned at her. "Right here."

Coming out from the far end of the greenhouse into the bright sunlight, she was for a moment dazzled by the glare but then saw just ahead, tucked away among pots of stunning flowering white lilacs (in *June*? Ah — right), a sumptuous purple and terracotta-coloured Moroccan tent, carpeted with a blue and scarlet kelim, elaborately decorated on the roof with gold appliquéd stars and hung with tassels and tiny tinkling bells. It was furnished with a low cushioned sofa draped with embroidered cloths sewn with little mirrors, and on an ancient-looking marble table ("Don't lean on that, it's only fibreglass," Greg warned) was a bottle of chilled white wine and — beneath a couple of protective mesh covers — a selection of flatbreads and dips. Pots of scarlet standard roses bloomed at each end of the sofa.

88

"You see, I promised you roses." He smiled at her as they sat on the sofa.

"Gorgeous." She sniffed at one. "And not pretend! Do you do this every day?" she asked as he poured her a glass. This all looked pretty special — it surely couldn't have been in her honour.

She put her hand up to stop him with the wine. "I'm driving, don't forget. Just the teeniest one for me."

"No problem — there's water here too. And no, I don't; but this tent is on its way back to a prop house after a Moroccan-themed wedding in Suffolk — I couldn't waste the chance to dress it up a bit, show off. Lunch is usually a cheese sandwich in the office if I can be bothered." He put his glass down on the table and turned to look at her. "But hey, tell me, Miss, Mrs or Ms Viola Hendricks . . ." And for the first time he suddenly looked serious. "How come you are still living with your mum?"

Viola was just drawing breath to answer when a lean, tanned woman with loosely piled curly red hair hurtled into the tent, looking thunderously cross. She was teenage lithe but thirties age, in faded, dusty jeans and a creased blue shirt that she'd tied, old St Tropez-style, so it showed a small, vulnerable piece of flat brown tummy. "Greg, what the hell are you doing? I did *tell* you," she almost spat at him. "They're coming to collect the tent at two. This thing's got to come down *right now.*"

"I hadn't forgotten, just give me half an hour," he said, leaning back comfortably and showing no inclination to move. She was now standing with her hands on her hips in a decidedly don't-argue stance. Greg was unlikely to be allowed three minutes, let alone thirty. But then, as if she'd only just noticed Viola, she put out a hand to her, smiled broadly, showing sparkling teeth like even slivers of bright ice, and said, "So sorry; how very rude of me — I'm Mickey. Mickey Fabian."

CHAPTER
EIGHT

"Miles says I should put my affairs in order," Naomi was saying to Viola. They were sitting at Naomi's old cherrywood kitchen table in the late hours of Wednesday afternoon, looking through a heap of paint charts that Marco had dropped off for Viola. The sun was reflecting little rainbows on the kitchen's creamy walls by way of the crystals Naomi had hanging at the windows. "I always think it sounds like something a bit filthy. I asked him if he meant that I should make a list of old lovers and did he want the order to be alphabetical or by date, and he got quite snappy with me. You wouldn't have, would you? You're quite different."

Viola laughed. "Miles is always *so* serious. And no, of course I wouldn't get snappy. It sounds a giggle — listing lovers. Not that I've had, um, many . . . and certainly not that you've had . . ." She stopped and gave Naomi a sharp look, realizing how little she knew about her mother's earlier years. Really, you couldn't assume, could you? And of course it was none of your business to.

"Yer mum's just *yer mum*," she remembered her friend Paula saying, back when they were fourteen and speculating on whether parents were allowed a past. Some parents might have been hugely, exuberantly promiscuous; others, virginal till the wedding dress came off. They weren't going to let on to their children, not unless they were drunk and being embarrassing, and even then you couldn't trust that they weren't just being showy-offy for the shock value. The two girls had eventually concluded that parents weren't allowed *any* sex life other than the minimal amount it must have taken to produce them and their siblings, and were quite relieved to leave it at that and never mention it again. Naomi had been a widow since Viola was very small, but if, when she'd gone out — and she was a social sort with many friends — she was with a man or men, the subject had never come up.

"You don't know," Naomi now teased, picking up a card of pink shades. "I could have had hundreds. I could have been a right scarlet woman in my day."

"Were you?" Viola had to ask, slightly dreading the answer and recognizing that even at thirty-five there was still a trace of that adolescent self who *definitely* didn't want to know about this. Rachel would probably feel the same.

"Well, no, not quite scarlet. Not even when I was young and free — it was before the pill, you know," Naomi said. "I was only about that shade, maybe a bit paler." She pointed a beautifully painted silver nail at a little oblong in stick-of-rock pink labelled Cupid.

"You must have missed Dad, though." Viola took the shade card and put it on the pile with the others she didn't want. She didn't much fancy the wall behind the dresser being the colour gauge of her mother's past love life. If she chose Cupid there'd be weird and unsuitable images in her head every time she reached for a plate.

Naomi thought for a moment. "I missed him as the man who was your father, but by then I didn't miss him as a husband. He drank — which is what made him ill in the end; he'd get nasty. He'd make bitter comments that put me down, especially in front of other people. But he'd been good with Miles and Kate when they were small. Less when they hit their early teens. He were so very old-fashioned, thought they should be out of school and working from sixteen, like he'd been. Especially Kate — he didn't see the point of staying on at school for a girl. He said she'd only get married and it'd be a waste, and that she'd do better getting a little job that had a skill, like being a florist or a hairdresser — something she could easily come back to when any babies were grown. I wasn't having that. He called me a silly women's libber. But anyway, as it turned out he were gone by the time she was doing her A levels. Funny though, she did end up working at something that was a practical skill. It wasn't her BA in Geography that set her up in soft furnishings."

"I know it's awful, but I can remember Uncle Olly better than Dad." Viola had a sudden vivid memory of the day they'd moved into this house. She'd been about four, and very confused with everything being in boxes and then not in boxes, furniture everywhere, a kitchen's worth of kit to be sorted. Books in heaps in the hallway waiting to be arranged on shelves, clothes in folded piles on unmade beds. The man she'd known as Uncle

Oliver had taken charge, telling the removal men where to put boxes, bossing Kate and Miles around and making them be helpful rather than slumping about sulkily. He smelled nice — sometimes even now in the garden when she caught the scent of lemon verbena she could remember him that day, his big warm hand taking her small one and quietly leading her away from the removal chaos to give her a tour of the rooms. He showed her the one that would be hers, with its high, curved-top window overlooking the big back garden, and the little flat at the side which Naomi later rented out to actors who were on tour at the local theatre.

She could recall hardly anything from before they moved in here, some months after her father had died. Oliver Stonebridge's paintings started turning up as they all settled into the house. Miles hadn't liked them and thought they were too big and overwhelming, so Naomi had hung them in the hallway and up the stairs where he only had to pass them, not gaze at them. She remembered Oliver had rehung two of them in the sitting room very soon after Miles left for university. Bits of plaster had fallen from the walls as he bashed the picture hooks in with a hammer, and she'd combed the white dust out of her hair in her room that night.

"That's not so awful. It can't be helped. Oliver was around when you were coming to that age when you start to collect the things in your head that you'll remember for life."

The sun through the window caught Naomi's eyes. They were glittery with tears.

"Mum? Are you . . .?"

"A little glass of something, I think," Naomi interrupted briskly, avoiding the hand that Viola reached out to her. "And yes, I know it's a bit early." She got swiftly out of her chair and opened the fridge. "White wine? Or a G and T? Don't let on to Miles and Kate that it's before six o'clock — they'll tell us we're doomed." Naomi bustled about with ice and glasses. "So — these affairs Miles says I've to put in order," she went on, quickly recovering her composure as she sliced a lemon. "I know it's just another term for 'Have you sorted your will?' I'm not daft, I know what he's like. Won't call a spade a spade if he can call it a metallic delving implement or something."

Viola laughed. "He means well. I expect he just doesn't want you to worry about the future. It's why he wants me and Rachel to stay on here."

"Ha! That's so *he* doesn't have to worry about the future! No, you two go back to your own house and don't let him bully you. I can see right through him there. But with the will, what's there for *me* to worry about? When I'm dead I won't be bothered about anything, will I? You can tell him when you see him that it's all done and dusted, though I don't trust him not to want to come and see for himself to make sure he's not been disinherited. No, on second thoughts," she put two generously filled glasses down on the table and gave a wicked giggle, "I'll tell him I've left it all to Battersea Dogs, then you and me'll have a bet on how long it takes him to suggest I give him one of those power of attorney things."

"I don't like talking about wills, especially yours," Viola said, feeling the room grow cooler as the sun went behind a fat rain cloud. Thoughts of death were always hugely unwelcome visitors in her head, but she knew only too well that those you cared about could vanish with cruel suddenness.

"Don't be so soft," Naomi said gently, patting Viola's hand. "I won't live for ever, but I'm not planning to go anywhere yet, not for a long time. That's the best any of us can hope for, isn't it?"

"First day of exams. Just look at this lot," Amanda said to Viola as they watched Viola's English pupils and Amanda's Business Studies candidates trudge sleepy and yawning into the exam hall to take their places at the allocated desks. Sandra Partridge, the principal, was bustling about looking nervous and rechecking that the entrants had handed over their mobile phones.

"She'd frisk them if she thought she could get away with it. I'm surprised she hasn't got an airport-style metal detector," Viola remarked, watching Benedict Peabody's pair of acolyte girls piling up their hair into scrunchies to keep it out of the way as they wrote. Each of them then pulled out a little mirror to check her reflection, tweaking at her fringe, pulling a curl into place and eyeing Benedict to see if he was noticing her. But Benedict lounged back in his chair, faced the ceiling and closed his eyes.

"He looks like he's been up half the night," Amanda commented.

"If he has, I bet he won't have been doing a last-minute read-through of the T. S. Eliot," Viola said. "All we can do now is hope they actually read the questions properly and have remembered a pen."

She wished her pupils luck and then had to leave them to the mercy of the examining board's questions. She was surprised how nervous she felt herself, as if it was her own future that depended on how well they did today, not theirs. She'd done her absolute best to teach them, to get them to kick-start their own brains when it came to literature, but with one or two it was a struggle, and you had to wonder why they had opted for English Lit when you were pretty sure that they'd never again choose to read anything except *Grazia* magazine and tabloid headlines.

"You didn't need to come in today, did you?" Amanda asked. "Effectively, you've finished for the term, you lucky thing. I've still got three more sessions with the Economics group."

"Sandra's asked me to supervise the first half of this morning with her, and also I thought I'd stop by to give them a bit of encouragement on all their exam days," Viola said. "I know they mostly seem cocky and don't-careish but one or two look like they could do with a hug, virtual though; it'd have to be. I won't be here when they come out though; Sandra's taking over and I'm off to have lunch with my brother."

"And that's . . . good? Bad?"

"Bit of both, I think. I know he doesn't mean to, but he somehow always makes me feel like a naughty child.

I'll let you know tomorrow. Are we still going out to see this band?"

"We are. I'll pick you up at about eight, OK?"

"Fine. I'm looking forward to it but, Manda, I'm absolutely trusting you *not* to be setting me up with anyone. You're not, are you?"

"No. I promise I'm not." Viola looked quickly at Amanda's hands — her fingers weren't crossed but then she added, "Well, not this time anyway."

CHAPTER
NINE

Lunch with Miles was going to involve a glass or two of wine, so Viola left the Polo at home and caught a bus. She sat behind two middle-aged women who were talking loudly and frankly about their love lives, giggling so much that their substantial flesh was shaking in a fascinatingly jellyish way. "So I'm lying there," the one by the window was saying, "feeling like a fat, frilly whale in my basque and suspenders, and he's there, bollock naked, by the bed with a massive hard-on and *carefully folding his socks!*"

"Could be worse, he could have kept them on!"

"Oh don't!" the other one howled.

"So it's over?" her friend managed to ask through her spluttered laughter.

"Over? What d'you think? If all he can think of at a moment like that is aligning his footwear, can you imagine what he'd be like to live with?"

The two women got off the bus, still happily shrieking with laughter, and Viola continued, more or less alone. She found herself thinking about Gregory Fabian, who, she recalled from Monday, hadn't been wearing socks at all with his tatty, dusty Docksiders. And when he did, she reckoned he was absolutely certain *not* to be a folder-upper when it came to moments of passion. Not that she was actually speculating. Not that she even wanted to. Especially as there seemed to be a Mrs Fabian. Would she ever see him again? Probably not, though she still had unanswered questions she'd meant to ask about the late-night gardening.

Mrs F. had effectively broken up the lunch. He'd been seethingly furious with Mickey for her stroppy interruption, but then what had it looked like to her? Her husband blatantly entertaining a strange woman on their shared work premises, in a gorgeously arranged tented bower with wine and food, surrounded by flowers? Ah but — why wouldn't it be surrounded by flowers? It was, after all, the family business. No, of course Mickey had every right to be thoroughly pissed off with him — the hell she'd have given Greg the minute Viola was off the premises wasn't hard to imagine. And no way did she ever want to be taken for some predatory Other Woman. If that was what Mickey had concluded, she couldn't be more wrong. But realistically, Viola probably wouldn't see him any more anyway. She'd sent a text to thank him for what had turned out to be an inch from the glass of wine and two pieces of pitta dunked in hummus, before she'd taken the hint from the glowering Mickey and fled. He'd apologized all the way to her car, but hadn't exactly pleaded with her not to go. Probably very sensible of him.

Miles was there first. Viola could see him through the restaurant window, over by the far wall, already at the table, flicking a napkin about at a tiny flying bug. It was a dark little place, all oak panelling and hushed voices and serious-looking portly men in dark suits. Women preferred somewhere brighter, more contemporary. Here there were way too many gloomy paintings of dead, unplucked, unskinned game. Surprising choices for decoration, she thought as she walked through to meet him: they'd surely put people off their food. You wouldn't much fancy the pheasant casserole if, while you were eating, you had to look at a picture of one of its relatives, all feathered and bloody with its dead eye accusing you.

"I was beginning to give up on you," Miles said by way of greeting, looking at his watch in an ostentatiously grumpy way.

"I'm not *that* late: only about three minutes. I had to call in at the college first, check the students in for their first A-level exam, make sure they'd actually turned up and then stay to supervise for a while," she told him. "Have you ordered any wine? I'm gasping for a drink."

"Car?"

"No car today. I came by bus."

Miles frowned. "You're not *drinking too much*, are you, Vee? It doesn't make anything better, you know."

Viola unfolded her napkin and gripped the edge of it tightly, stopping herself from snapping at him. Were all big brothers so bossy like this? Or was it the twelve-year age gap that made him treat her like a small child who was needing to be kept in order? He'd been lovely to her when they were younger, teaching her to ride her bike, how to fish, to play chess, patiently letting her join

101

in garden cricket games with him and his friends. He'd happily babysat for her and let her stay up watching unsuitable films way past her bedtime when Naomi had gone out. Kate had been sure she'd end up with an older man, entirely because of hanging out with her brother and his pals, but it hadn't happened.

"Don't be silly, Miles. I don't think fancying a couple of glasses of wine with lunch makes me a candidate for rehab, do you? I already know the balance, thanks. When you're feeling down it's the last thing that'll cheer you up, once you're past that first half-glass." Now she was sounding sulky and defensive. Maybe she should go out to the pavement, come back in and start again, breezy, smiley and determined to let any negative comments go straight over her head.

"Sorry," he said, looking round for the waiter. "I just don't want you to get any more tough deals in your life. After Marco and Rhys, the last thing you want is . . ."

"Hey, Marco doesn't come under 'tough deals'," she protested quickly. "We still love each other a lot."

"Yes but . . ."

"Let's move on, Miles, shall we? I know having a husband who went gay isn't the ideal, but he and I handle it quite cheerfully, OK? It's been sorted for years. Not an issue. Shall we order? And then you can tell me why you wanted to buy me lunch. And sorry I'm sounding moody. I don't mean to. I just keep thinking you've got me here for a big telling-off." She felt her eyes beginning to fill with unexpected tears. What was that about? She shook her head, telling herself to stop being so feeble.

"Oh, Viola darling, nothing of the kind." He reached across and patted her hand. He looked sweet when he smiled, she thought. Like an endearing polar bear in that floppy cream suit. He was losing his hair, she noticed. Did he mind that or did he rather welcome it? It did give him a bit of gravitas that his rather school-boyish face had always lacked. Her own face shape was more pointy, like Naomi's, and her hair was dark brown like Kate's and inclined to be disobediently curly like hers too, especially in damp weather, but you would never mistake round-faced Kate and sandyish Miles as *not* siblings.

Viola opted for a goat's cheese, beetroot and pine-nut salad, unable to face the fleshy menu after seeing the paintings. Miles went for calf's liver, onions and bacon, delighted to find it on the menu. "Serena won't have offal in the house. She says it's like having a post-mortem in her own kitchen."

"Really? I never thought of her as particularly squeamish." Serena's paintings were splodgy and a bit strange; nearly all of them were brooding, near-monochrome watercolours depicting stark, leafless trees against threatening skies. You wouldn't, Viola was sure, guess they were the work of someone too queasy to slice a kidney.

"Her pictures, they always make me think they could have been done by . . ." Viola stopped, realizing that to say "a potential murderer" as she so nearly had wasn't likely to go down well with her brother when describing his wife of twenty-two years. Viola had been a bridesmaid at their wedding, thirteen and smiling gritted-teeth-style through a mortified sulk at being seen in public in peach satin frills with a huge padded bow at the back. ". . . someone who could cope easily with hunks of bloodied meat," she finally said.

Miles laughed as he cut into the liver. "I know what you nearly said! *A tortured soul*."

That would do. Kinder than killer. "Er . . . yes. Something like that. Is she? Tortured?"

Miles shrugged. "Who knows. She doesn't say a lot these days, not now the twins have left home. She's forever out, painting or at an antiques fair, playing bridge, doing all her real living off the premises. Sometimes I think she only comes home to sleep and change her clothes. I expect it's what all marriages come to in the end. You've had a luc—" It was his turn to cut the sentence short.

"Lucky escape," she supplied for him. "I don't think Rhys would see it that way, do you?" Viola put down her fork, unable to eat any more.

"No, but hey, I'm sorry, really sorry. I didn't mean it the way it was coming out, honestly. But you and Rhys weren't going to make it to the bored years anyway, were you? Oh God, sorry, sorry. That's even worse!" He was flustered now. Viola noticed that gravy had splashed on to his white shirt. Good. It was all she could do not to follow it up by hurling the rest of his lunch down his front.

"No, you're right," she managed to say, calmly. "If you're telling me the upside of him leaving me after only fourteen months for some unknown woman and then dying was that we wouldn't end up bored rigid in front of the TV for forty more years with nothing left to say, then fine. I'm sure you're spot-on."

She reached across for the bottle of wine and poured herself a generous glass, not caring whether Miles thought this was a sign of impending dipsomania or not. She'd have walked out right now, but she quite fancied pudding. And besides, now he'd dug himself into such a huge hole, when the moment came for him to raise the subject of her return to Bell Cottage, he'd owe her at least a mile of leeway. She picked at the last of the beetroot on her plate and listened to the low thrum of male voices behind her, talking, it seemed, about mortgages. Her own was mercifully manageable; she and Marco had bought Bell Cottage when prices were in a dip, and the house had reeked so much of incontinent cats and needed such a lot of cosmetic work that all other potential buyers reeled away in horror, at both the stench and the thought of taking it on.

"Did you know Kate's working on the family tree?" Miles said eventually. "She wants to go back at least three centuries. She says it keeps her from going mad."

"Why would she be going mad?"

Miles made a face and went a bit pink. "Um . . . er," he pulled at his tie knot nervously, "nothing particular. Women's stuff, I expect. Age? Don't you all go funny around her time of life? Serena's showing signs."

She felt rather sorry for him. Serena and her angular paintings, her bridge cruises, and possibly the menopause. On their last anniversary, Miles had given her a tiny framed piece of something or other, like parchment, a little certificate that said "Serena and Miles, in love since 1988", and she'd immediately shoved it in a cupboard. Viola couldn't blame her for that — there were sweet gestures and there were ones that were nausea-inducing — but at least he'd tried. If she was heading into menopause madness, poor old Miles was going to be able to do nothing right.

"Now, about Mum," he suddenly said, turning businesslike just as the waiter handed out the pudding menus.

"She's fine, thanks. On great form," Viola replied, contemplating profiteroles or lemon tart. "We've talked all through our moving out of the flat and she totally thinks it's the right thing for us to do and the right time, no worries."

"But you don't *want* to go back to your house, surely? Wouldn't you rather stay where there's someone to look after you now and then? I mean, you are a bit prone to whatever trouble's going."

Viola was puzzled; surely the objection from Kate and Miles had been about *Naomi* needing care, not her? "I'm all grown up, Miles, I can cope — I thought you were worried about Mum?"

"Well, yes, yes. That's the big issue, isn't it?"

"Not for her. She's told me to go and get on with life. But — you're right about the house being a bit much for her. She hardly uses half of it. She could sell it for an absolute mint and be really comfy and safe somewhere else."

"No, really, she can't sell the house — think of the upheaval. She just needs more people in it. You see . . ."

106

He leaned forward, looking earnest. For an awful moment Viola thought he was going to take her hand. "Kate and I had this idea after Mum was so adamant that she wouldn't sell. We thought if you sold your place, and stayed where you are, you could invest in doing it up a bit. Then after the work was done, Mum could move into the flat where it's nice and safe and all on one level, and you and Rachel could have the rest of the house."

Viola considered this for a moment. It didn't actually seem *too* unreasonable, in theory.

"And then when she, er . . . passes on . . ." Miles half whispered. "Then obviously you'd sell up and it would be divided between the three of us, as per her will."

"Have you seen her will?" Viola asked. "Because she said to tell you she was leaving everything to Battersea Dogs."

"Ha! Just her joke — typical!" He chuckled.

"Or maybe not," she teased him, enjoying the hint of doubt crossing his face.

"So — let me get this right," she said slowly, doing calculations in her head. "You and Kate have got it worked out that I could live in the house for, ooh, maybe another twenty-plus years, given Mum's current perky good health? I keep the place going, right? Renovate it with the proceeds from Bell Cottage? Pay the bills, do the maintenance, invest everything I've got in it, have no option to move anywhere else, *ever*, even after Rachel's grown up and moved on and even if I met someone or just fancied maybe, oh I don't know, living in Spain for a bit."

"Spain? Do you like Spain?" Miles frowned.

"Oh, Miles, it was just a *what if*!" She continued, determined not to lose momentum, "And then at the end, when Mum's, you know, *gone*, that is after I've also been — possibly, and we all hope it would never come to this — full-time nurse and carer as well, I'm to be turfed out with a third of what it's worth so you and Kate can divvy up your share?" Said it, she thought, pleased even through her anger that she'd managed to get out into the open exactly what she meant, for once.

"Um . . . well, I'm sure we could come to some arrangement regarding what you've invested. A pro rata sort of thing. But don't you see, we're only looking out for *you*. Kate and I are concerned that you could do with protecting from yourself, that's all."

"Yes, I see, Miles. It's OK, I've got the gist. I'm so glad you invited me for this lunch and made it so clear that I don't actually count at all as a full-functioning *grown-up*. Now, for pudding I quite fancy the Death by Chocolate. Is that allowed, do you think, or are you going to tell me that I really shouldn't in case I make myself sick?"

Oh, the cool of post-thunderstorm air. While the atmosphere in the restaurant had been dry and stuffy and blunted every sound beyond the windows, outside a small, fierce storm had been and gone, leaving the streets with that wet-dog smell that they get after heavy rain on dust. Viola waited for the bus by the station, gratefully breathing in the soft damp air and wondering what had happened to the concept of a queue, as people milled around under the bus shelter in any old order. You could, she thought, tell the ones who really knew better, because they pretended to be looking at the route map on the pole and then casually forgetting to move away from the spot they fancied. Kate had once said it was getting like the French in ski-lift queues — everybody just pushing ahead and never mind who got there first.

Viola had never tried skiing, but Rachel had been on a school trip when she was thirteen. She'd fallen over badly on the nursery slopes, cut her head and been kept off the piste for two lonely days with suspected concussion. "That's just the sort of thing that would have happened to you, Vee," Kate had laughed when she'd seen Rachel with stitches in her forehead. "Like mother, like daughter." Viola hadn't seen any trace of a funny side to this and it had left her with a new worry — was Rachel going to be like her? A bit of a disaster area in the luck department? She hoped not — and she was doing her very best to let Rachel out and about freely without fussing over her, though sometimes, when she was with her on the street, it was hard not still to take her hand when they crossed the road, just in case.

"Mum!" Rachel and her friend Emmy now pounced on Viola as she waited. The lunch must have taken longer than she'd thought: it had run into school home time. All that time, all that food and nothing sorted. She could just see Miles ganging up with Kate, telling her that it would be all right, he'd get Viola on her own and make her see sense. *Their* sense.

"Can Em come home with us, Mum? Please? What's for supper and have we got any crisps and biscuits and that?" Rachel was post-school ravenous, jumpy and likely to get moody if she didn't eat soon.

"Supper . . . um . . . I hadn't really thought. What do you fancy? And yes, of course, Emmy's always welcome."

"You went out for lunch with Miles today, didn't you? You've been eating lots of top stuff and having wine while we had boring beans and chips in the school canteen. *So*, like, jealous!"

"OK, you choose then — and if you decide on something fairly quick and easy involving pasta, that would help." Viola felt tired from the lunch and she was looking forward to a peaceful evening, feet up on the sofa and some unchallenging TV.

The bus arrived and they fought their way on board through those clustered round the stop but disinclined either to get on the bus or to make way for those who wanted to. Rachel and Emmy got seats at the front — Viola was further back. She watched Rachel, trying to see her as a stranger would. She was taller than Emmy, thinner, all legs, as if she'd bolted, growth-wise, like a lettuce planted where it got too much sun. Emmy was more compact. Rachel had longer hair, blonde unruly stuff, parted just over her left ear and piled across her head in a wind-blown mess of haphazard backcombing. It was supposed to look, according to Rachel, like bed hair. Not actual just-woken-up morning hair, but just been shagged by your top rock musician or movie star of choice hair. Viola was as sure as any mother could be that Rachel didn't yet know this look from personal experience. She certainly hoped not — Rachel wouldn't even be fifteen for another few weeks.

Viola wondered how long Emmy would stay this afternoon — there wasn't much room in the flat for separate socializing, and although Rachel had the bigger of the two small bedrooms, it wasn't the most comfortable teen hang-out. Most of her clothes were hooked on to the back of the door, and the ones she was trimming up for Gemma's stall had ended up draped across Naomi's old piano in the sitting room. Her school books were piled on the floor and ended up scattered half under her bed.

Viola breathed in the warm damp bus air and longed and longed suddenly to have their own home back. They could spread out, be properly themselves again. Rachel would have plenty of space for her schoolwork, be able to have friends over who could actually stay the night instead of needing to be collected. They could play music as loud as they liked, talk freely without wondering if their every teen confidence could be overheard. Miles really couldn't have his own way with his bizarre plans. For one thing, by the time she'd sold Bell Cottage, reorganized her mother's house and got everything sorted to the rest of the family's satisfaction, Rachel would be working on her plans to whizz off to university. The least she could do for her, while they still lived together, was to take her back to the home that was completely *theirs*.

CHAPTER
TEN

"Have you got everything? Are you sure? You've got an awful lot of stuff to carry. How will you manage it on the tube?" Outside the school, Viola fussed and flapped as she helped Rachel unload her overnight bag, school books, and the bin bag full of the now beautifully renovated cardigans, from the back of the Polo.

"I'm on it. I can deal with it all, no problemo." Rachel somehow found a way to heap the whole cumbersome lot around her body, making it look as effortless as only a lithe teenager could. Viola had a sudden horrible vision of some of the bags tumbling on to the tube line at Ladbroke Grove, of Rachel thoughtlessly reaching down, trying to retrieve her scattered belongings just as a Circle Line train roared along. Stop it now, she told herself. All would be well.

"Have you got your Oyster card? And don't go leaving anything on the train, will you . . ." I must stop this, Viola thought. Rachel is quite capable. She won't accidentally shed possessions along the way like her mother does, or absent-mindedly take the wrong DLR train and end up getting off at Mudchute, curious to see if there actually was one.

"Oh, Mum!" Rachel laughed. "You should hear yourself! You're in full-on mother-hen mode. Cluck-cluckety-cluck! It's not like I haven't stayed over at Dad's before."

She was, Viola thought, in an unusually good mood for a school morning. Normally if she gave her a lift at that time of the day, Rachel, still dopily sleep-bound, could barely manage to dredge a word out of herself, let alone actually giggle and joke. Communication was reduced to a basic growl-and-scowl combination if you made the mistake of questioning whether she'd remembered all her books, whether it was a violin day, or dared to ask if she would be staying on late or going to a friend's place after school finished. At best there'd be a grunt by way of acknowledging a well-meant "have a nice day".

Today she was quite bouncy. Viola didn't expect this to be a permanent state of affairs but did put it down, mostly, to Rachel's delight that they would soon be returning to Bell Cottage. She'd already been talking about arranging her room with her bed against the far wall so she'd get a view out over the garden when she woke up, and, with the help of Emmy, she'd decided on the paint colour — a soft silvery grey. To Viola it looked a bit *too* grey, a shade that could feel cold on a gloomy morning. It was maybe more the choice of Emmy (whose wardrobe full of black and purple, lace and velvet headgear would have been the envy of any Victorian undertaker's mute), but Rachel insisted she was absolutely, *like, to'ally* sure it would look brilliant and she'd run it past her dad just to check — seeing as he was the designated Arty One. And anyway, it was *her* room. She was allowed to pick whatever she liked best.

"Give my love to Marco and James, oh and Gemma when you give her the cardigans. And don't . . ." Viola hesitated, stopping herself just in time from saying "and don't do anything silly". That sounded too like Naomi. Not just Naomi when Viola was a teenager, but Naomi now: Naomi in full kimono-on-the-doorstep mode. *Not* bearable when you're thirty-five, but at fourteen you had to hear these things — that was the deal. She modified it a bit, tried to be usefully specific. "When you're going down to the market tomorrow, hang on to your bag tight and keep it zipped up and be careful who you get talking to."

"It's fine, Mum! I've been down Portobello millions of times. And anyway, I expect Dad will come too, no worries. He likes to go to Garcias for posh ham and chorizo and stuff like that. He says we can have lunch at that little place with the roof garden."

"He lets you have a lot of freedom. I sometimes think he forgets how young you are," Viola said, worrying in spite of Rachel's reassurance. "Just take care, OK?"

"Yup." Rachel gave her mother a big, generous hug, which Viola found almost tearfully touching, considering that although Rachel's year group were forever hugging each other, preening each other's hair like fond monkeys and often holding hands, the idea of being caught showing public affection to a *mother* would be pretty much unthinkable.

"See you on Sunday then," Viola managed to say, feeling pathetic. Ye gods, Rachel was only going to stay with her dad. She'd done it often enough before. Also, Viola was, for once, actually going *out*, doing grown-up socializing, among strangers, just like she used to. Like real people, with real lives. She felt quite nervous, thinking about it.

As if she were mind-reading, Rachel said, "Yeah, OK, and, Mum? When you go out clubbing with your mates tonight, like, have a *really* great time." She turned to go, lugging her bag burden with her, and then she grinned and called back to Viola, "But be careful who you talk to and *don't do anything silly!*"

Rachel felt a bit guilty. She hadn't when she'd planned this and, really, it shouldn't be any big deal — other people bunked off school all the time. She went in through the school gates and waited for a few moments behind the hedge to watch the Polo drive away. She'd have to give it a while because the traffic was always slow in the mornings, and she didn't want her mum to get held up at the crossroads and catch sight of her legging it back down the road in the rear-view mirror. It was a terrible burden, being so trusted.

"What are you doing? Why are you here? Don't you have other plans?" Emmy made her jump.

"I'm waiting for Mum to be far enough away so I can escape," Rachel told her.

"You'll be seen. During registration there'll be one of the geeks who's stupid enough to say you're here somewhere. You're wack at this, aren't you?" Emmy laughed at her and picked up one of the bags.

"I haven't had enough practice." Rachel was worried now. Cutting a class occasionally was one thing, going missing for a whole day was a bit more serious. If she got found out, well — the school would go ape and give her the lecture about trust and safety issues, and as for home: grounded, for sure, for a long time. For ever, probably. At least till she was past voting age. Her parents would get together, and maybe even her gran too, and do that "disappointed" look, tell her she'd let them down on grounds of trust. *Everyone* hated that. It was the killer.

"You haven't had *any* practice. You're rubbish. Man up, Hendricks, you haven't a clue! Come with me, I'll show you the way. What are you doing about weekend homework? And where are you going to change? You can't work a stall in school uni. That would be, like, well weird."

Emmy led her round the side of the school, past the back of the lunch hall. Only a few smokers were hanging around. They wouldn't dob her in, she realized — they had their own school-rule breakages to deal with.

"Changing in station loos. Got the right books. It's always maths and there's a load of French about *Ma Famille*. I *hate* that. It's like they're wanting to know about your home set-up and they think that if they get you to write it in French, it's like not being so nosy. But it is really."

"Ssh . . ." Emmy slowed at a corner of the building, standing close against the wall and peering forward carefully.

Rachel giggled. "You look like a cartoon spy," she whispered. "This is so random."

"OK, over there, through the gate by the fence." Emmy piled Rachel's bags back on to her and gave her a push. "It's always open till just gone nine for deliveries and stuff. No one else ever uses it." Rachel hesitated.

"Go *on!*" Emmy said. "Just *go!*"

"I wish you were coming with me. Two of us would halve the guilt."

"No, it wouldn't, you moron, it would double it," Emmy replied, reasonably enough. "And anyway, *what* guilt? It's no biggie, it's only Friday. Have a great time, Rache. Hope you make loads of dosh."

By the time Rachel had reached the gate, Emmy had vanished as if she'd melted into the wall, though really she was probably behind the bins. She felt very alone — no turning back now. Her mum had once told her that when she was young she'd really loved the feeling that no one knew where she was. She'd got all misty-reminiscent about a holiday where she and her friends hitched all over Europe, backpacking on the cheap and hardly ever checking in with home. Rachel wasn't so sure. She must, deep down, be a total wimp. Emmy had been right — she needed to man up. Or woman up. Why did no one ever say that? She'd bet none of the candidates on *The Apprentice* would have fretted about bunking off school to get their first go at being a business big shot. If she sold just one of her renovated knitwear items on Gemma's stall, she'd be *massively* delighted.

And also — well, the longer she spent in the area, the better the chance of running into that boy again. OK, there were zillions of people in Notting Hill, and Portobello Road was going to be rammed, as always. But you never knew — and as a stallholder (she *loved* that thought — even though she counted as a mere work experience alongside Gemma) she'd be kind of on view, a bit like on a stage, not just a face in the crowd. If he were passing, he'd see her. Whether he stopped and talked, even remembered her face, that was something else. Reaching the station, aching under the weight of all her bags and starting to slough off the guilt, she thought, hey, you had to risk to win.

When she went into Med and Gib after leaving Rachel, Viola could feel a whole changed atmosphere in the place. Instead of being slumped on chairs thumbing nervously through last-minute notes or skulking on the courtyard benches, head in hands and looking terrified, the students seemed to have morphed into nonchalant old hands when it came to exams and were now sauntering in casually, some recklessly at the last possible minute. Benedict Peabody was being dropped off at the gate by a parent oblivious to the double red no-stopping lines, and he clambered out of the huge black Porsche Cayenne looking as if he'd rolled from his bed only minutes ago. Viola waited by the door as he ambled across the yard, fastening his ultra-low-slung belt a notch tighter. The belt had that unmistakable H of Hermès — Viola would have put money on it *not* being a fake.

"Those jeans," Sandra Partridge muttered to Viola. "Whatever idiot designs them so the crotch is halfway to their knees? He looks like a huge baby in urgent need of a nappy change. They all do."

Viola didn't say anything — it was well known that in Sandra's ideal world this college would be a hotbed of fast-track eager entrepreneurs in the making, all neatly turned out in suits and ties and properly shined shoes, not scuffed Converses. The girls would be in sleek, on-the-knee skirts, flesh-coloured tights and kick-ass heels. In reality, it was hard enough to get most of them to turn up at all, let alone start lecturing them on how they should dress.

"'Lo, Vo!" As he went inside, Benedict cherrily offered Viola a high five, which she returned.

"'Vo'?" Sandra's eyebrows were raised as far as Botox would allow. "He should address you as Ms Hendricks. They all should. You mustn't let them take liberties." She sighed deeply and would have frowned if her face had let her.

"Oh, he's all right, he's just being friendly," Viola said. "And most sixth-form-college staff are on first-name terms with their students these days. They'll mostly be at university soon, after all."

"In my day, it was either Sir or Miss Whatever-her-name-was. Respect and manners. All gone, now. Just chaos. *Chaos*." Sandra looked exasperated as the last of the stragglers scuttled in through the gate. "And also, while we're here, come and look what one of them has done. I suppose they think it's some sort of leaving joke." She took Viola's arm and pulled her round to the side of the building. Planted with professional care and expertly espaliered along the boundary fence in a border that had held nothing smarter than dandelions and ground elder were three young apple trees, neatly spaced and watered in.

"Oh — that's gorgeous!" Viola said. "But way too much like hard work to be one of the students, surely? Last year they just sprayed our cars with Crazy String."

"You and that little girl who teaches French are the youngest, so I'm guessing one of you has an admirer with easy access to a garden centre. Any ideas?"

Only one possibility came to Viola's mind, but she dismissed the thought — why would Greg go to all this trouble? And anyway, didn't he go for locations more public than this?

"Sorry, couldn't tell you," she said, nevertheless feeling a bit tingly.

Sandra shrugged and turned away, looking at her watch. "They just appeared overnight; at least, I assume so. I noticed them when I drove in this morning. I've asked the other tutors and the caretaker, but no one's any idea who did it. I suppose they can stay as they do cover that tatty fence, but other than guessing one of the brats or their parents has a massive crush on one of us, I really can't think where they came from." And with that she stalked off into the building to start another exam invigilation and to daydream of being head of an establishment where the pupils were thoroughly motivated, executively dressed, hard-working and certain to send her college to the top of the A-level league tables.

120

Viola, meanwhile, lingered with the young apple trees. Appeared from nowhere, overnight, had they? And did the donor also do a fine line in midnight quince-planting? Maybe he had put them there, but only for fun, not for more than a bit of a tease. Because Greg had got Mickey. And Mickey seemed to be as fierce and protective as a Jack Russell terrier, though with much prettier hair. Why would he waste his time on a gesture like this? If it *was* him, then it was obviously his idea of a joke. A nice edible one, but all the same . . .

CHAPTER
ELEVEN

I could never live anywhere else than London, Rachel decided as she and her collection of bags got off the 52 bus at Ladbroke Grove station and crossed the road under the flyover to walk down Thorpe Close to Portobello Road. She loved the dry, grubby heat, the mixed food scents. There was the occasional just-caught scent of dope from an unseen someone lurking among the banana plants on the green; the noises of traffic and reggae, air brakes and hooting, and people shouting to each other in languages she couldn't fathom. She liked the way one four-storey house might be divided into grubby bedsits with only old T-shirts tacked up to block out the light, yet the adjoining building could be a hugely palatial one-family home, the sort you'd see in *Elle Decoration*, with glimpses of vast creamy sofas, splashy abstract paintings and curvy chrome floor lamps. There was just so much energy, compared with the placid, pretty sameness of her suburban district.

Gemma's stall was pitched on the end of a row under a big canopy, just up from Portobello Green. The market was already busy, mostly with tourists looking a bit bewildered and anxiously taking photos of everything around them, as if fearing they would miss the one iconic thing they were supposed to be seeing. They'd heard there were treasures among the near-jumble castoffs, the ancient lace, the bags and jewellery, but they took some finding. A stall full of faux-fifties dresses patterned with teacups and daisies — did that appeal to a party of twenty-somethings from Canada?

"Rachel! Wow, you're early." Gemma broke off from hanging up a sequinned jacket and gave her a welcoming hug. She smelled of jasmine, sweet and light. Her fingernails were painted lilac and she was wearing a vintage rose-print dress and green suede pixie boots. Her beaded dreads were crammed under an old straw hat. Rachel liked the look on Gemma, but wasn't sure if it would be *her*. She wasn't sure, yet, what exactly "her" was, which meant she always felt she was wearing an unsatisfying mix of whatever was nearest in her room. Today she had grabbed what she could stash into the smallest space for the quick change at the station: jeans and a loose red and white spotted chiffon top over a little pink vest. Underdressed, compared with vibrant Gemma.

"Well, you know . . . no school. Um . . ." Rachel couldn't look at her aunt for fear of being caught out in the lie so turned away and tucked her bags under the stall, touching wood that they'd still be there at the end of the day. Ideally, she'd have dropped them off at Marco's first, but although she'd got a doorkey, she didn't want to run the risk of him or James being home and asking her what the deal was with school. Marco had said he would be back at about four, which would mean he'd be there when she was supposed to arrive — and with all her stuff.

"Is it a day off? What do they call it, an inset day?" Gemma wasn't to be fooled. When Rachel emerged from under the stall she met a look that was sharp and suspicious — not really what she expected from her aunt, who she'd assumed would think school was a tedious inconvenience.

"You won't say anything to Dad, will you?" Rachel pleaded. "And *please* don't send me away again. I've brought all the cardies — every one of them all decced up and ready to sell. My friend Emmy thought they were mint." She tipped them out from the bin bag on to the stall, spreading them on top of velvet hats and feathered berets.

"Hmm . . . well, I won't tell him, but you know, Rachel, this puts me in a tricky position with both him and your mum. All the same . . ." she picked up a pale grey bobble-knitted cardigan that now had silver buttons and a black and white gingham collar, ". . . you've done a brilliant job with these, I must say. I guess the least I can do is let you stay and help and see how they sell, but, please, no more skipping school. It's the summer holidays soon — you can come down any time then. You'll have plenty of time to get sick of all this by September."

By 2p.m. all Rachel's work had been sold except the old tobacco-coloured cashmere cardigan that she'd so carefully sewn pheasant feathers on to. Several potential customers handled it and commented, but it wasn't a

124

shape or shade the women seemed keen on, and the men passed it over as too fancy for them. As one of them commented to his friend, you'd have to be pretty upfront to wear it down the pub.

"Got it wrong, there, didn't I?" Rachel moaned to Gemma.

"Not at all. That guy had a point, that's all. It just takes a special, brave sort to carry this off. There'll be someone, you'll see."

"Someone like Dad, you mean." Rachel giggled. "You should see him preening in his new boots."

"He was always like that. We went to tap-dance classes as kids and he *desperately* wanted patent tap shoes, which no one sold. I don't even know where he got the idea they existed, but nothing else would make him happy. We had an aunt in New York — she found some and sent them over. He was in absolute heaven."

Rachel was just about to ask about the aunt when someone hoicked the cardigan down from its hanger to have a closer look at it.

"Oh, helloooo, it's you! From the tube steps — thought I recognized you!" The blond boy was talking to the garment, rather than to Rachel. She felt suddenly twittery and nervous. *This* was what she'd fantasized about all week, that somehow she'd run into him again. She hadn't really thought it would happen, only dreamed it up. Now what to say that wouldn't make him vanish again?

"Why don't you try it on?" Gemma suggested.

He gave her a look. "Like, *no*? I mean, can you see me in this? It's the colour of what's in my baby sister's *nappy.*" He grinned at Rachel. "Er, sorry — I'll hang it up again for you." And he did.

"Actually, it would look great on you," she said, desperate to make him stay longer.

"You think?" He took the hanger down again for a second inspection. "I like the feathers. Awesome."

"They were my idea," Rachel told him. "I designed the whole look for this piece." Euw — how did that sound? Pretentious or what?

"You did? Impressed," he said, pulling the old cardigan on over his Superdry checked shirt. "What do you think? Isn't it, like, totally pants?"

"Come round this side — we've got a mirror."

The boy gazed admiringly at his reflection, posing and laughing and pulling the garment round himself. "I quite like it actually, now it's on. How much?"

"I can let you have it for ninety-five pounds," Gemma cut in quite sharply. "It's cashmere, never been worn. And *not* the cheap supermarket quality."

"Yo, bargain then. Wrap it." He handed it to Rachel. "You want to meet up for a drink sometime, schoolgirl?"

Rachel looked at him. What kind of boy calls you "schoolgirl"? It sounded so cheesy.

"Sorry, cheesy." He looked a bit embarrassed. "Also you said you're from miles away, so you probably wouldn't want . . ."

"No, really, I would . . . could. I mean, I'm from here too. My dad lives on Lansdowne Crescent."

"'K, deal then. Mobies," he said, pulling out a white iPhone. She delved shakily into her bag beneath the

126

stall and, thankfully, her phone was in the first pocket she tried. Numbers were swopped and she gave him her name, just her first one. Her mum's experiences with mad people and journalists after Rhys had left her wary about giving too much information. Who knew who might turn out to be a crazy stalker?

"Ned," he told her. "Laters." And he went to walk away.

"Hang on, you! Payment?" Gemma called after him.

"Oh ya, soz!" he said, peeling twenty-pound notes from a roll in his pocket. "Nice kit you got on here."

I will neither giggle nor blush, Rachel told herself firmly, but did both the second he walked away.

"I'm off out for the night. You'll be all right, won't you?" Naomi was pulling on a jacket and was about to leave the house with her old leather Gladstone bag as Viola arrived home from work. She was tired and hot. The afternoon invigilating the Business Studies exam had been a nightmare, with one poor girl having to be accompanied twice to the loo to be sick and then weepily confessing that she might be pregnant, her dad would kill her and her boyfriend would dump her. Three people had pens that gave up the ghost and one boy finished so early that he put his head on the table and fell fast asleep, drooling on to what he'd written. Viola thought about making an excuse and cancelling her evening out with Amanda, but also thought that if she didn't make the effort she'd somehow never get back into the swing of a social life. It was time.

"I'll be fine, but what about you? Where are you off to? Have you been secretly meeting a man behind the crime shelves at the library?"

"Give over! Of course not. Monica's had a fall and she's feeling a bit frail. I'm going to stay with her and make sure she has some supper. She's not broken anything, thank goodness, but it's a shock to the system. You can die of that, a good shaking-up. Enough of us are kicking the bucket as it is. Those who are left have to get together and look after each other. The way the government's going there'll be bugger all anyone else to do it for us. Anyway, don't forget to lock up properly. And when you're out tonight," she said as she opened the front door to leave, "*don't do anything daft.*"

"That's the second time today!" Viola laughed. "Rachel said more or less the same. I'm not twelve!"

"I know, but think on. We're only looking out for you."

After much dithering in front of the wardrobe and wondering what had happened to her old instinct for what to wear to what, Viola opted for the not-making-huge-effort compromise of jeans but with an asymmetrically quirky All Saints top. She'd washed her hair and it had fluffed out in all the right ways for once, but she wasn't wearing a lot of make-up. If Amanda was being thrifty with the truth and had, in spite of her promise, tried to make this a foursome with some stray man (and Viola could just picture it: Amanda saying, "Oh, this is Steve, by the way. I forgot to mention he happens to be staying with us tonight, thought he might as well come with us . . ."), then he wasn't going to be encouraged to fancy her.

After all the thinking about it and dreading being set up, it was almost (but not quite) a disappointment when Amanda and Leo came to pick her up and there wasn't anyone else in the car. How contrary was that?

"Just to warn you, you and I'll be the youngest here by about twenty years," Amanda told her as soon as they arrived. "This lot are what Leo's mate once called SOGGS — otherwise known as *sad old gits with guitars*."

"They may be old," Leo, who was a good ten years older than Amanda, said, "but at least by now they can damn well play them. They've got years of music history in them, these guys."

"Here we go." Amanda rolled her eyes at Viola. "Now he'll start on the kids of today wasting their time mucking about on virtual guitar . . ."

"Well, you know I'm right," he said as they went into the pub and up the stairs to the clubroom. "If they spent as much time practising on the real thing as they do on the game version, they'd get bloody good."

Amanda hadn't been wrong about the age thing. The place was crammed with a mostly male audience: amiable, greying blues aficionados in ancient jeans, jackets proudly accessorized with rusting CND badges, wire-rimmed reading glasses poking out of top pockets. The women still had mildly exotic traces of old hippydom about them: Viola even spotted a couple of Stevie Nicks-style hanky-point skirts. At the bar people made way for each other; she heard the words please and thank you. It was a long way from the E-fuelled world of her own clubbing days, when an illegal rave in a field would be rammed with huge-eyed frantic dancers, beaming vacantly at their happy, happy world but totally unable to attempt a conversation.

"If you're looking for the older type, own bus pass, that sort of thing . . ." Amanda whispered as they made their way to a table alongside the stage area.

"I'll keep it in mind," Viola told her, settling into her chair with a spritzer.

And Leo had been right about the music. The thoroughly competent band played a selection of old blues standards mixed in with such eternal favourites as Eddie Floyd's "Knock on Wood". Down at the front, a few energetic sorts were dancing in the kind of Dad-dance way that would have had Rachel and her mates pleading with them to stop.

"That geezer keeps looking at you," Leo commented to Viola as the band stopped for a break. A grey-bearded man in ancient leather jeans and one dangling sword earring on the far side of the room caught her eye and raised his glass to her.

"Thanks for the warning, but leather trousers — nooooo! Didn't think they still existed." She half smiled politely back at the man, though, not wanting him to think (or rather to know) she was laughing at him. "I'll keep clear and hope he finds someone else to hit on. And hey, my turn to get the drinks." She pulled her phone from her bag in case Rachel had sent a text (she hadn't) and put it in her pocket, found her wallet and

130

hung the bag over the back of the chair. "Same again for you both?"

Viola took her turn at the bar feeling unusually happy, almost euphoric. It was good to be out; she'd almost forgotten how it felt just to have nothing to think about but enjoying the moment. Rejoining the real world: she'd picked the right time.

"You irk me," a male voice behind her said. She took no notice, assuming the speaker was having a conversation with someone else. The barman approached and she ordered the drinks.

"You are *irksome* to me." This time it was definitely aimed close to her ear. She turned to look and there was the leather-trousered man, too close and staring intently into her face. The silver-sword earring swung against his stubbly neck.

"Irksome?" she asked as she handed over money for the drinks. "You don't know me."

"You disturb me." This didn't sound good; she looked over to their table. Amanda was on her own — Leo was talking to the band's keyboard player. She put her wallet between her teeth and went to pick up the drinks.

"You can't carry all those on your own, let me help."

Before Viola could protest, leather man picked up two of the glasses and led the way to their table. Amanda raised her eyebrows at Viola. "Can't let you out of my sight for a sec . . ." she began, then stopped, seeing Viola's warning look. The man had pulled up a spare stool from the next table and now sat with them.

"Paul," he said to Viola.

"Hello, Paul." Viola wasn't willing to give her name but also wished she wasn't cursed with good manners; how did people ever tell anyone just to *get lost*? It wasn't in her nature to be that rude — you couldn't just tell a stranger who was only mildly annoying you to sod off. He was ignoring Amanda completely and was now staring at the floor.

"You have beautiful feet," he declared in a strangely flat tone. "They please me."

Viola looked at them, feeling as if her naked, pink-painted toenails at the front of her espadrilles were somehow indecently exposed. She could feel them trying to curl themselves out of sight, and she folded one ankle over the other and tucked her feet away under her chair.

"OK, how are we doing and who is this?" Leo arrived back at that moment; oh bless him, Viola thought.

"And this is her husband," Amanda said to Paul, quite loudly and slowly so he couldn't misinterpret or not hear and so Leo could pick up on the situation. The small lie made Viola swear eternal gratitude. "And I think he quite likes her feet as well."

Paul stood up, put his hand out and Leo shook it, both men looking almost comically solemn. "You are a lucky man. She is an irksome woman but has good feet."

"You see, Vee?" Amanda giggled as soon as Paul had vanished into the crowd, presumably to be irked by another cute-footed woman. "You've still got it!"

Pulling power she might have: if this was what she trawled she was glad she'd resolved to stay right out of the dating scene.

"Thanks, Amanda, that's so encouraging!" She laughed. "And it's made me even keener to stay away from even the *idea* of looking for a new man."

"Oh, now, never say never!" Leo said. "That's just defeatist! Haven't you been even slightly tempted to have a look at what's out there online?"

"Why, have you?" Amanda asked him.

"No! Of course not — not when I've got you, babe."

Viola saw a swift and loving smile pass between the two of them and felt a little tweak of envy. *Maybe one day . . .* she allowed herself to think, but not yet.

"I know exactly what would happen if I did online dating," she said. "I'd find someone who put up a photo of himself that was ten years old and two stone lighter and whose mum had written all his spiel. He'd have the dress sense of that Paul bloke and when face to face would communicate only in Neanderthal grunts."

"I'd better tell Charlotte that the Internet isn't going to figure in her manhunt for you, then."

"You can try — I don't expect she'll take any notice, though. You know what she's like."

It was only as they began to leave and Viola was about to put her purse back in her bag that she realized the bag had gone from the back of her chair. Her heart started to beat fast as she thought about what was in it, and whether anything was going to be the most massive hassle to replace. But she hadn't taken anything out with her other than her purse — which she still had, and one doorkey, which was in the pocket of her jeans. Only a small pack of tissues and a lipstick had gone, and the little bag had been an old one, brought out from handbag retirement because it had a long strap that she could wear across her body in a crowded bar and be safe from casual thieving. Well, that had worked well, hadn't it. On the plus side, the thief would be disappointed with such a meagre haul.

"So bloody unlucky!" Amanda looked stricken when Viola told her, as if by taking her out that night it was somehow partly her fault.

"Not really, just careless of me," Viola said. "I should know better than to let it out of my sight. I really *am* hopeless, aren't I?"

"Not at all," Amanda lied kindly. "But you are going to report it to the police?"

"No," Viola said. "There was absolutely nothing in it, and I don't want my family to know I can't even manage a night out without *something* going wrong."

"Well, Leo and I won't tell them. Just tell the barman, though — he'll want to know if people are thieving in here."

Viola felt relieved to be home as the Mini pulled up outside the house and she climbed out, hugging Amanda, who got out to move from the back seat to the front. OK, so something had gone wrong, but it could have been worse. She could have been about to spend hours on the phone cancelling credit cards or trying to get through to bank helplines.

"Thank you so much, both of you. Great evening."

"We must do it again," Amanda said. "Loved the music, just sorry about your bag."

"It's OK, honestly. And yes, let's do it again."

The Mini sped off and Viola, her doorkey already safely in her hand, waved till it vanished round the corner. Turning to go in through the gates, she tripped on a piece of loose paving and stumbled, the key flying out of her hand and clinking on metal. She didn't have to guess what had happened to it. She'd been here before, back when she was fifteen. The key had found its inevitable way down the nearest drain.

CHAPTER
TWELVE

As the saying went, the light was on but no one was home. Naomi's little Fiat was not in the driveway because it would be parked outside her friend Monica's house, where Naomi would probably by now either be fast asleep or reading Ed McBain.

Viola sat on the steps on the front porch wondering how to deal with yet another problem that was of her own making. So what to do next? At least it wasn't cold tonight — that was something. If the back door didn't give with the hard tug she thought was all she'd need, then trying to unscrew the catch on the flat's French doors would be a lot easier without frozen fingers. She picked her way carefully along the rutty path in the dark past the hydrangeas and went round to the back of the house to give the door a firm tug. But despite her best efforts, none of the doors budged, not even slightly. They might creak in a high wind and let whistling draughts through in winter, but the place was a lot tougher than she'd thought. The solidly built old house completely scorned her puny efforts, and the open but utterly inaccessible upstairs bathroom window was practically sneering at her. So it would have to be the heavyweight approach. But first to find a screwdriver and any other potentially useful tools. She switched on her phone to use the torch app so she could see her way to the shed in the back garden. At that moment a text flashed up, with the name Greg Fabian. She leaned against the porch to read it: "You still haven't told me why you're living with your mother. Am curious."

He was being quite persistent on that one, she thought, though feeling exhilaratedly pleased to hear from him, as if he were a little bit of welcome friendly company while she scuffed about in the garden, trying to break in.

"And you didn't tell me why you plant fruit trees in the night. Am also curious," she replied briskly, pressing send and immediately realizing she hadn't first checked the time he'd sent his message. It could have been hours ago. She should have waited till morning; by now he could well be asleep. The ding of the message alert might wake and infuriate both Greg and Mickey; after all, not everyone was up and about, prowling around wide awake. All the same, she thought, her question covered both the quince *and* the apples. This was his chance to fess up to that one — if it *was* him. It would be typical to presume and find she was completely wrong and make a total idiot of herself. Perhaps the world was full of night-time gardeners. Her phone dinged again. Not asleep then — either woken and annoyed by her text or still up and about.

"Apples for teachers = traditional. No fruit tonight tho. Sunflowers."

So it *was* him. Strange, loopy man! And he was out planting stuff in the night *again*? The thought made her smile, yet at the same time she also wondered if her nutter-alert radar should be kicking in here, just as it had with the foot-admirer earlier. Unable to resist her curiosity, she started tapping into her phone again.

"Sunflowers? Right now? Where?" She sent the message and switched the hopelessly feeble torch app on and set off round to the shed, thankful for a clear night with a good bright moon. With luck — if it wasn't in its usual short supply — she wouldn't trip over a tree root and break her ankle. As she rummaged through the old toolbox that had lived, more or less unbothered, in the shed for the past couple of decades, she suddenly felt desperately tired. It was nearly midnight. She was locked out and in urgent need of a pee. Well, at least that could be sorted, and she nipped round to the back of the shed and peed on the compost heap. Old Uncle Oliver would have approved — he'd once told her that all hard-core gardeners did that, something to do with uric acid being good for the mulch, though she wasn't sure what old Joe, the neighbour who took care of their garden in exchange for turning the far end of it into his personal allotment, would think of it. She was just hauling up her jeans when her mobile rang and Greg, yet again, caught her by way of the phone with her knickers down. Not that she was going to tell him that, she thought, as she quickly fastened her zip, one-handed.

138

"That dreary bare patch of earth by the library where the winos chuck their cans," he said, not even bothering with "hello". "It was crying out for cheery sunflower faces. The library's child clients will love them. I'm on my way home now, and I know it's late and your mum might be lurking in her curlers to clout me with a frying pan, but I don't suppose you've got the kettle on, have you?"

"Er, well, it's a bit difficult . . ."

"Sorry, sorry! I'm intruding, aren't I? It *is* too late and you're not alone. Why would you be? Sorry! I'll go . . ."

"No! No, wait, it's fine and I *am* alone. How far away are you?"

There was a small silence. "Well, actually, right outside. I'm not a stalker, I promise. It really is on the way home and it was just an off-chance thing."

"OK then, just drive in and park by the Polo. I'll come and meet you."

How threatening did it look? Viola wondered, as she approached the Land Rover wielding a big hammer and a long screwdriver. Greg opened the car door, but only a few inches.

"Have you gone back to your original opinion, that I'm a crazed killer on the loose?" he asked, pointing to her weapons. "Because I've done tonight's body-burying already and just fancied a friendly post-slaughter cup of tea, that's all."

Viola laughed. "No, this isn't self-defence. I'm locked out and I've got to try to break in."

He clambered out of the car, bringing with him a loamy scent of fresh earth and greenery. "Don't tell me you're home alone with no babysitter? Is that allowed?"

She hesitated, realizing she'd completely transgressed the basic rules on personal safety that Kate and Miles had been drumming into her head ever since the first demented Rhys fan had posted an anonymous piece of vileness through the Bell Cottage letter box. Too late now, though — she could hardly claim the house was full of lightly dozing occupants, or he'd think *she* was crazy for not having banged on the door or phoned someone to come down and let her in.

"Home alone is allowed, if I promise to behave. And so is going out, which I did earlier, but now I can't get in. I thought I'd unscrew something, somehow."

"Have you done this before?" Greg said, looking doubtfully at her tools of choice.

"Not since I was a teenager. But that time it involved a ladder and it didn't end well. The ladder is long gone and there's a paramedic out there who probably still wakes in the night reliving my howls of pain."

"Ew — sounds grim. But hey, I'm sure between us we can get in somewhere. Then you can tell me why you haven't got a key. Or Fort Knox-style security."

This last comment hit a nerve with Viola and "irksome", the word of the evening, came back to mind.

"Look, if you're going to tell me off, please go home right now," she snapped. "I *know* I shouldn't be able to get in without alarm bells ringing everywhere, the police swarming in and a big dog ready to take my leg off. It's all on the to-do list, OK?"

"Fine, I get it!" Greg backed away, laughing, which irritated her even more. "Just please don't wave that huge hammer at me. Don't you have a neighbour with a key?"

"If there is one, I don't know who it is. It's my mother's house, she's away for a night and I'm only staying here on a temporary basis. We can hardly knock on all the doors — the keyholder could be anyone or no one. And don't suggest I give my ma a call — I really don't want her knowing what an idiot I've been. Key down the drain, a bloody classic. And not the first time I've done it either." She assumed he'd say it could happen to anyone, but he didn't. She shouldn't have minded about that but somehow she did, a bit.

The ground-floor doors and window frames proved just as resilient to the tools as they had to Viola's early feeble tugging.

"Proper hardwood doorframes, that's the problem. You can't jemmy these open without doing serious damage to them," Greg said after investigating all possible entry routes. "Are you sure there's no ladder? I can see a little window open up there but I don't think we can risk drainpipes. Even in films they tend to come unfixed and fall down."

"Definitely no ladder, sorry. I'll have to break one of the small panes on the French doors. The key is in the lock on the other side so it'll be easy after that. I just didn't want broken glass all over the floor inside, but I guess it's going to be the price of getting in and to bed tonight."

"There needn't be glass. Hang on there for a sec, I've got something in the car."

Viola waited, beginning to feel quite chilly now. If she'd had a credit card with her she'd have been tempted to see if she could get a room at the local Travelodge and deal with all this in friendlier daylight, but she'd taken only the bare minimum out with her that night. A big fox trotted across the garden, turning to give her a dismissive sneer before leaping easily on to Joe-next-door's fence. She heard the animal jump down on to the dustbins and a bin bag being ripped by teeth. That would be a mess for old Joe to face in the morning. She crossed to the fence and banged the screwdriver hard and noisily against it, but wasn't surprised that the animal hesitated for only a few seconds before going on with his search for a chicken carcass.

"Gaffer tape!" Greg returned, looking pleased with himself. He ripped several long pieces of it and attached them to the glass pane nearest the lock so it was completely covered, then hit it firmly with the handle end of the hammer. It fell to the floor on the far side.

"There you go, there'll be nothing to clear up. If it hasn't even cracked, you can probably putty it straight back in the morning," he said as he reached in through the hole to find the key.

Later, Viola wondered how the two of them had managed to be so involved in what they were doing that they hadn't clocked the flashing blue lights or the sound of tyres whirling fast on the gravel at the front of the house. Before their presence had even registered with the housebreakers, two uniformed police officers with blinding torches were beside them. Viola had a very fast flashback to the last time she was in such close police company — the night they sent the sorrowful-looking policewoman round to give her some muddled information that — because the poor woman didn't seem able to use the word "dead" — involved the fact that Rhys wouldn't be coming home. Viola had replied, rather ridiculously it seemed afterwards, that she already knew he wouldn't because he'd just walked out on her, taking a very big suitcase and quite likely another woman with him. It had taken her many slow minutes to understand that he wouldn't be coming back to *anyone's* home. Ever again.

"You were saying something earlier about swarms of police?" Greg reminded her as they found themselves being bundled fast towards a patrol car slewed in at a dramatic angle that had left deep, dark skid tracks in the gravel, and trapped between it and the smooth broad fronts of Kevlar vests.

"What are you doing?" Viola tried but failed to wriggle out of a very firm grip. "I live here. We were just trying to get in because I was locked out and no one else is home," she explained, quickly looking up at the neighbours' houses for twitching curtains and bedroom lights. Which one had dobbed her in? Could it have been Joe? She might have woken him when she'd banged on the fence to scare the fox.

"So you'll have some ID to show us then?" one of them asked. He was overweight and overheated and breathing cheese-and-onion-crisp fumes into her face. Greg fumbled in his pocket and handed over a driving licence with a photo on.

"Er . . . hell, no, sorry, I haven't. Not a thing. Not out here anyway," Viola said. She wished she could back out of range, but he'd got her up against his patrol car. "I've been out for the evening and just took cash with me."

"Bloody Neighbourhood Watch," Greg, beside her, grumbled.

"Oy, enough of that. They do a good job," crisp-breath said. "Run a quick check, Sam. Name?" he asked Viola.

"Viola Hendricks."

Sam muttered into his radio for a while, then looked across at his colleague and nodded his head. "Him," he said, indicating Greg and looking pleased. "Oh yes! Got something on this one. But the lady, not listed for this address."

"Nothing? Right. Looks like we'll have to take you both in." Crisp-breath looked as if he'd won a major bet.

"I'm so sorry," Viola told Greg, unable to say more as they were bundled into the car. She was so tired that, like a child who's had too much excitement, tears threatened.

"No, *I'm* sorry. They'd probably have believed you on your own and you'd be in by now."

144

She felt him try to reach out to her, but he couldn't get far. You can't, she realized, in handcuffs.

Naomi finished the Ed McBain and switched the light off. She could hear Monica snoring evenly in the next room and she asked any available celestial beings to keep them both safe till morning. Strange evening, she thought as she settled down in Monica's spare room (one that smelled slightly of old shoes, but that was all right. Everyone had old shoes. The scent of them was quite homey). Monica had got a bit serious after the third gin and asked her if she had regrets. Well, who hadn't? As the song didn't quite go: too many to mention but no point dwelling on them now. Monica had told her she regretted never visiting South America, never having tried being blonde and also having only one child.

"It'll be a terrible burden for him, when I'm really crocked. You're all right with your three, they can share you out," Monica said, pouring just one small extra gin. "I don't want to be that burden. When it comes to it, I'll have to bow out early. You might have to give me a hand with that. I'd do it for you, you know, if the need arose."

Naomi said nothing, but thought of the old sign that used to be on the wall under the clock in the corner shop when she was a young mother: "Please don't ask for credit as a refusal often offends". Like Viola outside the locked house, she'd been here before.

CHAPTER
THIRTEEN

"Assaulting a police officer. Affray. Among other things." The desk sergeant glared at Greg with clear disgust and Viola felt scared. So it seemed he had a record and that meant he was forever to be treated with hostility and suspicion. Great, and all this absolutely wasn't his fault. Viola couldn't offer any evidence at all that she lived where she claimed. Greg's identity wasn't in doubt but, on the downside, if the two of them had been going to a fancy-dress party, he, with his old black gardening hoodie, earth-smeared face and roll of gaffer tape, couldn't have been more convincing as a putative burglar if he'd been wearing a striped top and a mask and was stuffing silverware into a bag marked Swag.

At the police station the handcuffs were removed, the custody sergeant booked them in and they were taken to separate interview rooms "just for a little chat". Greg was led away by a pert, smiley red-headed woman in pink trainers, while Viola was taken to a bleak, overlit little room by a short, rotund detective whose tight shiny suit had been bought a good many pies ago.

"So you didn't want to make a phone call then?" Viola's detective asked, smirking at her from across his desk.

"I didn't think I'd need to bother anyone. It's so late. This could all be sorted out so quickly." Or could it, she thought suddenly? Who would be best to confirm her story?

"Paperwork. We like our paperwork. Makes life tidy," he said, indicating a clipboard on the table, a form that had already been filled in. "Name?"

"Viola Hendricks. I already told the other officer."

"Address?"

"Thirty-six, Langmead Avenue." She wondered if it were possible to feel more tired without actually falling off the chair. "I can see it there on the form. Also your blokes just picked me up from there."

"Do you have any documents on you to prove you live there?"

"No, none," she said, wearily. "This is just a silly muddle. I was trying to get into the house, and I *do* live there — for the moment anyway — but I dropped my key and it went down the drain outside the house."

The detective smirked again. "Course you did, love. And what about your mate there?"

"Greg was only helping me, he was just . . . passing." It sounded thoroughly feeble and, even to her, unconvincing.

"He's your boyfriend?" This time she was treated to a leer. The detective lazed right back in his chair, podgy legs too far apart for comfortable viewing, reminding her of a giant panda sprawled, exhausted and full, against a bamboo clump.

"No. A friend." It crossed her mind that he was barely even that, but saying so would only complicate things. "As I said, he was just passing the house and stopped to help me."

He leaned forward again and tapped the clipboard with a pen. "You see, my difficulty is that we've run a check on the address and there is no listing of a Viola Hendricks living there. We did find one a few miles away, though. That would be you, would it? Or is Hendricks not *actually* your name just as *this* isn't *actually* your address? Because what with this and your *boyfriend* being what we call 'known to us', at the moment this is all looking very *untidy*."

"Oh — um, yes, it does look a bit confusing. I *am* who I say I am. I've been staying there with my mother for a while, that's all. She's called Naomi Challen so she'll be the one who's on the records, voting register or whatever it is you have to look at."

"Hmm. Well, it's still not looking *quite* as neat as I'd like. You said it's your house but it isn't. Then there's the little matter of the hammer and the screwdriver. Section 24 of the Theft Act: going equipped to . . ."

"I was *not* 'going equipped'!" Viola interrupted.

"No, but your 'friend' might have been. And he was the one holding them." He chuckled at his own wit.

"He was being helpful. Those things were in the shed, *our* shed, and I was just trying to find a way in! Are you really going to charge me with trying to get home to my own bed?" She felt snappish and irritable, which in the circumstances was possibly not the best way to come across. "Look, I know you're just doing your job and I'm *hugely* reassured that genuine burglars have to go through all this, but I'm *not* one."

"No — because *naice* middle-class *laydees* never commit crimes, do they? Well, believe you me, darlin', they do. I blame feminism. We get some right scum posh totty in here, up to all sorts then pleading big-eyed girly innocence, thinking they can have it both ways. Well, I've seen it all, and they can't."

"Please may I call my sister?" Viola felt thoroughly defeated and close to tears again. She could see herself on the wrong end of a five-year sentence, picked on in prison for being a know-nothing new bug and refusing to be some killer's girlfriend. If she called Miles she'd never hear the end of it, so it would have to be Kate.

The next couple of hours spent sitting in a bleak little cell felt more like days, and Viola had nothing to do but try to rub the fingerprint ink off her fingers. Where was Greg? She really hoped he'd been allowed to go, because none of this was his fault. She tried to imagine him coming up with an explanation for scary Mickey. How, at two in the morning, could you run "I'm so sorry, darling, I got arrested while breaking into a house with that woman I was schmoozing over lunch the other day" past your beloved?

It was noisy and cold down in the cell area, and not knowing what would happen next was terrifying. Viola sat uncomfortably on the hard bench-like bed, hugging the one thin cellular blanket round herself, hoping it wasn't rife with nits, lice or anything catching. It smelled clean enough, at least. And could anyone but comatose drunks ever sleep in these places? There were people shouting from behind closed doors, a woman alternately crying and shrieking, someone banging rhythmically on a door and swearing. A Friday night for the police must be like a constant A & E department: drunks throwing up and throwing punches, volatile muggers, end-of-week domestic violence, idiot pissed-up drivers. Absorbed in the cacophony, she was almost shocked to have her cell door suddenly opened and then to hear the detective with the pink trainers saying, "OK, love, the cavalry's here for you."

"Kate's here?"

"Your sister's here and your boyfriend's waiting. You can go — all cleared up now, no charges." It was all Viola could do not to kiss her as she left the cell.

Kate was waiting by the front desk, sitting very gingerly on the furthest edge of a bench away from two messily weeping, mascara-smudged teenage girls with their arms round each other and their high-heeled shoes off. Viola could just make out a third one outside beyond the sliding doors, being sick over the stair rail. Poor police, was it like this every night?

"Oh Vee! What have you done now?" Kate said, hugging her tightly. "Let's get you out of this horrible place and home. I've brought spare keys for you."

"Hang on, what about Greg? He's still here somewhere, I think."

"Greg? I thought it was just you on your own. Who's Greg?"

"Me," he said, coming in through the doors. He smelled faintly of cigarettes. "I haven't smoked for four years but tonight, well . . ." He looked across at the weeping girls and smiled at them. "Thanks for the ciggy, girls, you are lifesavers. And good luck."

150

"Do hang on here and make friends if you want," Kate said crossly to Greg as she bustled away from the bench. "But I want to get Viola home." And she stalked off through the sliding doors, glaring at the ill teen who was now draped over the stair rail, groaning softly.

Viola whispered, "Sorry," to Greg as they followed Kate out. He gave her hand a quick squeeze and murmured back, "Do you think she'll give me a lift back to yours so I can collect my car, or is she going to make me get a bus with all the sleepy teen drunks?"

"A lift, of course — and if not, we *both* wait for the night bus. That'll be OK, won't it, Kate? Greg's car is at Mum's."

"I suppose," Kate said as she started the car.

"I'm so sorry," Viola said. "I really thought they were going to charge me and keep me all night. I wouldn't have called you if I could have thought of anything else."

"It's all right. It's what family is for." Kate pushed her overlong hair back out of her face. She looked exhausted, as well she might, having been dragged from sleep by Viola's call.

"I suppose it was your idea to break in," Kate accused Greg by way of the rear-view mirror.

"Um . . . well, er . . . not exactly . . ."

"It's nothing to do with Greg," Viola told her. "He was just helping me out. He had a neat trick with the glass pane."

"I bet he did," Kate snarled. "So where had you two been this evening?"

151

Grumpiness began to cool the lovely warm gratitude Viola had been feeling. This was definitely more like a cross-examination of a naughty fourteen-year-old than a general social question. "Nowhere; well, not together. I'd been out to see a band in Fulham with Amanda and Leo. Greg had been . . . out somewhere else."

"Just doing a spot of gardening," Greg said. He and Viola exchanged a look and she wanted to giggle. Somehow she felt this wouldn't have gone down well with Kate. They'd reached the house now and Kate stopped the car in the driveway, behind Greg's grubby Land Rover.

"This yours?" she asked, looking unimpressed. Viola wondered if Kate would have perked up a bit if the car had been something a tad smarter. Probably. She'd been very impressed by Rhys's Porsche the first time she'd seen it, giggling flirtily and making him take her for a run round the block in it.

"It is. I'd better see if it starts. Sometimes it doesn't like damp nights. Also, cross your fingers I don't get arrested all over again for a dodgy tail light or something. I don't much want to go back to my cell, cosy and supremely luxurious as it was. Kate, thanks so much for the lift and, Viola, may I call you in the morning? Just to see if you're OK? I can come and do the glass for you if you like."

"I'll get my husband to sort the glass," Kate told him briskly. "No need for you to put yourself out."

"Kate, please don't be like that!" Viola protested. "Tonight *wasn't* Greg's fault! And yes, please do call, Greg. If only to reassure me that Mickey hasn't thrown you out on the street for this. I don't think I'd like to be a fly on the wall when you tell her."

"Mickey?" He looked puzzled. "Oh, she doesn't need to know any of this." He gave Viola a hug and surprised her with a brief kiss on the cheek, then said, "Goodnight, both of you. Kate — good to meet you. And thanks for the lift." Then the wolfish grin was flashed quickly at Viola. "Tomorrow," he said.

"How did you persuade them to let me go?" Viola had to ask as soon as they were inside the house and in the warmth of the flat's little kitchen. She filled the kettle and took mugs and tea bags out of the cupboard. Kate slumped into a chair and rested her chin on her hands, still looking doomy and somehow old, as Viola had noticed the other day. It was a reasonable question, although Kate was taking her time about answering it. After all, she wouldn't have had any more ID-proving documents than Viola herself. Eventually, she pulled her bag up on to the table and took out the framed wedding photo of Rhys, Viola and herself that Viola had seen beside Kate's bed.

"Easy. I took this along. They knew all about Rhys, from the night of . . . of the accident. So I showed the horrible detective this photo and they looked up something on the computer and found you, and some press stuff and other photographs too. Really, all they had to do was Google in the first place and I'd said so on the phone, but the sergeant said you seemed 'upset'. Think it's a euphemism for rabidly unbalanced. You could have told them you were his . . . widow."

"It never crossed my mind. And if they thought I was a bit loopy they'd probably not have believed me anyway."

Kate was quiet for a moment, then said, "You never did bother to change your name to his, did you? I always wondered about that."

"I wanted to keep my name the same as Rachel's, that's all." Viola wrapped her hands round her mug of tea, absorbing all the warmth she could. Three thirty in the morning wasn't a time she'd have chosen to be talking about this. In fact, no time was.

"Is it? Are you sure you didn't always kind of half wonder if you and Rhys would really stay the distance? I . . . used to wonder about it."

Viola's hands were trembling as she lifted the mug to sip the tea. Any more left-field questions and it would be all over the table. "Did you? Why?"

Kate shrugged and got up, fetching milk from the fridge and adding more to her tea. "No real reason. I . . . you . . . well, you didn't seem his type, somehow."

"He didn't have a type," Viola said grimly. "Unless you count female. *Any* type in fact, really. He wasn't fussy."

"He was, you know. Deep down. I always felt there was a side of him that longed for something, I don't know, *more* . . ."

"Oh, you knew that, did you?" Viola snapped. "Thanks for that, Kate, but you couldn't possibly know, not really. You hardly knew him."

"Don't be ridiculous, of course I did. You'd never have met him yourself if I hadn't." Kate gnawed a thumbnail, worrying at it hard between her canine teeth.

"Well, OK, but if you're going to tell me he only married me to look a bit less bad-boy, as a career move, then please don't. I think I'd already worked that out by the end of the honeymoon. And no, I didn't wonder about the 'distance'. Though I probably should have. Enough people warned me, and we did get married ridiculously soon after we'd met. And come on, even you didn't try to persuade me not to, did you?"

"No, I didn't." Kate sounded bitter, full of regret, and Viola felt softer towards her.

"Hey, you mustn't even slightly blame yourself. I made my own stupid mistake there, all by myself."

"I only blame myself for introducing you to him in the first place. It seemed a good idea at the time." She smiled.

"But honestly, Kate, if I *did* wonder if it would go the distance, which I didn't — because even though it was all too rushed and stupid and completely mad, if I'd had any doubts I'm sure I wouldn't have married him — I certainly wouldn't for a minute have imagined that distance would be so short or so abrupt."

"No. Well. None of us did, did we?"

CHAPTER
FOURTEEN

Four hours of restless sleep were nowhere near enough, but Viola needed to join every weekend DIY enthusiast on a trek to Homebase to find a tin, tube or jar, whatever it came in, of putty before Naomi got home from Monica's and started asking questions. She really didn't want to explain the events of last night, not yet anyway. That day would come — Kate would make sure Naomi and Miles knew all about it as soon as she got a chance. Just, not yet, preferably only when she was settled back in Bell Cottage and out of range of being fussed over.

Her text alert beeped as she was climbing out of bed: Greg. *This* early? In fact, at all? After last night she was very surprised he even thought of contacting her, ever, ever again. What was his excuse for being awake and texting before 8a.m., given the hour he must have got to sleep? Ah — *if* he'd got to sleep. She imagined Mickey furiously refusing to let him in after double-locking all the doors, swearing robustly as she flung his possessions out of an upstairs window and forced him to sleep in the office or the Land Rover under a heap of old compost sacks and fake banana leaves.

"On way with putty in about half hour," she read. "Request payment in coffee, also bacon sandwich."

She couldn't help smiling. She was about to reply when it beeped again.

"You do have bacon? Or are you a veggie?"

"Not a veggie," she texted back. "Coffee on, also bacon."

Rachel's room in James and Marco's big, light apartment off Lansdowne Road was a blissful place to wake up. The flat was on two levels of one of the huge white houses in the road, and her little bedroom and shower room were downstairs at the front of the building, with a door leading out to the porch steps. Marco kept that door firmly locked and had made her promise that even when she hit the most delinquent and sneaky part of teenagehood, she would never creep out and up these steps in the night. He said he'd always rather know where she was, even if she was sliding out to devil-worship classes. Behind her personal territory, the sitting room and kitchen at the back opened on to a bright sunny terrace which James had planted with lush clumps of agapanthus, and where he waged war on fat aphids that sneaked up every evening and attacked his favourite white lupins in their black granite pots. A gate led through to the communal private garden shared by the houses around the square, and when she took James and Marco's little spaniel Cyndi for a walk in there she always hoped to see somebody phenomenally famous playing with their small children. How cool would it be to drop into a school conversation over a copy of *Heat* magazine that (really nonchalant voice here), "Oh, yeah, *him*. Saw him on Sunday, pushing his baby on a swing, and y'know, he's quite short in real life."

Rachel was awake early, watching the passing silhouetted shape of a woman with a big dog breaking up the stripes on the wall where the sun sneaked in through the quarter-open plantation blinds. She was supposed to keep them completely shut overnight: Marco said the thought of some creepy snooper being able to catch even the smallest glimpse of her while she slept was just too horrific, and the scene in *Twilight* where the vampire boy had crept in to watch Bella sleeping had given him the shivers. (She had argued that this was *teen* fiction and not aimed at people's dads and their hang-ups, but all he'd said to that was she would get it, that and the not-sneaking-out thing, once she was a parent.) All the same, Rachel hated complete, disorientating darkness and needed a sliver of streetlight to give her a sense of life still going on outside overnight.

One of Oliver Stonebridge's paintings, like the ones at home and at Gran's, a scene of stormy sea and exaggeratedly angular pier at Brighton, was on the wall opposite her bed. It made, for her, a link between home with her mum and this other home here with Marco and James. There were other links too — the chrome Anglepoise lamp by her bed was the same as at home (*real* home, not Gran's), and her duvet covers were the same white waffly ones too.

The flat was stirring into life. She could hear muffled sounds from the kitchen TV and the whirr of the

Magimix, which meant James was up and about. He was always first in the kitchen, needing a caffeine fix the moment he was up, and he also liked making her breakfast treats — smoothies, waffles, the kind of thing you would never get on a rushed school morning. Marco and James always said she had to think of their place as home, just as she did with Viola, but sometimes it felt like being at a luxury villa or a boutique hotel — or, at least, what she'd read about them in magazines. They were taking her to Ireland in a couple of weeks, for a holiday in a horse-drawn gypsy caravan. She was looking forward to it, but couldn't help wondering how the two men would cope without their fantastic multi-way shower and their espresso machine.

Rachel, now wide awake and scenting coffee, had a quick shower and pulled on her denim shorts and a T-shirt. The sunlight through the blind slats told her the day was going to be a gorgeous one, and she wanted to be outside.

"Hi, James!" she greeted her father's partner, who was now out on the terrace at the ironwork table with *The Guardian* and a dense-looking cup of coffee. "Shall I take Cyndi into the square?" she asked. The little golden spaniel, guessing what she was saying, bounced to her feet from where she'd been lying under James's chair.

"Hello, darling, sleep well? And yes, please, do take Cyndi for a run around — if you don't mind being on poo duty. They are *very* strict here and quite right too. Bags are under the sink. I've whizzed up pancakes for breakfast — fancy that?"

"Yum! Ten minutes? I'll take Cyndi's ball — she loves that."

The garden square was empty and so silent Rachel almost felt like tiptoeing around. The pink and yellow roses climbing the perimeter fences showed off their full-bloom glory only to her. No children were yet scrabbling about on the climbing frame or fighting over the swings. There was no litter, no discarded cans, no graffiti, no branches pulled from the trees like in the park and on the riverside at home after a hot summer night. Only the scent of an unseen somebody smoking nearby spoiled the perfect morning. Cyndi, excited at the space and freedom, bounded around on the grass, chasing the raggy old tennis ball Rachel threw for her, then finding a spot under a buddleia bush to deposit a neat pile of crap.

If Rachel was for a moment tempted to leave it where it lay, one look at the hundreds of windows surrounding the garden told her that there'd be sure to be someone who noticed her negligence. She took the plastic bag from her pocket and approached the heap, wrinkling her nose.

"Aww, so who's a good little schoolgirl then?" A taunting voice came from a bench just beyond the bushes. Rachel straightened up, her bag of dog shit dangling from her fingers. She held it away from her body, conscious that it was still repellently warm. Terrific — just what any girl would choose. To come across the boy she's been fancying when she's carrying a bag of dog doo.

"You can't just leave it." She went across to the bench and sat beside him. Ned was in an old white T-shirt with a black and white Debbie Harry on the front, not wearing the tobacco-coloured cardigan he'd bought from her. This disappointed her, which was ridiculous, as who would want to wear wintry cashmere when it was already so hot out? His hair was all over the place and he looked as if he'd just got out of bed, which he probably had. She wondered about his room, whether it was an untidy heap of clothes, trainers and electronics or if he was a neat-nerd. She'd guess the first one.

"I could," Ned said, flinging his cigarette end under the roses. "But then, me, I wouldn't have a dog. I might in the country, not here."

"She's my dad's dog." She instantly felt a bit disloyal to lovely Cyndi. She sounded as if she were disowning her for the sake of agreeing with this boy. She threw the tennis ball and Cyndi sprinted off after it, tongue lolling and glossy golden fur rippling. He'd called her schoolgirl again, she noted, wondering if that was because he'd already forgotten her name. And only yesterday he'd been sort of asking her out. She slid the bag of dog poo under the bench. She had to deal with it, yes, and take it with her to put in the garden's dog bin, but she didn't have to be clutching it in her hand while they had a conversation.

"So, Schooly," he said. "You live on this square too. Which house?"

"Over there." She pointed. "And you?"

"Back that way." He nodded vaguely in the direction of the far side, where the houses were on an even bigger scale. "Usual thing, folks, sister, baby sister, *people*." He shrugged as if disconnecting himself from his entire family.

"So can you get in here from your own garden or do you have to go round to the gate?" It was a totally lame question but she didn't really know what else to say to him. Why didn't sparkling conversation come instantly to her head? But it *was* very early in the morning.

"Huh? Not sure what you mean . . ."

What was so hard to understand? For a moment she considered that he might be really a bit dense. Not good and potentially so disappointing. "I mean, my dad, he's got the lower-level apartment with the garden, so . . ."

"Oh it's a *flat*?" He looked rather confused, as if he'd *heard* of people who lived in apartments but had never actually met any. Perhaps he hadn't. How exotic would he find Emmy, who lived in a council flat? "Right. No mine's, like, you know, like a *house*. So yes, garden. Gate. All the usual."

"Nice." She took another look across the gardens, at where he'd indicated earlier. What was it Marco had said about that side with the massive, stupendously expensive houses? 'Banker wankers' was the term he'd used, she was sure. Ned's dad must be one. Or his mum. Probably both.

"I don't live here all the time," she said. "I live with my mum mostly."

"Hang around here long enough and you'll get scouted for a model. Or has it happened already?" He reached across and picked up a hank of her hair, twisting it up behind her neck in a knot. "You look OK. Nice legs. A camera would love you."

She laughed. He'd forgotten her name, sure, but he was definitely flirting. "No, it hasn't happened! Why would it? And anyway, I don't want to be a model. I want to be a . . . oh, I don't know, a doctor or a vet or something."

"A vet? That is, like, *so* gay!" He was laughing at her. But what was so funny?

"So 'gay'?" she challenged. "You can't say that. It's wrong to use it like that. Like it's insulting."

"No, it's not! Course it's not. What's your problem? It's just *something you say*. Not an insult."

"I don't say it. Not ever. Not everyone does! It's . . . it's *gayist*?" She couldn't think of the right word. Typical.

"Gayist? What, like homophobian or wha'ever? But I'm so not!"

"Well, don't say it then!" Whistling to Cyndi, who trotted up beside her, she got up from the bench and stalked off, back towards James and Marco's flat.

"Rachel!" he called after her. She refused to look back in spite of an involuntary inner tingle that he had, after all, remembered her name. Hell, what would she be like if he ever actually kissed her? Not that she wanted him to now. Not ever, not after what he'd so carelessly said. She heard thumping footsteps coming after her.

"Rachel?" He stood in front of her, forcing her to stop. He looked into her eyes, his face so close to hers she could see all the tiny individual flecks of colour in his grey eyes.

"You forgot this." He handed over the little plastic bag of Cyndi's shit as tenderly as if it had been a bag of rare birds' eggs.

"Thank you," she said solemnly, taking it from him, then flounced past him and continued her walk of protest, trying to keep her head up and some dignity. Not easy when you're carrying a bag of excrement and trying, in spite of stubbornly insisting on making your point, so damn hard not to laugh.

"It looks like I owe you again, Greg. You keep rescuing me and I can't thank you enough, but you don't have to, you know. I was going to fix the window myself, *should* have done it myself, being a capable twenty-first century woman," Viola said to Greg later as he finished reattaching the window pane.

A sparkly look and the raised eyebrows told Viola that Greg wasn't entirely convinced. Given her track record with him so far, it wasn't really surprising.

"But it was me who broke the window in the first place. It was me who screwed up our lunch thing the other day — Mickey can be such a bossy cow, but deep down it was my own fault. I knew that marquee had to go back but I wanted a bit of time with you. As for the window, you've paid me for it royally in bacon rolls and coffee."

"Yes, but it was my idea *to* break the window. It was me who was locked out, not you."

"Hey, what does it matter?" He looked up at her from squidging in the last of the putty, treating her to the playful-Alsatian smile again. "It's all sorted now."

"So did you get a lot of grief from Mickey last night?" It was a question Viola had been dying to ask since he walked in, looking amazingly well rested and with the curled ends of his hair still shower-damp. So he hadn't had to sleep in the Land Rover, then. He cleared the last smear of putty from the glass.

"Mickey? No — I haven't seen her." Viola had a vision of a cross half-woken woman, head firmly lodged under a pillow in protest at her husband staggering into the bedroom and disturbing her in the dawn hours. She pictured her sliding out of their house before seven to take a long run along the riverbank and across the common so she could come panting in later before Greg was even awake, all smugly exercised to make a point about how *some* people didn't carouse about all night. Except he wouldn't have been there . . . he was here, with someone else. Not that she counted as *that* kind of "someone else". Absolutely not.

He was sniffing at the greyish sludge of putty that was left on his thumb. "I love the scent of this stuff, don't you? Linseed. Clean, luscious oil. Here, have a whiff." He offered up his thumb under her nose and she put her hand on his wrist, steadying it while she inhaled the smell, not quite trusting him not to smudge it all over her nose and think it hilarious.

"Mmm — it's giving me a déjà vu," Viola said. "It's a real flashback to something from years ago. There was this family friend we used to call Uncle Oliver. He was a painter and Mum took me to see him in his studio sometimes. I must have been about six, I think. It was really messy there, the kind of seriously untidy that really impresses a small child. There were paint tubes and pots of oil everywhere, the floorboards were all spattered with paint and canvases were leaning against the wall. Mum kept telling me to be careful and not to touch and he said none of it mattered, I could do anything I wanted. He gave me a brush and a bit of board and squeezed dollops of oil paint out on to a palette for me. So I could paint while they drank wine and talked." Viola stopped for breath, thinking how much this must *not* be of any interest to Greg. Why would it be?

"Sorry — I'm rambling." She turned away to collect up their coffee mugs and take them to the kitchen.

"No, go on, what did he paint?"

"Landscapes, sometimes seaside scenes as well. Turbulent stuff. He was called Oliver Stonebridge; quite well known in his day. There's a really scary, stormy one that Mum keeps on the top landing. I always used to run fast past it when I was little, trying not to look."

"I've heard of him, vaguely. Dead, isn't he?" Greg was loading his tools into their box. He'd be gone in a few minutes and the day — with Rachel over in Notting Hill — would be all hers.

166

"Yes, years ago. Mum wore scarlet and purple to his funeral because he'd told her — she said — that she looked terrible in black."

"Who looks terrible in black?" Naomi strode in through the French doors at that moment, clutching her bag from the night before. "I know you," she said, not waiting for Viola to answer, jabbing a finger towards Greg. "That car out there — you brought our Vee home in it after her puncture." She turned to Viola and asked, "So is this going to be a new friend?"

"Possibly," Greg answered warily.

"You're here very early. It's only just gone nine." Naomi looked past the two of them, glancing round the room, expertly checking for evidence of some kind and then seeming distinctly disappointed.

"If you're looking for signs of . . ." Viola was going to say "a night of passion", but thought better of it.

Greg looked at his watch. "Yes, it is early, isn't it? How was your evening? And have you only just come home?"

He was teasing Naomi. A dangerous game, Viola wanted to warn him. She could feel the words "walk of shame" about to come up in the next sentence. She managed to suppress a wave of laughter and gave Greg a warning prod. Naomi didn't do humour in the mornings, only suspicion.

"I have just come home, thank you. I could hear voices so I thought I'd come and see who it was. But if you're going to stay around, Mr New Friend, you'll want to get something different to drive," Naomi told him. "Green's very unlucky for cars. Anyone'll tell you

167

that, especially this one." She nodded towards Viola, then stalked grandly across the flat's sitting room and through the door to her own part of the house.

"You nearly accused her of having a naughty night, didn't you?" Viola said, trying not to smart from the reference to green cars, as soon as Naomi had gone.

"I very nearly did," Greg agreed. "And as a reward for *not* saying it, you have to promise me something."

"I do?"

"You have to come out planting with me one night, just so you can see for yourself there's no murder involved."

Viola felt a bit torn. Yes, she was madly curious about his nocturnal gardening and, yes, she'd admit there was a thrill about the idea of seeing him again, but — there was the Mickey factor. Although . . . digging a hole in the ground and stuffing in some hardy perennials was hardly a hot adulterous date.

"But . . . why do you do it? It seems, well, *weird,* to say the least."

He shrugged. "Just something I got into, something I read about in one of the Sunday papers — guerrilla gardening. There's so much that's bloody wrong with the world, wars and bloody banker bonuses and stupid governments making the poor even poorer. I mean, you can go on any number of protest marches and sign petitions, but they don't make *everyday* stuff less bleak. Who can't be a tiny bit cheered up by seeing flowers in a wilderness? *Real* plants, not the tat I rent out for the day job to the make-believe con industry. Sorry, sounds so fucking worthy."

168

"Protests, then — is that how come you've got a police record?"

"Yep, anti Iraq war. Not proud of the record, but the cop lammed me with a truncheon so I pushed him away, hard. Six of them were on me in a millisecond. *All* with truncheons. Anyway, did the crime, did the community service and now I'm into planting flowers where no one expects them. Got to be the safest form of subversion ever, hasn't it?" He grinned at her. "Go on, tell me I'm a wuss."

"You're a total wuss," she said. "An activist with a trowel."

"So will you come out and plant something with me?"

"Won't your wife mind?"

"I doubt it. My wife is my ex-wife and lives with her new husband and three-year-old son in Vancouver, and I've got no current plans to offer the vacancy to anyone else."

"OK, then. Yes, I'll come out. So long as we don't get arrested again."

"I'll give you a call. And when we're out in the dark and I smear your face with mud, just think of being a kid again with your Uncle Olly."

CHAPTER
FIFTEEN

By Wednesday, the Bell Cottage hallway and kitchen were already painted, the sitting room ceiling was done and there were three lads painting walls with fat rollers, covering the space in double-quick time.

"Talk about fast," Viola said to Marco when they'd called in to check on the progress. "They've done almost all of downstairs already. Didn't they only start on Friday?"

"They're scenery boys, that's the trick. They're used to squeezed time limits," he told her. "And there wasn't a lot of preparation to be done so it's kind of instant result, which cuts the costs. What do you think of the pink kitchen wall?"

"Fabulous — I love it. I can't wait to have all my own stuff back in the house. I keep feeling, and I know this is mad . . ." She hesitated.

"No, go on, what?"

"It's like getting another go at everything, starting grown-up life all over again. Another chance to get it right. No more screw-ups."

"Ha! You think? What about Friday night?" Marco was laughing at her. She felt a bit hurt.

"I wish I hadn't told you now!"

170

"I wish you'd told me on the night, Vee. You know I'm always here for you."

"I didn't want Rachel to worry. What would you have done, woken her up and said I won't be long, I'm just off to bail your mum out of jail?"

"OK, when you put it like that . . ."

"Exactly. And she *definitely* doesn't need to know I spent hours in the cells — it'd be all over her Facebook page in minutes and her friends would look at me funny. It's bad enough I had to involve Kate. It's even more ammunition in her battle to keep me shacked up with Mum and out of harm's way. Also, Mum hasn't stopped raving about Monica's flat since she spent the night there, though she did say there was too much beige in it. I'm hoping that she'll come round to the idea that moving isn't such a terrible thing after all."

"Hmm . . . good luck with that. How will you run it past her?"

"I won't. Not directly. It'll have to be her idea, *just* hers, or she'll think she's being manipulated. If anything, a bit of opposition might help to persuade her. For that I'd need Kate and Miles. But, well . . . you've seen how they are. It won't be easy. I just wish . . ."

"Wish what? That we'd gone for Dead Salmon in the hallway?" Marco asked.

"No . . . that it could be something other than her having to be on her own again for a while to persuade her that she'd be happier and that life would be easier up in the retirement flats. To come round to that way of thinking — as she's so determined at the moment to

171

stay put — she'll probably need to feel lonely, or something negative anyway. I don't want that for her, I really don't."

"I know, and it'll be something she won't admit to easily, either. Your ma can be stubborn to the max."

"She wouldn't say she was stubborn, she'd just insist she wants to be on home ground, with her own things around her. I know how she feels." Viola sighed, happy just to be in the cottage again, even though its furniture hadn't yet come out of storage.

"You'll be back in here soon — and hey, look, this was on the doormat when I got here." Marco handed her an envelope. "Looks like a card, hand-delivered anyway, no stamp."

Viola didn't recognize the writing and slit the envelope open. There was a greetings card inside, a painting of a cute rural cottage. Inside, the sender had written the words "Welcome back", but hadn't signed it. She felt cold and shoved the card back in the envelope quickly.

"Who's it from?" Marco asked. "One of the neighbours?"

"No. Well, could be, I suppose. I don't know. They haven't signed it." She handed it over to Marco and he took a look and frowned, then said, "Probably just forgot. Must be from someone round here who's seen you coming and going lately. Nice of them, isn't it?"

"I hope so. You don't think . . ."

"If you're thinking it might be one of those crazy bats who used to chase Rhys, then no, I don't think.

They've long moved on, haven't they? Grown up at last, maybe."

Viola tried to feel reassured but didn't, quite. Rhys's fame had been pretty fleeting in the long-term scheme of things, so Marco was almost sure to be right. But all the same, this was a bit unnerving.

"I'd rip it up and bin it, but if it *is* a neighbour that would be horribly rude, wouldn't it?" she said, taking the card and stuffing it into one of the kitchen-dresser drawers.

"And even if it isn't, it's no one who can really hurt you now, is it? Look at it this way, if it *is* one of the crazy ones, at least it says something nice," Marco told her, giving her a gentle squeeze.

"Yes — you're right. Positive thinking — only way forward. Just . . . please don't mention it to anyone in my family, will you?"

"Not a chance. No worries on that."

The book group was going to take a summer break, but Charlotte had been the one to choose their next read and insisted on one more meeting before the holidays took over their lives, which meant they'd only had three weeks to read the whole of *Middlemarch* — Charlotte's ambitious choice.

They were meeting at Amanda's and Amanda hauled Viola into the kitchen before letting her join the others. "The barman at the club phoned Leo this morning, so I've got good news and bad news about your stolen bag," she told her, as the two of them sliced up the cake while the others settled in the next room and made a start on the discussion.

"So someone found it?"

"Yes. It was found on a window ledge behind a blind. That's the good news."

"How can there be bad news?"

"Um . . . Leo brought it back here. It smelled funny and had a water mark-type of stain. I think someone's peed in it."

"Wow — talk about expressing disappointment at the lack of profitable contents. That's gross."

"I actually chucked the bag. Thought you might not . . . you know . . ."

"Thanks," Viola said, feeling a bit flat. "Who would do such a horrible thing?" She thought about the man who had followed her to their table. It might or might not have been him. Probably not. The point was, you couldn't tell anything about anyone. She thought briefly of Greg, out there in the night transforming old patches of scruffy ground into little pieces of living colour, for the pleasure of strangers. Did he ever wonder if it was worth the trouble, when the world was full of random, careless nastiness?

"No idea." Amanda shrugged. "I wish I hadn't told you now. I thought there might be a funny side, but . . ."

Viola smiled. "Oh, give it a month or two and there might be. For now though, it's just a bit vile. Depressing. But hey, I can hear Charlotte giving them hell in there. Let's go and rescue them with cake."

174

"So — OK, so I got it wrong." Charlotte wasn't happy. "I should have realized most of you wouldn't be able to read all the way through a huge — huge and *important* — book like *Middlemarch* in less than our usual month. It was just *too* big an ask. Wrong choice, mea culpa." After a second or two's pause, Charlotte then added, "My fault." She obviously felt that if they couldn't read the entirety of *Middlemarch* in the time allowed, then no way were the book group going to understand a bit of basic Latin. She wasn't exactly sulking, but her lips had gone thin and she briskly waved away the piece of cake (coffee and walnut) that Amanda offered her. It was only a gesture, Viola could tell. Her eyes followed the plate quite longingly as it was passed to Jessica, next along on the sofa, who took a piece eagerly and downed half of the generous slice in one groaningly voluptuous bite.

"Did *you* get through it, Char?" Viola asked, feeling a new sympathy for her Med and Gib pupils and their never-ending work-avoidance excuses. "It's massive — how on earth did you find the time?"

"Well, obviously I've read it before. I assumed we all would have and that really we'd just need a skim through, a bit of a reminding catch-up. Didn't absolutely everyone do it for A level?"

"Not me," Jessica said, licking smudged icing from round her mouth. "But then I was all Maths, Physics and Chemistry. It's why I enjoy book groups like this one that do the more classic stuff — you get to go over all the things you missed out on at school. We scientists had a limited education."

"Except you're one of those who didn't finish reading it, Jess," Charlotte pointed out.

"OK — well, let me give you my take on what I *did* read of it, then." Jessica rose to the challenge. "For starters I couldn't really find anyone to like, which is a bit of a put-off, in any kind of book. I hated prim old Dorothea. I couldn't for the life of me imagine why she married dry, dull old Casaubon in the first place unless it was for, oh, let me see — could it be the massive house, the land, the cottages, the money? But no, we're not supposed to feel like that because she's the *nice* worthy one in this book, isn't she? All sacrifice and good works and yet too dim to realize that her old man's great work wasn't worth all those hours wrecking her eyesight to write up."

"Oh, I think she realized that, quite early on probably. Do you think they ever had sex?" Amanda asked. "There didn't seem to be any hint of love or intimacy at all in their relationship. He treated her like a useful servant, as if he'd married her because that was the only respectable way to keep a secretary on permanent duty on the premises, and she behaved, at least at first till the disappointment kicked in, with ridiculous deference."

"So much of the book was about disappointment. Sounds like home!" Lisa said. They all looked at her in some surprise; Lisa was usually a quiet, shy sort, and her contributions to book discussions were usually barely above a whisper and accompanied with a nervous blush.

176

"That's it *exactly*, Lisa!" Charlotte perked up. "*That's* why a book like *Middlemarch* is still so relevant. Expectation versus disappointment. Who couldn't relate to that? I mean, look at Viola."

They all did. Viola felt as if she'd been pinned up on a noticeboard for close inspection. Did Charlotte expect her to come up with an instant three-line homily on how to avoid being a hopeless failure when it came to relationships? Because she couldn't, obviously, because, well . . . she was one.

"She is the ultimate triumph of hope over experience," Charlotte went on, somehow making it sound like a wonderful thing.

"I am?"

"Well, yes! Aren't you? I mean, look at your track record. But you're still up and about and functioning *and* starting to go out again, which is positive, isn't it?" Charlotte gave them all a moment to ponder this, while she got up and went to help herself to a slice of cake. The collective failure to finish the huge novel seemed to have been forgiven: cake could now be taken.

Hostess Amanda handed Charlotte a napkin and fork, and then went round the group topping up their glasses with wine.

"It's not that much of a track record," Viola protested. "I've only had two husbands. Loads of women have more than that."

"Ooh yes, and quite a lot of them have other people's as well, don't they, slotted in among their own!" Jessica's dirty laugh somehow managed to make adultery seem like a jolly hobby, up there with Zumba classes and making sock puppets.

"Yes, they do. Bloody health risks," Viola said, then wished she hadn't, as all eyes were suddenly wider with curiosity. "What? Well, it is, isn't it? A health hazard. Sex with other people's husbands. Unless you're really careful? Look — are we done with the book? Because one thing I want to tell you is that at last I can be host for the next book club. Rachel and I are moving back home soon." She hadn't meant to say this right now, but having seen the collective nosiness she definitely didn't want Charlotte (and it *would* be Charlotte) asking awkward questions about Viola's experience of sexual health hazards. Charlotte would cosy her down, secretly add wine to her glass, do her we've-all-been-there thing but carefully not actually tell anything about herself, so that Viola would end up being the one lured into exposing all.

Before she knew it, she'd be turning her one long-ago trip to the GU clinic into something for them all to laugh at. She thought of how she'd opted — for the first and last time — to use Rhys's surname there, which meant the nurse had squeaked, "Ooh, you're Rhys Llewellen's wife! I saw a picture of your wedding in *OK!* I used to love him in that band, years ago. Can't even remember their name now, ha ha, way it goes." An unlucky bit of recognition, considering there'd just been the one photo shoot, the lack of any more having so infuriated Rhys. And the whole waiting room had looked up from behind newspapers to give her a

178

thorough staring-at. So much for patient confidentiality. And after all that — and a lot of uncomfortable tests — she'd only got a touch of thrush, nothing too serious. But with Rhys, she'd realized just the wrong side of the wedding ceremony, you could never be too careful.

"That's great about you going home. Not before time, too. Much longer and you'd have been a permanent mummy's girl. *Now* you can concentrate even harder on getting back your real life." Charlotte was approving, as if it had all been her idea.

"She's got a real life, Char," Amanda said quietly.

"Yes, but . . . look, what I meant was . . ."

"You meant a man." Lisa was nodding as if a huge burden of new wisdom was on her. "A man is a comfortable thing to have around the place."

"Ha! Not always!" Viola laughed. That was progress. It was a laugh without bitterness, without resentful memory. "I might be in the market for a kitten, if anyone knows of any going, but I'm not looking for a man, thanks."

"No, sweetie. Best not to," Charlotte agreed, rather unexpectedly. "But now it's the holidays, you must come out with me. I have a *thing* to go to and I know you'll love it, so don't even think of saying no. My friend Abigail, she's singing at an event and she is *just* wonderful. Voice to die for. I mean, er . . . she sings like a dream. Anyway, it's invites only and I'd love you to come with me as my Plus One. What do you think?"

What did she think? Well, not every trip out had to end in loss of property, arrest and a sleepless night, did it?

"Where is it? Is it night, day or what?"

"Daytime. Mid-morning, next Thursday, and then we can go for lunch. Very simple and civilized." Charlotte glared at Amanda at this point.

"Hey!" Amanda laughed. "Don't give me that look, Charlotte. It wasn't my fault Viola had her bag nicked!"

"You told Charlotte?" Viola asked.

"Sorry, I just mentioned it in passing. Sorry."

"Nothing like that will happen on *my* watch," Charlotte told Viola. "You'll be fine with me, sweetie. There will be no thieving rabble at *this* event, so there is absolutely no need to worry on that score."

"Oh, I won't," Viola said, although in the face of Charlotte's excessively fervent reassurance she was already starting to feel a slight dread and reluctance to go anywhere at all. Wasn't it always the way? She'd go. In spite of the bag and pee thing she'd go to everything, absolutely everything, anyone invited her to. If she didn't, it could be next stop agoraphobia.

CHAPTER
SIXTEEN

She should have realized. Of course she should. What an idiot. Viola could have kicked herself for being so trusting and unquestioning. After all, the clue had been right there in Charlotte's slyly brief instruction: "It's quite a formal little do." She'd dropped this into their phone chat that morning when she'd called to check Viola was still on for their outing and to tell her what time she'd pick her up, casually adding, "Maybe wear something pretty, you know? Simple, kind of *summer-flowery*, sort of thing?"

Viola should have picked up on the "formal", but somehow it whizzed right over her head because at the time she was talking to Charlotte she was on a very quick early visit to Bell Cottage, and concentrating on making sure that in her bedroom's bright sunlight the shade of palest Caribbean-sea-colour paint Marco had recommended was that essential bit more blue than green. Honestly, though, for what other possible event could you be ordered to come up with "formal", clotheswise, unless you were up in court, possibly? The woman, for brutal thoughtlessness, really took your breath away. Now captive in Charlotte's car, she tried a last-minute protest and resolved that if all else failed, she would just refuse to go in, glorious unmissable voice this Abigail woman might have or not.

"Char, I *really* can't go to this. I don't even know the . . . the . . ."

"The happy couple? Oh, neither do I, but Abigail said it'll be fine," Charlotte supplied with a breezy lack of either hesitation or qualm, as she swung her little Audi convertible into a space in the car park outside the hotel. Ribbons, flowers and balloons decorated the doorway and people were collecting in silkily dressed groups, chatting and laughing.

"You *don't*? You don't have an invitation? Jeez, let's just go home."

"Don't be silly, darling. Anyway, legally I'm sure all weddings are public. We won't even see the bride and groom till after the ceremony and they'll be fairly easy to avoid, trust me."

"Charlotte, I absolutely *don't* want to go gatecrashing strangers' weddings. I mean, *why*? Doesn't this Abigail sing at other events we could have gone to?"

"Well, she does quite a few funerals, but I didn't think you'd want to go to one of those." Charlotte switched off the engine and took hold of Viola's wrist, possibly more to stop her doing a runner than to reassure her. She even had the grace to look a tiny bit shamefaced. "But weddings, they're such *happy* events. You must remember yours — it wasn't that long ago."

"Of course I bloody remember. I'm *so* not doing this."

"Oh, but Abigail . . ."

"Abigail? I don't even *know* bloody Abigail! I don't care if I never, ever hear her phenomenal sodding voice! How could you, Charlotte? This is ridiculous. I thought we were going to a . . . oh, I don't know, a private view at a gallery or something. No wonder you were all mysterious about it." Viola unfastened her seat belt, grabbed her bag and opened the car door, very nearly smashing it into someone who must have been waiting to pounce on them.

"Hello! So glad you could make it. I'm Daniel Fields." A tall and unbelievably glamorous man, one who would certainly come under the heading of "Older" — lustrous long silver hair, a fabulous purple velvety jacket and black silk opera scarf — took Viola's hand and helped her out of the car. "Bride or groom? Sam or Jack?"

"Well, neither," Viola replied firmly, taking back her hand. "Not any . . ."

"Oh! Both — that's even better. May I escort you both into the marriage room?"

"Thank you. So kind," Charlotte said to him, pushing her hair back so her diamond earrings were at maximum twinkle and treating him to her most radiant smile. She even had the nerve to wink at Viola across the back of Daniel. Suddenly, it was a done deal — no backing out, especially when, after her initial fury subsided a bit, Viola considered the distance back up the hotel's long, long gravelled driveway and how much her feet would hurt In These Shoes if she abandoned Charlotte and strode off in a huff to catch a bus home. Also, on the hotel steps the group was now quite a large one and any huff gestures would be seen by all of them. Even though none of these people had ever met her, she could imagine (and oh, how she could imagine . . .) the speculation if she suddenly ran away, probably along the lines that she was a thwarted fiancée or something, come to put a curse on the day.

"Glorious day for it, the photos on the veranda after will be gorgeous," Daniel murmured to Viola as the three of them approached the hotel steps. He smelled lovely, she thought, something floral yet sharply mannish as well.

"Sorry, that's such a stupid thing to say, isn't it?" he chuckled. "But someone at a wedding usually does, if it's sunny. Happy the bride, and all that."

"They do, it's true. As if it makes a difference." Thinking about it though, she considered perhaps it did. The day she'd married Rhys, the rain had poured on the steps of the Marylebone register office. Naomi had said perhaps they shouldn't go through with it, but Rhys had told her he couldn't plan his life on the whims of the Met Office forecasts.

Now as she walked between Charlotte and Daniel, Viola surreptitiously slid her hand inside her jacket and hitched up her knickers through her dress. That had been, she now realized, the morning's first mistake — she'd forgotten that this particular silky pair, unless held firmly in place by either trousers or tights, had an unnerving way of sliding down her hips as she walked.

Inside the marriage room, Viola tried to make Charlotte go into a row at the back so they could escape quickly at the end, but Daniel seemed to have taken on the role of minder, leading them further forward and ushering them into more central seats. A few people nodded and murmured greetings, the groom and his best man gave them a welcoming wave and Viola managed to respond politely, feeling she was on some kind of autopilot.

"If there were hundreds here I wouldn't mind so much," she whispered to Charlotte, "but there's only about fifty. We'll be busted, soon as."

"Smile, darling; just be nice and all will be well."

It was too late anyway as music started, everyone stood and the bride, a woman of about Viola's age, came in, with two young boys of about ten and twelve, dressed in kilts. She was wearing a short, strapless cream dress and carrying the darkest red roses, with a small rose-trimmed tiara on her head.

Viola found herself fishing for tissues in her bag. What was it about weddings that brought on the tears? Little else moved her so easily. Even at Rhys's funeral she'd found it impossible to cry, although there was, around her, plenty of heartfelt sobbing from everyone else, especially Kate, who had howled from the moment the coffin entered the chapel and clutched her arm throughout as if to prevent either of them from falling down in distraught prostration. All the time Viola had felt such a sham — angrily counting the seconds till the ordeal was over and she could push her way out of the church, go back home and lie under a duvet, wishing she'd never, ever, met him.

"There's Abi." Charlotte nudged Viola and pointed a silver-nailed finger at an elfin young blonde woman in a pink taffeta cocktail dress, sitting at the front with her harp, facing the congregation. Abigail caught sight of Charlotte and flickered her fingers discreetly at her, smiling gently as the vows were exchanged. Viola's eyes kept filling as she looked at the couple's faces, full of love and hope.

"Abi's got her professional face on," Charlotte whispered loudly, causing three aunt-like figures in front to turn round with a loud "ssh" chorus.

Abigail only sang at the end of the short ceremony. She played a few seconds of quiet harp and then she began to sing "Love Is All Around" in a clear and soaring voice. Viola had run out of tissues by now. Daniel pushed a perfectly ironed white cotton handkerchief into her hand and she dabbed at her leaky eyes. Charlotte squeezed her hand but she wriggled out of her grip. She wasn't going to forgive her for this so easily.

And it was over. "I'll just play some 'going to the bar music' now," Abigail announced, and the guests started to make their way to the door.

"Can we go now, Charlotte?"

"Just a little drink with Abi first, sweetie. Anyway, you look like you need one. Who knew you were such a softie about weddings?"

"No, really, let's just *go*. Before anyone clocks we shouldn't be here."

"They won't. Who's to know? *Lovely* ceremony, wasn't it?" Charlotte smiled, turning to a guest, one of the aunts who shushed them earlier on. "And such a sweet dress . . . And wasn't the singer . . .?"

"Marvellous!" the aunt replied. "To the bar, now, I think."

"See? No one's going to say anything. Just a quick hello to Abi and then we'll go, I promise. Hang on, that's my phone . . ." She scrabbled in her bag and Viola hesitated. "No, sweetie, do go on ahead with Daniel, I'll catch you up," Charlotte gushed, almost pushing Viola at him. He took her arm and firmly led her across the lobby to the bar that opened on to a veranda overlooking the hotel gardens. Oh joy, Viola thought as she hauled up her floor-bound knickers again, wondering, as she walked with this man, had she been set up? It wasn't easy to tell. Charlotte and Daniel didn't give any clues they knew each other (and Charlotte would have been hopeless at disguising it), so she had to assume not. He, at least, seemed quite happy to accept the two of them as genuine guests, so that was something.

"So how do you know the bride and groom?" he asked.

"Er, well, I sort of don't exactly. We're really only here for Charlotte's friend . . . the er . . . singer. We'll be going in a minute, honestly. Don't want to crash the reception. Obviously. How about you? Are you . . .?"

"Well, like you, I'm another of those who are rather on the edge, shall we say." He was smiling as if there was more to give away than he was admitting. She let that go because, really, if he didn't feel the need to tell her, then fine. If there was some mystery, she didn't need to be at all involved.

"No receiving line. That's good. They're always tricky," Daniel said, looking quickly round. The bride and groom were by the windows, surrounded by family. "Champagne?" he asked her as a waiter approached with a tray.

"OK, yes, I will, thanks." She looked around for Charlotte. There was no sign of her. "Actually," she said, feeling her knickers slide another inch floorwards, "I'll just visit the loo for a sec. Won't be long."

"I'll be right here," he told her. "I'll guard your drink."

"Very *gallant*, isn't he, your companion?" One of the guests, a woman in a feathery fascinator that glistened with gold sequins, commented.

"He is, isn't he? Not that I actually know him," Viola said, catching sight of the sign for the Ladies.

"Ah, well — always the way at weddings," the woman replied with a knowing grin and the hint of a nudge. "They're quite the places for making *new friends*."

Viola wasn't sure what was being implied here, but right now the most important thing was to deal with the sliding pants, which were in immediate danger of making an appearance at the party. It wouldn't do to upstage a bride, she thought. Once safely locked in the loo cubicle, she took them off, rolled them into a ball and stuffed them into the far corner of her handbag. She felt a bit exposed and would be glad to get home and find another — more reliable — pair, but unless she had a horrible falling-down-with-skirt-over-head

188

accident, no one here would be any the wiser. And besides, the moment she found Charlotte she was going to make her take her straight home, no arguments, before they were hauled off to line up for the photographs.

She'd half expected to find Charlotte in the cloakroom, but there was no sign of her there. Viola made her way to the front door of the hotel and looked out, wondering if she was already in the car. It would be just like Charlotte to have gone out already, leaving Viola to talk herself into confusion and ignoble eviction from the festive crowd. Charlotte's car had gone. Not a word had she said, she'd just vanished. Viola checked her phone but there was no message. Thanks, Charlotte, she thought.

"Your champagne. Not a bad little number either." Daniel was waiting exactly where she'd left him and handed her the glass, along with a mushroom vol-au-vent. "Are you all right? You look a bit nervy, to be honest."

"Thanks. Um . . . it seems my friend has left me in the lurch and *gone*."

He eyed the crush of guests. "Did you want to mingle for a while, as she's not here?"

"Er . . . not particularly. Sorry if that sounds harsh, but I don't actually know anyone."

"Me neither," he admitted. "The trick is to bluff it out till they summon the troops for photos and then bolt. I'll give you a lift, don't worry about your friend buggering off."

"So . . ." The fascinator woman lurched up to them. "Enjoying the party?"

"Er . . . yes. It's, er . . . lovely. And they look very happy."

"Well, of course they do. They've waited long enough for this. Well, you'll know that, obviously."

"Absolutely. But then with marriage, it's not something to rush into, is it?" Daniel laughed.

Fascinator woman's smile faded. "Rush? *Rush*? After what they've been through? Afghanistan? The *leg*?"

"Absolutely. The leg," Daniel concurred, though faltering slightly and looking unsurprisingly puzzled. But fascinator's voice had cut right through the rest of the room and most people were now staring at Daniel and Viola. "Are you *gatecrashers*?" she demanded.

"No, not at all," Viola lied fervently. Her phone dinged through the silence and she fumbled in her bag to fish it out. Why did it always go to the far corner, especially when you were searching one-handed while holding a glass? The phone tumbled to the floor but no damage was done as it landed on something soft. Ever polite, Daniel bent to retrieve it and handed Viola her phone with one hand and the black lacy knickers that had broken its fall with the other. Fascinator woman grabbed them from Viola's hand and waved them in the air at the watching crowd. "Blimey," she laughed. "Were you planning to gatecrash the honeymoon suite too?" The guests cheered and whistled and Viola backed towards the door.

"That's right, you two, time to go," fascinator woman then hissed, shoving the knickers down the front of

Viola's dress and grabbing her glass from her. "You can bugger off."

"Well, that's a first. I've never been evicted from a wedding before." Daniel was giggling like a boy fifty years younger than he actually was as the two of them whirled out of the hotel by the side door. "Have you?"

"No!" Viola couldn't help laughing too. "And it's not as if I wanted to go in the first place. But hey, I suppose it is quite funny really, isn't it? They probably thought we were a pair of habitual drunks, hanging out for the free booze." Once safely out on the pavement, she checked the message on her phone. "Home emergency. So sorry to abandon," it said. Somehow Viola wasn't too amazed. Had Charlotte had *any* intention of joining them for the do?

"Oh terrific!" she said. "No Charlotte. No surprise. Oh well." It was going to be quite a trek home and her shoes weren't getting any more comfortable.

"I'll be happy to drive you home, as I said. After all, being chucked out was completely my fault so don't even think of refusing," Daniel urged her.

"No, really, I've already had use of your handkerchief and you've looked after me at the party as well. Honestly, I'm sure there'll be a bus stop just somewhere near." A breeze had got up while they'd been in the hotel. She held her skirt down firmly, bunching it into folds so it couldn't escape and blow up to expose her naked nether regions. It was like being back at her nursery school when she hadn't quite made it to the loo and the school nurse, having had a run on the spare-clothing cupboard, made her spend the rest of the day knickerless. One of the boys had spent every possible minute finding excuses to be down on the floor, trying to look up her skirt. It was the first time it had occurred to her there were aspects to her body that might be in some way a bit *rude.*

Daniel grinned. "I think you might be more comfortable in my car," he teased.

"Actually, a lift would be very welcome. Thanks. And those were just spares, by the way." Another lie. In the back of her mind she could hear her mother going completely ballistic: not only was Viola getting into a car with an unknown man, but he was one who knew she had no knickers on.

"Of course they were," he agreed diplomatically as they arrived at a little black convertible Mercedes and he opened the passenger door. She climbed in rather gingerly and told him her address.

"You didn't know those people any more than I did, did you?" she asked Daniel as the car sped away. "So, you know, kind of what were you doing there? Were you there to hear Abigail singing too? That's my excuse — Charlotte dragged me along because Abi is a friend of hers. Bloody Charlotte."

Daniel didn't reply for a moment, negotiating a tricky roundabout. "Well . . . OK, I'll come clean. This might sound odd but it was just something I read about in a magazine. Weddings can be rather a good way to meet people." He looked at her quickly, grey eyes sparkling. "Women. Ladies. You know . . ."

"What, like, to *pick someone up*? Is that what you mean? *Really*?" How bizarre. She'd heard it all now.

192

"Er . . . in a way. And why not? I'm single right now and I don't particularly want to stay that way. I don't much fancy Internet dating, and everyone in those newspaper ads lies. All that 'slim, attractive, GSOH, likes country walks and theatre' and so on. They all turn out to have been to a musical as part of a coach party in 1976, drag a smelly Labrador round the local rec every day and have the figure of a steamed pudding. I don't want to hang around in bars and I'm not going to meet anyone new and interesting at the golf club, so . . ."

They were at the traffic lights now. He turned to look at her, his expression rather unhappy. "You think I'm a sad old git, don't you?"

She did, slightly, though not so much sad as a bit desperate. She couldn't help it.

"No, of course not."

"It's the celebratory atmosphere, obviously. At the do after, people can get very lively, if you know what I mean."

"Well, yes. Everyone expects a good time at a wedding. Don't you find it tricky, with seating plans and so on?"

"Not really — you just check out the lie of the land, plump for those that are more a casual effort than a formal do. And please don't think I just do it to get . . . well, get . . . er, sex," he said. "No, it's not that. Well, not entirely, I mean that would be a welcome bonus. No, people really open up and talk at these things, so if I meet someone interesting who I can take out for dinner, or see a few times, maybe see how it goes, so much the better. It's a huge improvement on something like going for the evening in a bar where everything's a bit contrived. And of course I do like cake." He laughed. She felt flustered now as they approached Naomi's house. Was he going to want to see her again? How did you deal with that asking-out thing? She could barely remember. Daniel was, she reckoned, far too old for her. He went such a long way back that he would know all about early Stones music and Bob Dylan in the years before he went electric. He was ideal for someone bang in the middle between her mother and her sister. If she were actually to be with someone ever again, she'd prefer a man whose formative years included the Lemonheads and the Cure.

"I'd love to invite you out for supper sometime, but I think two things." Was he reading her thoughts? "The first is that you'd be sure to say no, and the second is that, sadly, you're a bit young for me, to be honest." Daniel turned and smiled at her as he pulled up outside the house. Unreasonably, she couldn't help feeling slightly deflated at this. "Though I do so admire a woman who takes her underwear off even *before* the first date," he added, laughing.

Viola laughed too. "Well, it was that or have them fall off."

"Which could be open to misplaced misinterpretation of a certain eagerness," he said. He was looking at her in a slightly questioning way. Was he having second thoughts about not inviting her out? She half hoped he was. He had turned a potentially miserable day into a completely fun adventure, and you didn't get many who could do that.

"Thanks so much for the lift," she said, surprised that he sprang out of the car, whizzed round and opened her door for her.

"My pleasure." He smiled. "I do hope the bride and groom will forgive us. I'm sure they will — I got the impression they quite enjoyed it." For one tricky moment she thought he was going to kiss her but instead he simply patted her arm like an awkward uncle, got back in the Mercedes and drove away. She felt quite sad about this, as if she were waving goodbye to a good friend she'd never see again, rather than the casual acquaintance of an afternoon. Mad, she thought, opening the gate and catching sight of something she hadn't noticed before: a huge clump of dark-leaved nasturtiums nestling by the gatepost and spilling out across the gravel.

The masses of flowers were a rich deep bronze shade, the kind of colour you want to stroke in case it really is warm, like soft fabric. Self-seeded from up the road, she told herself firmly. Not newly appeared from nowhere *at all*. And of course she hadn't noticed them before — you didn't spot every road-level plant in the neighbourhood and, after all, they weren't exactly *inside* the garden. But all the same . . . her heart did a few extra skippity beats. Equally mad, she concluded. Plants just *do turn up*. It didn't have to mean that someone you are rather liking, someone who is almost certainly *very unavailable and must not even be thought of,* had nipped along and planted them. After all, why would they?

CHAPTER
SEVENTEEN

Naomi carried the basket of courgettes and baby leeks up from the vegetable patch at the far end of the garden. Old Joe from next door wouldn't be thrilled that she liked to harvest the crops he'd planted for her when they were still quite small and at their maximum tastiness, but if he wanted to carry on having shared use of that big patch at the end, that was the deal. In return, she didn't go near his planet-sized cabbages or the marrow he was cultivating for the local produce show. She remembered her old father, all those years ago, growing giant vegetables for competitions, and how nothing he'd bring home for the family to eat ever tasted anything but woody and a bit stale. Joe probably preferred the taste of over-mature veg, going by the expression on his face when he caught her snapping young, tender pea pods off and eating them raw. Maybe it was a man thing; something Viola and Kate would dismiss as willy-waving. She sympathized with both viewpoints, but when it came down to it, you couldn't beat flavour over size. In leeks, anyway.

As she walked back up the path she had a good look at the roses. The ones Oliver had planted against the fence for her when she'd first come to the house were at their best just now. He'd smile about that, she thought, the fact that his gift was at maximum splendour just at the anniversary of his passing. She would take some to the cemetery on the day, as she did every year. Not that she believed anyone's spirit would choose to hang about in a place of ultimate loss and sadness, but because, in a macabre, literal sense, it was the closest she could get to the physical presence of him. She didn't think too much about the reality of what was down in the ground, but she knew full well that there would be splintered wood, a worm-chewed corpse, a gape-grinning skull. All the same, a few times a year, it cheered her own soul to sit on the cold granite grave, weed out the stubborn dandelions that grew between the cracks and remember the many past good times.

Thank goodness for mobile phones. Would she dare call Greg if she had to phone the nursery office? All the same, Viola's heart was beating much faster than usual as she clicked on his number in her phone. From just that one brief meeting at the nursery, she knew that Mickey — who was *not* his wife, so that was something — was one scary woman. She'd be willing to bet that if Greg had left his phone on a desk in his chaotic office, Mickey might be the one who picked up this call. She could just imagine her barking "And who IS this?" at her in a cross-at-being-interrupted sort of way. Viola knew that although her call was all innocence, she'd fluff and bluster and manage to make herself look like the worst kind of desperately pursuing woman. Luckily she got Greg.

"Nasturtiums?" Viola decided a blunt one-word accusation should do it. She had to know.

"Bless you!"

"No, you eejit — the great mass of nasturtiums by the gate. When did those go in?" Oh Lordy, suppose it wasn't him after all. Suppose Old Joe next door had left them, maybe as a love token for Naomi. She almost switched the phone off.

"Last night, just after 1 a.m. And honestly, Viola, how come it's taken you more than half the day to see them? Don't you take *any* notice of the abundance of nature around you? Another time I'll dig in a row of great tall runner beans right across your gateway so you can't miss them."

"Sorry — I've been, er . . . out. Just got back."

"Out having fun?"

"Out, yes, but not that much fun really, since you ask. I went to a wedding."

"Oh, right. Well, I can see weddings might not be everyone's idea of fun."

"Not this one. But, hey, I love the flowers. You do realize you're completely barking mad, don't you?"

"Am I? Yes, probably. But it's peaceful, harmless mad. I'm glad you like them. I was going to say, if you're not keen on nasturtiums — and not everyone is, they're martyrs to blackfly — just rip up the flowers and scatter them in a salad. Delicious and peppery. I'd wash the blackfly off first, though."

198

"No, I'll leave them. I love them. So where had you been out gardening at one in the morning?"

"Council offices — they've given up on the window boxes. Something to do with the cuts, I suppose, and no one's so far been Big Society enough to take them over, apart from me. People are such lazy bastards. I had a few plants left over, which you've now got."

"You'll get arrested one day, going around doing illicit digging."

"I've already been arrested, remember? And more than once now, too." He was teasing her again. Why did he always seem to be laughing at her?

"Yes, but . . ."

"Yes, but . . . wait till you come out and try it with me. It's fun. Gardening is so much more fun when it's the secret variety, and not just lawn-mowing duty and boring old weeding at home. This way, you get a sense of adventure about it. It's a bit more Famous Five than SAS, though without the big dog and the lashings of ginger beer, obviously. You did say you were up for it, so when shall we go?"

The mention of boring old weeding made Viola think of the plant-strangled tangle and the out-of-control lawn that was the Bell Cottage garden. It was going to be quite an undertaking to sort out. Perhaps Greg could advise her whether she should deal with it in small manageable doses or take the equivalent of a flame-thrower to it.

"Well — I know I said yes but, you know, I'm not really sure . . . What about your wife?"

"*What* wife? I already told you, I don't have one."

"I meant . . . Mickey. You've got the same name." It sounded feeble. "Is she your sister, then?"

"*Sister?* No, she's my aunt." He was laughing at her. Mickey had looked younger than Greg. "Auntie Mickey and I have totally separate lives. End of story, nothing to add. So come on, you know by now I'm not really a crazed axeman. You can even bring your mother if you'd feel safer."

"Er . . . no, I think not! And what do you mean, 'Auntie' Mickey?"

"Exactly what I said. But don't ever tell her I call her that. So are we on? I mean, just say no and I'll leave you alone. But I'm only inviting you to bung in a few bulbs; if you're worried about your saintly virtue, I promise the only filth will be the earth under your fingernails." He was sounding sarcastic now, running out of patience, and she didn't blame him.

Well, she had promised herself she'd accept every single invitation . . . and he did come firmly under the heading of Just a Friend, so it wouldn't be like a *date*. Also, grovelling about in the dirt under cover of darkness wasn't exactly the fast route to becoming an adulterous woman.

"OK. I'll come. Let me think . . . I'm moving back to my own house at the weekend," she told him. "So . . . maybe after Tuesday or later in the week, once I'm actually in and organized?"

"Fine," Greg said. "Give me your new address and I'll pick you up, say, on Thursday night? Wear something dark, bring your own dibber."

Something dark. What-to-wear instructions ... again. That was where the day had started. But she felt pretty sure that this promised to be a lot more fun than a wedding that involved Afghanistan and something catastrophic about a *leg*.

CHAPTER
EIGHTEEN

"Your mail's here on the table," Naomi said to Viola as the two of them crossed in the hallway. Naomi was dusting — very gently, as if tending a delicate baby — the tops of the three Oliver Stonebridge paintings that hung there. "You'll want to hurry up and get it redirected or it'll be coming here till next year. You know what they're like. Red tape and bureaucrats." She spat the last words with the kind of much-relished disgust that she also kept for the local council's ever-changing rules on recycling, adults who ride bikes on pavements and the ineptitude of every farmer in *The Archers*.

"You're right. I'll sort that in the morning," Viola promised. "And, Mum? Are you really sure you'll be all right here on your own again? Maybe Miles has got a point. Perhaps . . ."

"No!" Naomi almost roared at her and raised her lime-green feather duster as if she intended to shove it down Viola's throat. "You and Rachel, GO! Shoo! I'm more than happy with my own company and when I decide I'm not then I'll get someone into the flat; maybe one of Kate's boys would like it if they get a job that needs an easy commute into town. It would suit me, that. And then if I ever get properly doddery I'll be able to get someone a bit medical in — some care in exchange for free accommodation. Bills excluded, obviously. I've thought it through, don't you worry."

Viola was having serious second thoughts. This seemed all wrong, leaving Naomi alone in this increasingly ramshackle house. But she also understood the attachment to the much-loved and familiar.

"And before you start on about that place of Monica's again," Naomi went on, "yes, those flats are very nice. But I can't sell this and I don't intend to. *And,* like I said before, I don't want a bunch of workmen poking about in here looking for things to mend, so don't send any in, whatever Miles and Kate say. Everything works fine just now. Once you start mucking about with it, every last thing'll pack up. Houses do that. They get cross with you for prodding."

"But it must cost a fortune to run this house. However do you . . ."

"Never you mind." Naomi cut off her question and waved her away, dust wafting from the green feathers. "Do I ask you about your finances? No, I don't. Family money, is all I'll say." And she tapped the side of her nose like an actor playing the kind of dodgy car salesman who's being wily about mileage.

"Ah well, Kate's doing the family tree, so maybe she'll find out where it all came from," Viola teased her, flicking through the little heap of post. Dentist reminder, a gas bill for Bell Cottage and what looked like a birthday card, except it wouldn't be hers for several months. She'd seen the handwriting before, on the card at the cottage. Had the sender signed this one? Maybe now she'd find out who to thank.

"Kate shouldn't go meddling," Naomi said, dusting briskly between the banisters. "What does she want to go rooting about in the past for? It's no more than making a useless list of the dead. She'd do better to look to her future, that one. She could do a lot worse than go to Shape Sorters and yoga and trim herself down a bit. Everything you eat at her age tends to stick. And there's plenty sticking on her at the moment. Comfort food, that's her trouble. And I'll tell her if I'm asked, which I hope I'm not. We don't want any more disasters."

Only half listening, Viola opened the white envelope and pulled out a greetings card — a cutesy black and white photo of two tabby kittens curled up cosily together in a bathroom sink. She really must make a list, she thought, and getting her mail redirected back to Bell Cottage would have to be near the top of it — she was starting the moving process in the morning.

"*He'll always be there*" was written inside the card. No signature. Viola looked at the sweet kittens on the front as if half expecting them to spit and snarl at her. But their innocent little faces remained the same and they just stared back prettily. Rereading the message, she felt rather sick and clammy and went and sat on the stairs, her legs trembling. A little detached part of her wondered why the sender hadn't gone the whole anonymous-drama hog and cut out individual letters from a magazine and glued them on, like something from the kind of crime novel her mother loved. So what was this — was it all going to start again, like before? Who would do such a cruel, spiteful thing?

Whoever it was must have been watching her going back and forth from Bell Cottage and put two and two together about her moving back in. Hellish. What would be next? More ugly plastic-wrapped carnations tied to the magnolia with florist's raffia? Prayer flags that would quickly turn to muddy shreds? Curled-edged photos of Rhys smouldering at the camera for all he was worth in his *Doctors and Nurses* costume scrubs?

"Anything nice in the post?" Naomi had stopped dusting and was eyeing the assorted papers in Viola's hands.

"No, just the usual junk, nothing special," Viola managed to say, getting up and moving towards the door of the flat. "I'll just do a bit more packing," she mumbled, needing to escape, but Naomi was now adjusting the Staffordshire dogs on the hall table, giving each of them a pat after she'd dusted, her interest moved on. Good — because she didn't want to talk about this. Naomi would only worry, and she might say something to Kate and Miles and accidentally load them with a chunk of ammunition to keep Viola from moving on with an independent life.

Viola went into the flat holding the card between the very tips of her thumb and finger, reluctant to have closer contact with it. She should, she knew, keep it somewhere safe, in case there was worse to come and it would add to evidence of . . . what? Stalking? Harassment? And yet — the urge simply to rip it up and bin it was overwhelming. She folded the kitten picture to the inside, for who but the hardest sort could tear those tiny furry faces to shreds without a qualm? She was just about to make the first rip when the flat door opened.

"Hi, Mum! Is it OK if I just pick up some stuff and go over to Emmy's?" Rachel's eyes were bright, expectant, hoping for a "yes" answer.

"Er . . . hmm, I don't know. Let me think." Viola watched Rachel's face fall. What kind of excuse could she come up with for "no"? The truth was she just wanted Rachel to stay close and safe beside her. But this wasn't about Rachel; it wasn't fair to involve her. She made a little more effort, just managing to overcome the feeling that, really, she was about to keel over.

"Yes — OK, why not? Back later this evening though, OK? I need to move some more things back to the house before Marco's lot bring the vanload from the storage lock-up, and you've got to sort out what to keep separate from the house-packing for when you go to Ireland."

"Ace! And thanks!" Rachel bounded across and hugged her mother. Viola pushed the card behind her back and gave Rachel a hard, fond squeeze.

"Ouch, Mum! You're squishing me!" Rachel laughed, breaking away.

"Sorry — just affection." Viola tried to laugh along with her, but could feel her mouth twisting all wrong. "Off you go then, and say hello to Emmy's mum for me."

"I will! Hey, we're going home soon! Yay, can't wait! And more yay for holidayyy!"

So there it was, Viola thought as the door slammed shut. She couldn't back out of the move now, even if she wanted to. And she definitely didn't. She glanced at the treacherous kittens again, then took the card into her bedroom and stuffed it into the pocket at the back of her laptop bag. She just hoped there wouldn't be any more joining it. But there probably would.

"I still think you're mad," Kate told Viola as the two of them unpacked a boxload of cutlery into newly scrubbed kitchen drawers at Bell Cottage. The whole of the downstairs area seemed to be a jungle of cardboard boxes. Viola couldn't believe how fast Marco's team of helpers had unloaded everything from the hire van, but now she could also hardly believe she'd ever get through the sorting process. Somewhere around Christmas would be her best guess. Rachel was still out with Emmy doing whatever important teenage things always mysteriously come up when a bout of hard physical graft is needed, but had promised to turn up later in the afternoon to unpack the boxes that were now waiting in her room. All she'd done so far was hang up the latest selection of knitwear she was trimming up for Gemma's stall and leave a heap of clothes on the landing for the laundry fairies to deal with.

"I know you do. And looking at this lot that needs doing, I'm half inclined to agree," Viola told Kate as she cut another drawer liner to the right size and smoothed it into place. "But this is my real, proper home, the only one I've ever actually put together myself, and I want to get on with living in it again. For over a year now it's been like a limbo thing, waiting for something, escaping from something. If I don't give this a go I'll just be a . . . I don't know, a *blob*, something passive and lifeless for ever. I also made a promise to myself to go out as much as I can, accept every invite. And I have been, just lately. No more hiding under a stone and letting life drift by. For one thing, it's not a great role model of Strong Capable Woman for Rachel, is it?"

Hmm, she thought but didn't say: and look how well *that's* turning out so far . . . A stolen bag, an arrest and a gatecrashed wedding with her knickers off. Top entertainment by anyone's standards. But, the lurking Pollyanna in her brain encouraged her, surely it can only get better?

"Yes, but *here*." Kate sliced open another box and started on the crockery. "Why does it have to be *here*? You could live anywhere. Somewhere new, for a fresh start. It would still be all yours, even more so. I mean, even apart from . . . *Rhys* . . . this is still a bit Marco too, isn't it? Much as I'm fond of him, he's *past*, surely. Yet his paint-colour suggestions are all over it, I can tell."

"Oh, leave it, Kate, *please*! Rachel and I just want to come back home and get back to some kind of normal. Can't you just be the teeniest bit positive for us?" She'd felt so excited about moving back home — in spite of the sick-making card in the post — till Kate had turned up, volunteering to help. The house was all new paint and a feeling of bright optimism. She didn't need or want any kind of downer.

"It can't ever be completely normal, though, can it?" Kate persisted as she loaded plates into the rack on the wall beside the sink. "Not really. Don't you still see Rhys in it, everywhere you look? Don't you half expect to see him on the stairs or coming in through the front door? Won't you feel utterly, hugely, heartbroken that he *doesn't*?" Kate's eyes were wet with emotion, as if she were trying to show Viola what *she* should be feeling.

Viola stopped rifling through the box, a colander in one hand and her favourite conical sieve in the other.

"No, Kate, I won't. Look, I never told you this before, but the last thing he did before he took off with whoever was his next idiot victim was to hit me. Very hard. Even if he'd come back safely after that night, I wouldn't have wanted him back. The whole thing with him was a stupid mistake, beginning to lousy end."

"He *hit* you?" Kate's eyes were wide and glittery, challenging. "Why? What had you said?"

"*What?* Kate — how could you? How could you even *ask* that! Does it matter what I said? If I tell you, are you going to decide whether I asked for it or not? I mean, please!" Her own sister. Shouldn't the support on this one be pretty much unconditional?

"No, no. Of course not. Sorry."

"Good — and you'd better bloody mean that or just . . . just piss off home to your nice safe golfy husband and all your sodding *cushions*."

209

Furious, Viola opened the garden doors and stepped out on to the terrace to breathe in some fresh, calming air. The house was just about perfect — she didn't want Kate polluting the atmosphere with bad thoughts, so, if she couldn't physically chuck her out through the front door, she'd stay outside for a while till her anger subsided. The garden was still an exuberant wreck of weed-choked perennials, deliriously overgrown shrubs escaping over the fence and grass long enough to make a winter's worth of hay for a pony, but it didn't matter — there'd be time to sort it, some peaceful day soon. And the garden would do its best to recover, just as she was.

She walked slowly along the side border, pulling out a few dandelion plants but leaving the pink campions because they looked so pretty. It felt good to wrench out the weeds like that and was safer than her first urge, which had, in the kitchen, been to grab the nearest heavy saucepan and batter her nagging, infuriating sister into silence, a swift but bloody death by kitchen utensil. The dandelions snapped off as she pulled; she wasn't getting the long tap roots out and they'd grow back, tougher than ever before. The whole long, soft-tipped quivering root needed to be excised. Forks and trowels, she thought, where were they? Still where she'd left them in the little green-painted shed down by the bins?

She went on down the path, treading the overgrown buttercup-strewn lawn out of the way, and pulled back the bolt on the shed door. It was stiff and rusty, and so were the hinges. No one had been inside since she and Rachel had left, and it was full of old spider-webbing and dead flies. A can of oil was on the shelf so she took it down and pulled off the cap, then drizzled a few drops over the bolt and the hinges. The garden tools were hanging where she'd left them. Which one was the dibber thing that Greg had told her to bring on their late-night gardening outing? She'd had to ask Naomi, find out that it was something for making holes. Maybe the long skinny pink-handled trowel would do just as well? She took it down from its hook and went slowly back up the garden, removing a few more dandelions on the way before feeling calm enough to go in and carry on sorting the kitchen. Small starts, she thought. Small steps. All would be well, whatever any stupid ill-wishers hoped. Breathe.

"I'm sorry, Vee," Kate said, stirring tea bags round in two steaming mugs.

"It's OK. Just, you know . . . leave all that old past stuff, will you? I'm trying so hard to do the new-beginnings thing. Maybe I *am* clinging to the house when maybe I shouldn't, but it's got to be easier this way than completely starting again somewhere new. Anyway, I couldn't afford to, so it's not as if there's really a choice."

"I know. So, new beginnings, huh? Here's to lucky bloody you." Kate raised her mug in a toast.

"*What?*"

"Sorry, sorry! Ignore me. And I'll make those new bedroom curtains for you if you want me to. Only . . ."

"Thanks, Kate, and I'd love you to, but 'only' what? Are you all backed up with other orders? Because it's OK, I can hang up the old ones for now."

"No, it's not that. I'll have to find a new workroom. Rob and I are . . . well, it's not so cosy, dull and safe as you think. Fact is . . . um . . . we're splitting up. Selling the house as soon as we can and divvying up the cash." Kate reached into the fridge for the milk Viola had brought with her that morning.

"But you two have been together *for ever!*" Viola had a flashback to Kate's bedroom and the solitary pillow, the snappiness with Rob over that last family lunch. So that was the score. "I thought once you got to that many years, you were, you know, *cooked* as a couple?"

Kate laughed, but not in a particularly amused way. She pushed her over-long hair back away from her face, taking, Viola thought as she watched, a good five years off her age. "It doesn't work quite like that, Vee. I don't think you ever get to a safe zone. Just a sort of separate-islands type thing. You're co-existing in the same cage but with hardly a word to say. Who wants that?" Then she did laugh, properly. "Anyway, I thought I was the one who'd been fretting to be free but it turns out Rob's been seeing the golf club's lady captain. If he'd only done all this two years ago; how sodding different it might all have been. He tells me they're moving into her place up by the seventeenth tee, and they're very excited about it apparently. He couldn't resist telling me, all bouncy and showing off like a small boy around Christmas. They're planning to build a

212

practice bunker in her garden so they can have hours of fun with their sand wedges."

Viola was confused for a moment, having immediately pictured the bunker as some underground haven from nuclear fallout and mishearing the last bit as sandwiches. A very claustrophobic picnic was in her head but the mists cleared eventually, luckily before she said something completely loopy.

"Why two years ago? Would you have *wanted* him to go off with someone then?"

"No, of course not. I was just a lot more together then. Now it's all, you know, all what's-the-point-ish."

"Menopause?" Viola wondered, as the word came out, if there was a more tender way she could have put that.

"Probably. It doesn't help. I'm all over the sodding place," Kate said, turning away and shoving tea towels into a drawer.

"Do the boys know?" Viola asked. "What do they think? Don't they want you two to try and work something out?"

Kate shrugged. "They're OK about it. We told them together, but it all seemed rather ridiculous. They just looked embarrassed and shuffly, the way boys do when you expect them to be emotional and they can't manage it. They were a bit 'yeah, like, well, whatever'. They've got their lives going on and it's not as if they can't still see us both. I haven't told Mum yet. Dreading that — she'll probably tell me to go back and try to make a go of it. Like she did back when . . . well, I mean like she just would."

"Back when? Have you and Rob split before?"

"Er . . . no, not as such. Just a wobbler, ages ago. Nothing." Kate was flapping her hands as if they were wet dusters, waving Viola's questioning away.

"You should have told me at the time, Kate. I hate to think of you all unhappy and keeping it to yourself. And do you really think Mum would say that? I'm not so sure. Because it's Rob leaving you, so . . ."

"That won't make a difference with her, will it? She'll still be thinking it's my fault, a bit like she did with you, with Marco going gay, as if you could have turned him if you'd put your mind to it. And after Dad died, there was never anyone else, was there? Loyalty even to just a memory. But then that's the way it is, isn't it, when it's the absolute love of your life. And there's no saying when those will turn up, out of the blue. Maybe early on if you're lucky, maybe later. Maybe never. Either way, I've had my go at it. Much good it did me."

Kate's eyes filled with tears. Viola put her mug down and went to hug her but Kate fended her off, dashing tears away with the back of her hand. One fell on the black granite worktop, flashing in the sun like a fallen diamond. "No, don't," she said, opening another of the boxes. "Don't be nice or the floodgates will open. Just tell me where you want these pans stashed."

CHAPTER
NINETEEN

"So he, like, texts you all the time?" As the two girls sidestepped a bunch of dawdling tourists wielding big, lethal backpacks and walked down the first part of Portobello Road, Emmy's look of frank envy was massively gratifying. This Ned thing was just such a totally cool thing for Rachel, the best thing that had happened this whole year, possibly even *ever*, and it made her feel on an equal footing with her best friend for once. Emmy was usually the one who had boys flocking to her like urban foxes round café bins. Emmy's boys were all a bit gothy, of course, always scarily skinny and grim-faced pale and wearing droopy black all the time, which was the part Rachel wasn't jealous about, but at least Emmy and her Camden velvet and lace and bluey-purple hair got male attention from that clan wherever she went.

"He does. Just tells me stuff like where he is and where he's going. Don't know why, sometimes. I mean, like if he's texting me that he's hangin' with a mate in the Met, does that mean he wants me to go there too?"

"Does he ask you to?" Emmy asked, sounding slightly puzzled, as if nothing needed analysing and agonizing over. Perhaps it didn't. How, Rachel wondered, did you learn to take everything at the simple just-as-it-seems level?

"Not really. It's just, like, *information*. Lots of contact. Maybe the Met is kind of impressive? I don't know the place, don't even know if it's a pub or club or what. I can't tell."

"Ask him? Google?" Emmy's face was all screwed up with confusion. It crossed Rachel's mind that if her gran saw her she'd tell her not to pull that face or it would stay like that if the wind changed. She'd miss having Gran around, but only a bit, and anyway they weren't going far away from her. Naomi was great but, maybe it was all the detective stories she read, she always seemed to be keeping an eye out for more information than you actually gave her. Unless that was Rachel's own guilt showing . . . She had never really had secrets till now. She hadn't had any practice at keeping them from people. Even here, miles from home, she felt watchful and nervous. At the Kensington Church Street end of Notting Hill there was the danger she'd run into Gemma. Anywhere past halfway down Portobello Road she risked bumping into her father or James.

"I already Googled, Emmy — course I did. I got the Metropolitan Police and the Met Office with some weather. No help at all. If I ask, especially this long after, I'll just be looking stupid. Like I should *know*. He's loads older than us. Not that he knows that, cos he hasn't actually asked how old I am. If he does," she suddenly felt panic about this, "can we be, say, sixteen? Otherwise he might just *run*."

"Hmm, yeah OK. Tricky, innit, life?" Emmy laughed.

Before Ned, Rachel had begun to think she might be invisible. Now she was getting some attention she was thinking more about looking like *who she was*. She knew she looked like just about every other tallish, thinnish blonde London girl of nearly fifteen, wearing the flowery cut-off shorts that were this summer's version of last year's denim ones, just as everyone else was. Same long messy hair, same little Topshop long Ts, same OK face, but she so wanted something that made her a one-off. Gemma had given her a gorgeous 1940s floral tea dress, but when she put it on she just felt like a little girl dressing up in a grandmother's outfit. Also it had smelled a bit funny. A lot of what Gemma sold had that same pong, which Gemma said was from being too long in musty wardrobes with worn-out mothballs. Whatever the reason, it wasn't a smell you'd ever want to wear. She and Emmy now stopped to look in a window at fringed cowgirl-style skirts and thick leather belts studded with turquoise.

"Is *that* me, do you think?" she asked Emmy, who understood Rachel's need to find her defining image.

"Dunno. You'd look OK, but then as you're not completely fuggerz, you'd look hot in anything. Do *you* like it? Wouldn't you have to know about, like, Dolly Parton and country stuff?"

"Suppose," Rachel agreed. "Can't see me going for all that yee-hah country music. I only know a couple of Taylor Swift songs; don't even know if she counts. I'd end up getting looked at by blokes who only listen to songs about dead dogs and Nashville. Dad likes all that, but then he loves rhinestones and cowboy boots."

"So where are we meeting these people? Is it far? These shoes are a bit of a killer." Emmy winced as her ultra-pointy-toed boot caught the edge of the pavement.

"No — he said it's not far down the road. Actually, look — that's it, over there." Rachel pointed, reading the sign Gold, big letters running from top to bottom outside the pub. She felt nervous, her heart rate sky-rocketed and she fluffed up her hair quickly and licked her lips. It was too late to delve into her bag to find a mint and she hoped that if (and oh please . . .) Ned actually kissed her, she'd taste all right. She was definitely a slow starter compared with some of the others in their year; she'd only snogged two boys before, both of those at last new year's party when it didn't really count as anything but practice. This one mattered.

"So, do we, like, go in?" They crossed the road to the pub, but hung back. There were a few quite old tatty looking men hanging around the doorway, smoking and laughing, clutching pints of beer and looking as if they'd been there a while, possibly years. As the girls lingered on the pavement, two of the men finished their drinks, took the glasses inside and yelled goodbye to the bar staff.

"I don't know," Rachel said. "He just said to meet him here, him and some mates. Or, rather, his *bredrin*." She felt odd with Ned's vocabulary. Country music might not be her, but neither was this. Nor, she suspected, was it really Ned. Some of the urban expressions he used sounded as if he were just trying them on, like he'd heard them but didn't own them.

Emmy snorted. "*Bredrin*? Is he, like, a *rappah*?"

"No — well, I don't think so. He said it's the 'local vernacular'."

"He sounds stupidly posh. Or poshly stupid. I bet he doesn't talk like that at his swanky boarding school. It'll be all fagging and Matron." Emmy sniffed. She eased her aching foot out of its tight boot and back in again, wincing with pain.

"Shut up, Em, you haven't even met him yet. You don't know what kind of school he goes to, neither do I. You can't prejudge."

This was a huge mistake, involving Emmy. Rachel should have kept him to herself, her own private non-school, non-home life. But he'd said, almost ordered, "Bring a mate." So she had. She didn't want to look like she hadn't got any.

The two girls hovered outside an antique shop beside the pub, looking at old silver clocks that were of no interest to them, nervously putting off the moment when they had to venture, well underage, into an unfamiliar bar, with each of them pretending to the other that they were perfectly nonchalant about this.

"Yo, schoolgirl!" And there he was, in between two boys with hair just like his. "These are Baz and Jaz. And ooh look," Rachel tried not to feel a tweak of jealousy as he gave Emmy his very best smile, the one she thought was just for her, "a little gothette! Are your knickers all black and velvety as well?"

"Frig off, that's to'ally gash," Emmy told him, showing him her middle finger.

"Soz. Didn't mean to vex you."

"Well, you did. You well jarrin' me, man." Emmy was scowling.

"Safe!" Ned nodded, approving. Rachel felt unexpectedly troubled by this exchange, somehow left out. Emmy didn't usually talk like this. Was she laughing at him or genuinely looking for him to like her?

"Drink, girls?" he asked, suddenly sounding, Rachel thought, like someone who'd just come offstage and was back to normal. That was fine by her — she felt he was back with her again. "Shall we go in or hang outside here?"

"Out here," Baz (or possibly Jaz) said, producing a pack of cigarettes from his pocket. The other one carefully pulled out chairs from under a metal table and motioned the girls to sit down.

"Me and Baz'll get the beers. You two want wine? They have a bracing little Pinot Grigio."

Emmy giggled. "Just Coke for me, please."

"And me, please," Rachel said.

"You sure? You got ID with you?"

"Er, no. Forgot," Rachel said, feeling a potentially disastrous age-revealing moment creeping up. "Anyway, I really do just fancy Coke. Hot day."

They spread themselves out on the small veranda in front of the pub. Rachel could see the flickery eyes of Baz and Jaz looking her and Emmy up and down as if absorbing every physical detail. She pulled the front of her little vest top up so they couldn't peer down her front and find her inadequately endowed. Emmy was curvier and the lacing on the front of her dress pulled her in and up, basque-style. This was all going a bit wrong. It wasn't supposed to be a competition. Emmy was, for once, meant to be the one who was tagging along, just there to be fun and friendly but not to take over the attention. Rachel wanted Ned to claim her, to put his arm round her, say something that was just between the two of them. Not that she was his girlfriend or anything.

"So you cotchin' at your pater's place?" Ned turned just to her and asked at last.

"*Pater*?" Emmy scoffed, accepting a cigarette from Baz/Jaz.

"Yah. And? What do you call yours?" Ned challenged.

Emmy shrugged. "Just, y'know, Dad?"

"Ordinary," Ned drawled. "The 'rents like exaggerated respec'. That way they never know if you're ripping the piss." He laughed and helped himself to one of Jaz's cigarettes. Baz flicked his silver lighter at him.

"Why would I want to rip the piss? I like my dad."

"Me too," Rachel chimed in, "though it's hard only living with him part-time. But I'm going on holiday with him at the weekend. We're going to Ireland."

"Funny place to go for a holiday," Baz drawled. "Doesn't it, like, rain a lot? What's wrong with the Maldives or something?"

"We're going in a caravan. Horse-drawn, you know?"

"Just you and your dad?" Ned asked.

"Well . . . me and him and . . . a friend of his."

Later, Rachel told herself that this was easier, quicker, than explaining in detail; that she wouldn't have minded Ned knowing (Emmy already did), but she didn't see why she should explain the sexual orientations of her various family members to a bunch of total strangers. It was none of their business. All the same, at the time she felt like she'd betrayed Marco and James, hugely.

"I'll miss you," Ned said, squeezing her hand and leaning closer to her.

"It's only a week."

"A whole long week." He pushed his chair back and stood up, pulling Rachel with him. "Come with me for a sec, just down the road. Got something to show you."

"Oo er." Baz and Jaz snorted and leered. Emmy gave them a look and they stopped, instantly.

"I'll bring her back, no sweat," Ned said to Emmy, who shrugged. "I know my way home if you don't," she told him.

Just down the road and round the corner, Ned drew her into the doorway of a closed-down shop and put his arms round her, pulling her close. She snuggled into him, scenting fabric conditioner mixed with coconut hair conditioner, the same one she used.

"Don't forget me while you're away," he said to her, running his hand down the side of her hip and sliding a thumb just under the hem of her flowery shorts. When he kissed her he pulled her in hard against him, jolting her so that her lower lip crashed against his teeth, and then his tongue stroked against her mouth, soothing and exciting at the same time. "Mmm . . . nice," he murmured into her neck, kissed her some more, then let her go, rather abruptly, taking her hand and leading her back to the pub where Baz and Jaz were smirking at her. She could feel herself going pink and still trembling from Ned's kiss.

"That was quick," Jaz said, leering.

"Well, you know . . ." Ned grinned at him. "Gotta go," he told Rachel, his hand on her bum. "Folks are having drinks and they've booked me and Baz to dress up and do the waitering. Cheap labour. See you when you get back?"

"Oh, er . . . yes. Will text."

"Yep. Oh and party time, on eighteenth at mine. Results day and folks away. Celebrate or commiserate, your choice. Have you two got A-level results coming as well?"

"Not really. Big stuff is next year," Emmy replied quickly.

"Oh, right. Just ASs then — doesn't really count so much, does it?"

Rachel rather thought it would, when the time came, but let it go in the interests of Ned and his friends not discovering that she and Emmy hadn't even taken their GCSEs yet.

"Eighteenth is my birthday too," she said, deflecting the subject.

"Oh, is it?" He smiled. "Extra celebration all round then."

"Hey, he, like, so wants to shag you," Emmy declared as she and Rachel walked back up to Notting Hill to catch the train home.

"He wouldn't if he knew I wasn't even fifteen yet." Rachel felt a bit scared.

"Well, there you are then. If it all gets difficult and you decide you don't want to, that's your way out. You can just tell him your age."

"Yeah, course I can," Rachel said, unconvinced. "Easy as that."

CHAPTER
TWENTY

Because Viola was so occupied sorting the house (in which every surface immediately fuzzed up with clouds of dust from nowhere the moment she unpacked a box), she was just about managing to keep at a distance the horrible dread that each day's post would bring more evidence that there were still crazed Rhys admirers determined she should never have the chance for a peaceful life. Saturday's delivery had given her a scare in the form of a bright pink envelope landing on the doormat, but it had only contained a Happy Moving Day card from Amanda and Leo, which was sweet of them. Over the weekend and through the first night she and Rachel slept back at Bell Cottage nothing had gone horribly wrong, apart from Rachel wailing that she'd left her hair straighteners at the flat.

Now, as darkness fell, Viola was trying hard not to see hostile shadows lurking in the gloom. When she came back from that night's planned illicit gardening adventure with Greg she would be sleeping alone in the house, and it was going to be quite a test as to how safe and secure she felt, not just on a purely physical level. Rachel had decamped to Emmy's for the night, smiling an awful lot at nothing in particular and looking almost plumply stuffed with teenage secrets, but not even remotely suspecting that her mother might have one or two of her own. It occurred to Viola that back in her own youth, she hadn't ever wondered about Naomi, either — she was wondering now, though. Mothers, when she was younger, used to be just *mothers*, though hers had always looked a bit different, a bit like photos she'd seen of Juliette Greco from the fifties, wearing a duffle coat, lots of black and (in one picture) carrying one end of a banner on an anti-nuclear march. But at some point Naomi had given up the drab look. She'd started dressing in bold colours and still did, several times over the years accidentally becoming completely on-trend fashion-wise with her habitual blocks of bright shades.

The recently revived memories of Uncle Oliver had made Viola think about him, too, in a way she had never bothered to before. He hadn't been a blood relative — so what had he been to Naomi? *Just* a friend? Someone who liked to help with the blokey stuff like changing plugs and car tyres, out of kindness to a youngish widow? A gay "walker" to go out with for fun? Or her lover, and, if that, why hadn't he moved in or married her? She didn't remember any other apparently unattached men being around so much in her childhood. Lots of female friends: Naomi was always out and about with those, off to galleries and parties, but not any particular man.

Oliver had even been with them on Viola's first day at the local infants' school. She had a hazy memory of him and Naomi all big and tall each side of her, holding

226

her hands, doing that counting to three and swinging her in the air thing to make her giggle. She had a memory that as they'd swung her she'd swooshed against her mother's full, flower-patterned skirt, which she'd now think of as wonderfully vintage 1950s. It must have been quite something back in the 1980s, when everyone else was probably going around in navy blue shoulder-padded power suits.

Naomi and Oliver had seemed more nervous about her starting school than she had been. She had a vivid mental picture of the two adult faces (her mother's hennaed hair topped by a green hat with cherries on it, Oliver's long black hair curling over his forehead), peering through the half-glazed classroom door looking worried, while she greedily inhaled the thrilling scents of Play-Doh and wax crayon. Other than Oliver, she only remembered Naomi's wide and chatty circle of women friends who left vivid lipstick marks on coffee cups and smoked in the garden. She would ask more about Oliver. Surely her mother would at least want to talk about the paintings? Or maybe Kate, being so much older, would have some idea about him.

There was something to be said for a garden full of impenetrable nettles, brambles and waist-high weeds, Viola considered as the night closed in and she reluctantly (given that the house still felt pretty damn hot) fastened and carefully locked all the downstairs doors and shutters. Only the most determined lunatic would clamber through that lot to get at the back of the house. As for the front, short of moving right away to some soulless gated community, there wasn't much she

227

could do about anyone who was inclined to tie memorial ribbons to the magnolia. You just had to feel sorry for whoever it was, really, she told herself, trying to find a generous side to being an obsessive's target. And she was sure it was just the one person — was that more or less scary than the previous gang of idiots?

The late-evening air felt barely cooler than the scorching day had been. Viola had needed a long, cool shower after another day of sorting and putting away; she had, finally, folded the last of the cardboard packing boxes and stashed them in the garage, not quite able to send them off to the recycling in case she needed to move again in a hurry. If she hadn't had that stupid kitten card, she'd have happily consigned the boxes to the recycling and cosied herself into Bell Cottage for the long foreseeable. However, although she didn't really anticipate a whole lot of trouble (the cards, in bright, unthreatening daylight could be construed as quite a feeble, last-ditch gesture somehow, compared with the immediate post-Rhys onslaught of spite, though it was still depressing and hurtful), she still felt wary. So *please*, she'd appealed to whichever gods were on duty at the time, as she stripped the tape off the final box and flattened it down for storing, could you possibly organize it so there are no more hassles? Is it too much to ask that Rachel and I have a peaceful life, the sort other — *normal* — people have?

Soon after 10p.m., Greg was leaning on the Bell Cottage doorframe, head to foot in black. "So — are you ready to come out and subvert the Highways Department's massed-begonia plans?" he asked. He

228

was looking just as when Viola had first met him, that mad night on the roundabout, except that this time she knew his eager smile wasn't that of a crazed murderer spotting the perfect victim. Or at least she assumed not. You didn't — she guessed — plant a row of beautifully espaliered fruit trees and a mass of nasturtiums as a friendly gesture towards someone you planned to garrotte, unless this came under extreme and perverse softening up.

In the doorway the sun-gilded ends of his hair sparkled under the porch light, and he was framed by a mass of overhanging and overblown white roses. It flashed across her mind that this would make a glorious photograph — the contrast of the tender and the tough, shining beneath the Bell Cottage lamplight. Except it was the thorny roses that could inflict the most pain, not Greg. "Just Friends" may or may not have described what her mother and Oliver Stonehouse had been, but it was definitely going to be her own mantra from now on. She wasn't about to go through any kind of man angst again, not in this lifetime.

"Yes, I'm ready! And look at us both, kitted out for horticultural warfare, all in black, though I think you're short of one Che Guevara beret," she told him, carefully double-locking the front door after her. Should she have invited him in for a drink first? She felt strangely shy about the idea of having him on her premises. This house was intimately *her* in a way the flat at Naomi's simply hadn't been. She could imagine him padding about the place, looking at the books on her shelves, checking out her CD collection and mocking her mixture of Puccini and vintage punk.

"I may be a well-tough guerrilla gardener, but it would crush my coiffeur, darling," he said, running his fingers through his hair as he opened the car door for her. "And you have to have a certain youthful *insouciance* to carry off a beret with style."

"The way you say that reminds me of . . . oh, just someone I know." She laughed, thinking how like Marco he'd sounded. Very fleetingly she wondered — maybe Greg was gay as well? No, she didn't think so — not that either way affected her, in any case.

The Land Rover had a damp earthy smell of rich loam and wet dog.

"Sorry about the niff — Mickey's had her stinky old spaniel in here," Greg said as he drove out on to the road.

"Mickey's dog? Not yours?"

"Hell, no. I like dogs but I wouldn't want one. They're so damn needy, always looking at you with those huge wet eyes, and just when you think they *lerve* you they go and eat your shoes."

Viola managed not to blurt out that she'd had a husband who'd been a lot like that, though it was on the tip of her tongue. Damn Rhys — awful as he'd been, she couldn't bring herself to say something so heartlessly frivolous. He'd been someone's beloved son, a brother and — for some poor unknown woman — a lover worth running off with.

"So — where are we going?" she asked as she braced her foot firmly against the side of the door. The Land

Rover didn't seem to have a lot in the way of suspension, and it bounced and bumped its way over every tiny pothole.

"Tesco's," he said, turning briefly and giving her the smile.

"*Tesco's?*" It sounded too ordinary, surely. "Right. So not a spare patch of earth outside Buckingham Palace? Not the hanging baskets of Downing Street?"

"Yep. Tesco's. Hey, are you disappointed? Sorry. I know it's not *the* most romantic of venues to take a beautiful woman for a night out, but it is the big Tesco's, not the titchy little Express by the station. So please don't think I'm not pushing the boat out for you here."

"Oh, I don't mind," she replied, overlooking the reference to "beautiful". After all, he'd seen her at three in the morning after half a night in a police cell, so he could only be joking. "I mean it's not as if it's some kind of . . . *date* exactly, is it?" When she thought about it, Viola felt quite relieved to be heading somewhere both nearish and fairly public. She hadn't told anyone where she was going, or even that she'd be out. Rachel was over at Emmy's so she didn't need to know, but Kate and Miles would have been appalled. Even Marco would have done his best furrowed-brow look. Ever since the Rhys fans had started tormenting her they'd been insistent that her personal safety had to come first, that she should let someone know where she was going *at all times.*

It made sense on one level, but with Kate too frequently reminding her that "you never know who's out there", as if every moment of darkness were loaded with peril, she often felt as if she was expected to ask permission before so much as putting the bin bags out. No wonder her default setting was, until so recently, to stay at home. Tunnelling out could be such a palaver. If she'd told Kate about tonight there'd have been a whole long list of questions, starting with Who with, Where to, and eventually . . . *Why?* To be honest, if she had to explain this quest, she wouldn't blame Kate for that last one. Random gardening in the dark wasn't really the sanest thing to do.

"It's *not* a date?" Greg said. "Ah, now I'm disappointed. And I got all dressed up for you too."

"Don't tease me!" She whacked him on the arm, realizing at the same time it wasn't the wisest thing to do to a man who was about to change gear. She really must learn to *think*.

"Who's teasing? This is my very best old hoodie. And also, it may lack the usual clichés of romance but the Tesco's car park has its charms. Those recycling bins make a stunning silhouette against the night sky. And it is *such* a beautiful evening. See, the magic lights!" He pointed to the vividly lit sign over the Tesco 24-hour garage and sighed, thoroughly overdoing the drama as he turned the car off the road and into the car park, which was deserted apart from a few vehicles dotted around the edges and someone in a Mini with L-plates practising parallel parking.

"Need to trust to luck a bit here," he told her, crossing to the farthest corner where there were sheltering trees. "There'll definitely be CCTV, but I reckon it won't be pointing at the bit we're heading for. They're not going to be wasting footage on a scruffy little patch of neglected ground by the valet car wash, now are they? It's not exactly in brick-lobbing distance of the main doors."

He pulled up at the back of the little car-wash marquee and they both climbed out, Viola wondering if she should have brought a scarf to tie round her face, looter-style. "The trick is," Greg was saying, "to keep the car behind us so we're pretty much hidden from view."

"I hope we are." Viola suddenly felt a bit unsure. "I really don't want to spend any more time being interviewed by that vile detective. Do you ever get challenged when you're doing this?"

"I haven't been so far. I think people generally steer clear of men digging holes in the ground late at night. Apart from you, that is."

"Yes, well — it's not as if I knew you were there. I'd have run a mile if I had. But there's always a first time, though . . ."

He got closer to her, took hold of her hand and gave it a squeeze. "Hey, we can abort the whole mission if you'd prefer. I can take you straight home or we could rush to the pub before it shuts if you'd rather not do this. I thought . . . you know, just a *laugh* . . ."

Leaving now would certainly be the sensible option. Playing safe, taking the adult, no-risk course, just as Viola had promised herself she would do for the rest of her days so as to avoid havoc and chaos. But that didn't exactly go with her determination to accept every invitation on offer and get her life back. So here she was — and she could feel it as an almost physical euphoric rush — actually for once knowing that excited flicker of *really* enjoying herself. It was as if backing out now would mean she'd never let herself have any silly, spontaneous fun ever again. She could picture herself months later in the spring, coming here to shop and spotting the rogue bed of flowers that would remind her of this night. Something good, something positive for once.

"No, it's fine — I really want to." She reached back into the car for her bag. "See? I've got my trowel all ready to go. What are we planting?"

She pulled a scrunchie out of her pocket and crammed her hair back into a ponytail, not caring how messy it looked but wanting to be able to see what she was doing without stray tendrils trailing in her eyes. Greg was leaning on the car bonnet, smiling at her and watching. "Hey, it suits you like that. Shows off your cheekbones."

"Oh — thank you. It's probably the Croydon-facelift effect, hauling all the loose skin back really tightly."

He reached across and smoothed a finger down her cheek. "Come on, learn to take a compliment, why don't you? And if you're embarrassed by it, you can return the favour and make us even."

"Oh — OK. You've got, um . . . quite nice . . . er . . . eyes? Aaagh!" she laughed. "You're winding me up, aren't you?"

"Totally." He nudged her gently in the ribs with his trowel. "And it's *so* fantastically easy! Come on, let's get on with the planting. It's way too early to be putting in tulips really, because too much heat once they're in the ground isn't good for them, but this is a shady little patch so we'll plant them deep and risk it. I'm sure the plants I put out in the wild know they've got to make a bit of a special effort to thrive, so we'll let them take their chance against the dreaded tulip fire. Perks of the trade — I was given a whopping big free-sample bag of those parrot ones, pink tinged with green." He opened the back of the Land Rover and pulled out a small sack of bulbs and a garden fork.

"Oh, I love those frilly tulips; they're completely mad-looking. Like regular ones but dressed up in really fancy frocks. But aren't they wasted on a tatty old bit of supermarket ground?"

"I don't think so at all," he said. "I mean, you might think I'm just sweating the small stuff, if you like, but an unexpected random flash of beauty in this sad suburban wilderness will gladden a lot of hearts, even for a few seconds. Isn't it worth it for that?"

Viola felt that hers was gladdened already. Greg's committed belief in his mission almost made her want to cry. How come some people could be so damn *nice*?

He looked down at the sack of bulbs. "I spend all my working days renting live plants out to be used as fake scenery, then bringing them all back again, a lot of them damaged because they're just there to be functional and no one's bothered to take care of them. And then when I drive through the areas the powers that be have allowed to rot with neglect, places that collect nothing but filthy litter and nobody cares, sometimes I just want to dig the real thing in and make a bit of a difference," he said, stabbing the fork into the ground and beginning to turn over the earth.

"Ah, that's such a lovely thought." Viola was touched by his admission.

"Is it?" He turned and grinned at her. "I thought it sounded vomit-inducingly worthy, myself. But this kind of thing is a worldwide movement. You should Google guerrilla gardening and have a look. My personal buzz comes when I drive through the area and see strange little subversive plots of greenery that I've been responsible for. Gives me a silly, secret tingle."

"You're a kind of Banksy with a spade, then?"

"I completely am. Here, I've turned this patch over; now you can start making the holes." He stopped forking and handed her his dibber. "Put them in at around four inches deep and only about the same apart; there's nothing worse than sparse tulips. We're going for the de luxe massed version, like you would if you put them in a big pot. They probably won't come back the year after. In fact, if I remember, and if they're still here, we could come back and lift them after they've flowered."

Viola set to work as he'd directed, getting completely absorbed in what she was doing and feeling exhilarated by the now-cooling night breeze and the shared adventure. She and Greg knelt on the well-dug earth and planted the bulbs together, working silently and fast. The scent of fresh earth made her forget all about the madly incongruous location. It was only when they'd nearly finished and she heard a dog snuffling at

236

the car wheels and saw a beam of feeble torchlight weaving about that she remembered that they were in a highly public spot. Greg didn't seem to have noticed so she reached out and took hold of his wrist, giving it a warning shake.

"Someone's behind the car," she whispered.

A short, stout man wearing a shiny football shirt and a hand-knitted beanie hat, with a fat Labrador on a lead, was peering in through the Land Rover's open back door.

"Looking for something?" Greg stood up and asked politely. The man jumped back, looking nervous and a bit furtive.

"Er . . . no. Sorry. I just thought . . . I mean, you had the interior light on so I thought . . ."

"Thought the battery would go flat? How kind of you to worry." Viola smiled, deciding that the friendly option would be the safest. The last thing she wanted was some suspicious bloke doing a concerned-citizen act and reporting them to the police. Or maybe he'd just intended to rob a bag of compost from the back.

"Well, not exactly, I just . . . er. Yes. Sorry. My mistake." The man wouldn't look at her but kept his gaze firmly floorwards. He tugged impatiently at his dog's lead but the dog was taking its time, having a copious pee against the rear tyre. Viola saw Greg quickly scan the rest of the car park, then grin at the man. "Ah . . . Now I know what you thought! Jeez, is this one of the sites for it, then? If only we'd known." He pointed across at the far side. "Look, mate, there's a

Volvo estate over by the bottle bank, with its headlights on. I reckon you'll have more luck with them."

The man started to shuffle away, looking embarrassed. "Well, like I said, my mistake." He grunted, then turned back. "But if you don't mind me asking, what exactly are you doing here then if you're not . . . you know . . .?"

"We're gardening." Greg told him. "And no, that's not a euphemism. Goodnight!"

The man frowned. "Gardening? At this time? Oh, I get it. A wind-up." And he stomped off crossly, pulling the reluctant dog after him.

"What on earth was that all about? And this place is known for *what*, exactly?" Viola asked as soon as he was far enough out of earshot. Every last tulip bulb was planted, and Greg was treading the ground to make it look less freshly dug and to dissuade neighbouring cats from taking advantage of soft earth.

"Dogging!" he laughed. "Poor bastard didn't know where to look once he realized his mistake."

"*Dogging*? Oh, yuck! And he thought . . . we were . . . um, *at it*?"

"Yep! He was all geared up for a bit of lecherous watching. Interior light on, you see. Apparently it's a sign — and before you ask, that's just info picked up along life's way. I *definitely* don't know from personal experience. Poor bastard!" He laughed. "Talk about looking disappointed."

"That's *gross*!" Viola squinted through the dark in the direction of the far side of the car park. A couple of cars *did* have their lights on. If she hadn't been told this, she'd have assumed their occupants were reading a map or choosing a CD track or something equally innocent.

Greg stowed the fork in the back of the Land Rover, then smiled at her. "Well, it wouldn't be my choice for an evening's entertainment, but each to their own. And you have to admire the fact that he did actually have a dog. Attention to detail, you see." He slammed the back door shut. "Shall we go now, or did you want to check out the, er . . . players?" He nodded in the direction of the lit cars.

"No! I mean, yes, let's go!" Viola clambered into the car and pulled her scrunchie off her hair, shaking it loose around her face. She could feel she was blushing. This wasn't a conversation she'd ever expected to have, certainly not with Greg. Well, not with anyone. The stuff you learn . . .

"Excellent — let's leave them to it and get out of here. Some people do have very strange pastimes, don't they?" he said, starting the car and heading out towards the road.

"You're so right. But they'd probably say the same about us," Viola replied, looking back at the neat patch of ground where no one would suspect that months from now there would be a stunning display of exuberantly frilled tulips. That she and Greg were the only ones who knew they were there made a special bond between them, she thought.

"Would you like to come in for a drink when we get back or . . . do you have to get home for . . . er . . . anything?" she asked.

He stopped at a red light and looked at her, his face serious for once. For a moment she felt quite nervous. What was he going to say?

"There is no 'anything'. I already told you I'm divorced, Viola, if that's what's bugging you. My only connection with Mickey is a family one. And the business, obviously."

"Oh, right. But it's OK, I only wondered. Sort of idly, the way you do, because it doesn't matter either way, does it? It's just you've not really said anything about yourself. I don't even know where you live. Not that I need to know." She was waffling. Was the evening going to be a total ruin now? It had been such fun. Appalled, she realized she could almost cry, but mustn't. How pathetic would that look? But even if she did, it wouldn't be about *Greg*. It was just that for once an outing seemed to have gone right and been something she could really enjoy, without all the past *stuff* getting so much as the tiniest look-in.

"I don't know much about you either," he said. "I like it that we are a pair of pretty much blank pages, don't you?"

"Well — yes, maybe, I suppose so." That told her. He might as well have said, "No more questions." The lights changed and Greg crunched the Land Rover into reluctant gear.

"And yes, please, thanks for the invitation, I'd love a drink," he said, which rather surprised her. She'd imagined he'd now want to drop her at the gate and screech off fast into the night. "But first I have to pick something up on the way — it's only a teeny detour. Is that OK? Do *you* have to get home for . . . anything?"

"No, I don't and yes, it's fine." Viola could hear her voice sounding flat and small.

They drove a mile or two further, over the river bridge and on towards a row of shops. At the corner, Greg turned off into an alleyway at the back of the parade where there was a delivery road and bounced the car over a series of pits and ruts, avoiding carelessly placed rows of wheelie bins.

"The back of the police station is just up here. This is the bit where they keep the patrol cars," he said, switching off the main headlight beam and squinting into the darkness. He slowed down and stopped the car in the small goods yard at the back of the M&S food store.

"*Not* the place I'd choose to hang out, to be honest," she whispered.

"It's OK, we won't be caught. There's just something I need to get. Stay here a sec." And before she could ask any more, Greg had got out of the car and crossed the yard, vanishing into the darkness. Viola closed her eyes and leaned back against the headrest, suddenly feeling incredibly sleepy. It must be close to midnight, she realized, feeling both her body and mind relaxing and drifting off.

"Look at these!" Viola jumped as her door was flung open. Greg was waving two enormous cucumbers at her. "Harvest!" he said, pushing them into her hands. "They're a bit overgrown, hazard of absentee farming, but you can have these if you want. If you like them, that is; a lot of people don't."

"Oh, but I do — thanks!" She looked nervously at the shuttered back door of Marks & Spencer. "You didn't . . . No, you wouldn't. Even you wouldn't break into M&S just to nick a couple of cucumbers."

He was climbing back into the car now and starting the engine. "No, even I wouldn't," he told her with mock solemnity. "I've got a patch of them growing over there in front of the wall. It's nice and sunny and they get plenty of water because the security bloke is a mate of mine and he shares the crop. There are chillies too, but they're not ready yet."

"You're growing *vegetables* out here? Why don't you get an allotment like anyone else?"

"Why? There're plenty of discarded patches of land in every town, ripe for the planting. The people's plots."

"Don't people just find the stuff and take it?"

"Yeah. That's OK."

She laughed. "You're a bit . . . I don't know, something between ecologist and communist."

"In a good way, I hope. And anyone with a little time and energy can do it. Why hand over all the money to the Man when you can grow your own food?"

"I've only ever grown a few herbs and some lettuce. I must try harder," she said.

He turned and looked at her. "Sorry, you're tired, aren't you? I should have taken you straight home. We didn't need to stop here really, I was just showing off. Being a bloke."

242

"That's all right. You can be a bloke, it's allowed." She settled back against the headrest and closed her eyes again. "But yes, I am tired. Not too tired to give you coffee or a glass of wine back at mine, though."

"Sounds like a good plan," Greg said, speeding up as the Land Rover finally lurched out of the potholed alleyway on to the main road. "Especially as this time your mama won't be on the doorstep, waving a rolling pin at me and shouting the odds about your honour."

"I'm all grown up and left home now," she told him. "Being at hers was only ever temporary." She sensed him turn to look at her and waited for him to ask her why . . . but he didn't. It was quite a relief, to be so anonymous. How long would that last?

Greg didn't pick through her CDs or comment on her bookshelves that contained the complete works of Jane Austen, Thomas Hardy and Charles Dickens alongside bright-jacketed rows of contemporary writers. Instead, as she was in the kitchen making them both mugs of tea, he had a good look at a framed black and white photo of Viola, Marco and the then-baby Rachel which hung on the wall, all of them smiling and looking as if nothing could ever be better in their world. She glanced at the photo — that had felt so true at the time.

"Am I allowed to ask?" He pointed at Marco.

"Yes. That's Marco. My daughter Rachel's father. Divorced but friends." So here it came, trickles of information-sharing.

"Best way to be," he said, nodding. "I didn't know you had a baby."

"Baby! Not these days. She's a teenager now, staying over with a friend for the night." There was a short silent moment while she — and possibly he — took in that this meant that whatever happened — or didn't happen — now, they weren't going to be interrupted. As she reached into the fridge for the milk, Viola contemplated the mad idea of actually sleeping with Greg. As she wasn't going to have an emotional entanglement ever again, it would have to be on a sex-only basis, none of that getting-involved, complicated stuff. The idea seemed brutal, cold and absolutely *not her.*

"This is the point where we should . . . um . . . make a decision," he said, looking serious.

"Is it?" She thought she knew what he meant. Her decision had already been made.

"Yes. Are we to stay in here or shall we take this tea and sit on that lovely squashy sofa?"

"Well — we could . . ."

There wasn't time for the rest of the answer because Greg moved close, put his arms round her and kissed her. And God, it felt good.

"Sofa?" he murmured when they stopped to breathe.

She'd been too close to choosing a third option of "bed". That close, she realized, to rushing towards potentially wrecking a good friendship by taking her old if-it-can-go-wrong-why-don't-I-let-it route. A whirl of common sense somehow made its way into her exhausted brain and she nodded.

"Sofa."

CHAPTER
TWENTY-ONE

The storm painting halfway up the stairs would be one that Naomi would definitely keep, when it came down to the last few of them. That and the big nude portrait of her that had so horrified Kate and Miles when they'd been young teenagers. "Mum, you actually *posed* like that?" Kate had been wide-eyed with shock, adding, "Gross!" Miles had said nothing, just blushed and tried not to look. Back then, she'd told them — as a tease — that she intended to hang it in the sitting room, big, brazen, rude and bold over the fireplace, and they'd been so gratifyingly horrified that she'd very nearly done just that. "You are disappointingly bourgeois," she'd told them, which had given them a bit of a surprise. It wasn't a word that usually featured in her Lancashire vocabulary. Viola had asked what it meant and Naomi had told her not to worry about it, it was something she'd never be. And of course she wouldn't really have hung it there. Never mind her children's embarrassment and the blushing, speculative glances from their visiting pals, she didn't want her own friends making comments and doing a lot of wondering either, especially Monica, who'd ask no end of questions. In the end it had stayed forever out of public view up in her bedroom, where the only visitors for the past few years had been the window cleaner and the man who steam-cleaned the carpets. If they saw any resemblance between the voluptuous, sofa-sprawled floozy with the generous mass of auburn curls and the brisk, brick-shaped matron with a penchant for purple and a collection of gory novels, they were discreet enough not to comment.

She would call David the dealer sometime in the next few days, let him know that one more rare Stonebridge was about to come on the market. In spite of the recession it would fetch a top price, because she'd been as careful with the selling as Oliver had trusted her to be, and his pictures had a still highly desirable value of rarity. When it came to the art market, he'd told her, slow release would be the trick. Like the tablets he'd been prescribed for the pain.

They were all coming for a celebratory supper at Bell Cottage now Viola had had a few days to make sure everything was working and she and Rachel had settled in. It had to be today, as Rachel would be off to Ireland with Marco the next morning. Marco, James, Kate and Rob (hmm — that would be fun, not), Miles (but not Serena — it was her reiki night), and Naomi would all be there. She would have family round first, friends later, Viola had decided, as she was feeling ridiculously nervy about putting together a meal for people again after so long. At her mother's flat, cooking had been reduced to the bare essentials, and she sometimes felt guilty that the most labour-intensive home-cooked food

Rachel had had over the past year had been a simple roast chicken. Her excuse had been that the flat's kitchen had been basic, to put it kindly, and she'd simply got out of the catering habit. The best meals they'd had there had been courtesy of Naomi and her skill with a tasty Lancashire hotpot and sumptuous shepherd's pie.

Today, Viola was going to remind her ever-doubting family that she could not only live perfectly capably without constant backup, but could actually get by more than well enough in the food-and-foraging department. From now on, she resolved to make a real effort and do the efficient working-woman thing — filling the freezer with home-cooked pasta sauces and casseroles and fishcakes, so Rachel would be able to come home to real food instead of pizzas and ready meals. For one thing, without the rental income, that kind of instant food would be out of their price range. "Move over, Nigella," she murmured as she parked the Polo at the supermarket, switched off the *Woman's Hour* chirpy discussion on Whatever Happened to Herpes and took her enormous shopping list out of her bag.

The store was full of exhausted-looking women with superactive school-holiday children in tow. Every aisle contained at least one infant having a tantrum, another child crying and a third racing round, arms stretched out for maximum crashing-into potential while they whooped fantasy-animal noises. Any sensible woman would have shuddered and been glad her child was past this stage, but Viola was surprised to find she was feeling a bit envious. It hadn't really hit her before, but now she couldn't help a piece of important knowledge burrowing into her brain uninvited: she wasn't likely to be needing the babycare aisle at the supermarket ever again. She shook her head sharply for a second, almost consciously trying to dislodge and evict the thought, but it wouldn't go away and it brought with it a little seed of regret. Rachel wouldn't have the support and love of a brother or sister when she was older.

Suppose something terrible happened (and how easily Viola had seen vibrant life wiped out in an instant), and Rachel hadn't a sister to turn to, as she had Kate? But, she reminded herself, Rachel had cousins closer to her in age than a sibling could now be, an aunt and an uncle on her mother's side of the family, both of them fond of her. And best of all she had her father and James, and her lovely aunt Gemma. All would be well. There were plenty of only children in the world and they got by absolutely fine. And where had this thought come from, anyway? It wasn't as if she was planning on having another relationship, let alone another baby. Kissing Greg had felt wonderful — she'd forgotten how blissfully her body could respond to a much-wanted touch — but he had done the sensible thing and left soon after. "Bloody reluctantly", as he'd put it, with a final delicious doorstep snog.

Viola pushed the heavily loaded trolley along the petfood aisle and wondered again about a cat. Whether to get a kitten or a rescued adult? The stripy one on the Whiskas packaging was very cute, but it must have been the woman pushing the trolley ahead of her who made her think a big lazy ginger one would be a good choice. It was the woman's hair, wild and red and curly . . . and not unlike Mickey Fabian's. Viola hung back, reluctant to go nearer in case Mickey (and one glance at that pointy profile told her it *was* her) recognized her and gave her a verbal going-over for causing Greg to get arrested. What did he mean by all that "Auntie Mickey" stuff? She still didn't know. Even the other night he'd been pretty slippery about explaining the set-up. "Family connection" could cover just about anything, but then his vagueness fitted in with the "blank pages" that he seemed to prefer.

She liked him a lot, so far. But she really didn't feel she could say she knew him, because he wasn't letting her *in*, exactly. For now, she slid her trolley a discreet few yards behind Mickey, having a sneaky look to see what she was buying. She wasn't sure what she was looking for, maybe a cosy selection of ready meals for two? She was startled when her phone rang, and she turned the trolley as sharply as a London taxi driver and whizzed off towards the laundry products, fumbling in her bag for the phone as she went.

"I'm *so* sorry, sweetie. Polly fell off a swing and the nanny texted me in a panic. I *had* to go. Did you get home all right?"

Viola didn't bother to wonder why it had taken Charlotte so long to call, to come up with an apology and an explanation for abandoning her at a wedding she'd never wanted, or been invited, to go to in the first place. Charlotte was a to-do list sort of woman; she'd have only just worked her way down as far as "Call

Viola", well below buying Polly's next-term uniform and having her roots done. That was fine, really. With Charlotte you knew what you were getting, so you knew what not to expect.

"So was Polly OK? Any damage?" Viola remembered the child squealing in a wake-the-dead kind of way once at Charlotte's, just over a tiny nettle sting.

"Cut her head open, screamed the place down, but she was all glued back together in A & E. Heads do *bleed*, don't they? And her dress was ruined — Nadja put it to soak in hot water instead of cold, silly girl. So tell me — did that lovely man ask you out? Are you going? Have you already, actually?"

"He was rather lovely, wasn't he? While I was still waiting for you — without a clue you'd buggered right off out of there — we got busted for gatecrashing and then he drove me home. But no, I'm not seeing him again. And, Charlotte . . ."

"Sweetie, I know what you're going to say, and no — I *absolutely* didn't know him, had never met him before that day. Honestly. Well . . . all right, I'd met him just the once, briefly, at another of Abigail's . . . er . . . engagements. But it was *not* a set-up. I truly promise. Shame you're not seeing him again, though. Was it the age thing? I mean, older men, you know, they're well worth considering. So long as they still have teeth and a functioning bank account."

"Hmm. Actually, Charlotte, that isn't what I was going to ask." Viola had her, bang to rights. She couldn't mind, not really — Daniel had been quite a find and she'd have liked to see him again on a friends-only level. Just as every other man would be in her life from now on. That way there could be no more disasters.

"You know, you could do worse than Internet dating, Vee." Charlotte clearly wasn't going to let Viola escape into permanent singledom without a fight.

"You do love a project, don't you?" Viola laughed. "I'm not looking for anyone! I'm going to concentrate on living in my own house again, being a good, supportive mum to Rachel and see if I can persuade Med and Gib to give me more hours' work per week. I shall also get myself a cat."

"A *cat*? Oh but, *darling*."

"Yes, a cat. It's all right, it'll be just the one, not a mad-woman houseful of them, Charlotte. Also, what I was going to say was, how about next week for the book group at mine? Not to talk about a book; I know we agreed to take a break until September. I just thought more of a moving-back-in gathering? I'm a bit out of catering practice but I'll see if I can remember how to make a cake."

"Ah, book club. Now, *Lisa* has been Internet dating," Charlotte persisted, blithely ignoring Viola's invitation. "She's got one of them taking her to Paris later this week, so, yes, if we meet up the week after, she can tell us *all* about it. It would suit you, the Internet thing. You can be anyone you want, keep yourself as private as you need to. In fact, I'm going to call her *right now*, get her to give you the website details . . ."

Viola had lost sight of Mickey, so never did find out whether she was cramming her trolley with ready meals for two. She finished her shopping, paid at the checkout and idly skimmed the newspaper headlines on the rack on her way out. The front page of one tabloid had a photo of teenagers partying with bottles and cans on a Cornwall beach, with a disapproving headline about Ya Ya Yobs who were apparently pretty much nightly trashing the small seaside village they'd taken over, and upsetting the residents and the young-family holidaymakers. It was the kind of story that turned up in the press every other year, whenever more than five teenagers with beers gathered after dark on a beach. And there among the revellers was Benedict Peabody's cheery face. He was wearing a dinner jacket over a wetsuit, had his arm draped round a curvy bikini-clad girl with the usual teen mane of tumbling golden hair, and was grinning and waving a champagne bottle at the camera. Viola wasn't remotely surprised to see him in the shot but decided that, no, she wouldn't turn to page five for the Full Story. It was all too predictable.

At last, outside in the humid sunshine, Viola found her car and started unpacking bags into the Polo's boot. Reaching back to grab a twelve-pack of loo rolls, she felt her pulse rate rocket as she recognized a Fabian Nursery van parked about forty metres away. Mickey's, she told herself. Greg was probably miles away, delivering huge painted polystyrene toadstools to a hyper-expensive children's party venue, or a hundred yellow standard roses to a fashion shoot. That he hadn't called her didn't matter *at all*. It had only been a casual snog, not a lifetime commitment. So, no, it really didn't matter. Much.

She lingered a bit after the shopping was all loaded. Mickey appeared, and she saw her approach the van, but it was the boot of the blue Peugeot next to it that she unlocked. Then the van door opened and Viola half hid behind her own car as Greg climbed out, carefully carrying a small baby, holding it safe and close against his chest. She watched as with his free hand he helped Mickey load her shopping, then he kissed the top of the child's head and placed it tenderly in a car seat in the back of the Peugeot, hugged Mickey, kissed her briefly and climbed back into the van. Mickey then watched him drive away, waving and smiling, still looking decidedly fond.

Well, he'd been right in one way: you couldn't get more of a "family connection" than being a co-parent with someone. How much she'd believed, or *wanted* to believe, that Mickey really wasn't a partner after all. He'd said she wasn't, and Viola had been wary. Maybe at last she was learning not to be so gullible. After Rhys, how else *could* she be other than wary? But this tender little scene was quite an ouch. It shouldn't have been one, because she had no claim on him other than that he had been very sweet to her. Like a friend. A sexy, tempting one who kissed like a dream. She didn't want it to be an ouch at all, but it just was. It meant she couldn't see him again now — even if he *did* call — because if she did, well, the kind of all-round trouble and pain it could lead to would be unbearable. Her phone rang as she was stuffing the last of the bags into the Polo's boot.

"Help!" It wasn't really a surprise that it was book-group Lisa. "I've done a *stupid* thing!"

"Haven't we all," Viola said, feeling horribly low, slamming the car boot hard. For a terrible second she thought she'd locked the car keys inside with the shopping, because that was exactly the sort of thing that *would* happen, but in a rare piece of good fortune they were safe in her bag. "So tell me yours." She had no intention of telling hers — there were just too damn many of them.

"I have this Internet date, for Thursday, it's Paris. Right? I know you know because Charlotte's just called and told me she told you. And I was *so* excited. But it's a weird thing, this dating site. All in the interests of safety, which is mad as we're all grown-ups, aren't we, it's supposed to be a foursome. And I'm supposed to provide the other girl! I don't suppose . . . I know you've said . . . and I know Charlotte's also said . . ."

"I'll come," Viola told her immediately.

"You *will*? I promise I won't let you fall off the top of the Eiffel Tower or anything. It'll all be really safe."

"Yep. I've said I'll go to everything I'm invited to and I'm . . . well, I'm free on Thursday. Rachel is away on holiday with her dad. Just text me some times and stuff."

"Great! Eurostar, St Pancras. 7.30 a.m. Oh, fabioso! It's only a day trip, just for lunch, not an overnight, but it'll be *mega* fun."

254

Well, it might or it might not, Viola thought. But it had to be better than letting herself brood about a completely impossible someone she absolutely shouldn't have grown to like rather a lot.

CHAPTER
TWENTY-TWO

"Eh, you've got it looking nice in here. It were always a pretty house, this." Naomi roamed the downstairs areas of Bell Cottage, sniffing the fresh-paint air which mingled with the scent of Viola's lasagne that bubbled away in the oven. She tweaked at the sunflowers in their vase on the front window ledge.

"You'll want to move these flowers when it gets dark," Naomi said, giving Viola a look. Viola let it go. She didn't need to be told to close the shutters once the sun went down. During the day, she liked to leave them folded right back so she could enjoy the sight of the roses around the windows, but when darkness came she didn't plan to be alone in the house wondering if the sender of the cards had got together with the crazy people who'd left all the memorial flowers, so they could lurk by the gate and stare in through her lighted windows, putting curses on her.

"Here, have a shot of fizz, Mum," she said, handing Naomi a glass of celebratory champagne. "I'll see if I can weasel Rachel out of her room. Or . . . why don't you go up and find her? She'll want to show you her new colour scheme — try not to point out that it looks a bit grey though, she loves it like that. I'll go and get on with the salad before Kate takes over and starts cutting tomatoes into fancy shapes."

"You mean I should get a look at the room while she's still got it tidy." Naomi laughed. "You were just the same at her age."

"But we've been back here for a few days now, so there's no way it'll be tidy. Also, she's been packing for Ireland so she'll have scattered stuff everywhere. Marco and James are joining us for supper and taking her straight off with them after, so they can leave early tomorrow." She had a moment of worry about Rachel. They were travelling to Ireland by ferry. She didn't want to come over all fussy-mother but she wanted to make sure Rachel knew to stay away from the boat's rails, not to lean over too far. Not to . . . oh . . . not to do *anything* on this trip which would lead to death, damage, disaster, anything even remotely unlucky, just in case it was all in the genes.

"It's good she gets on with her dad so well," Naomi said.

"Well, of course she does. Marco's a top dad and James loves her too. And people generally do, don't they? Get on with their dads?"

"Generally." Naomi looked a bit awkward, put her drink down on the window ledge and headed upstairs to check out Rachel's territory.

James and Marco arrived in a flurry of more flowers and more champagne. "Happy new old house," James said, hugging Viola.

"Absolutely," Marco added. "Blessings on the place." He put the bottles in the fridge and then asked, "And did you find out who sent that moving-in card, by the way?"

Viola felt cold, thinking of the card with the kittens on it that now lurked in the drawer with the other one. She could have confided in Marco about them both, but he'd be away for a week from tomorrow and she didn't want to send him on his way with her problems on his mind. There wasn't much he could do apart from worry, and that never solved anything.

"No — not yet. It was probably a neighbour, like we said. Someone a bit forgetful."

"Ah — that good old standby, lasagne," Miles said later. He was opening a bottle of red wine as Viola, fully armed with oven gloves, carefully lifted the steaming dish out of the oven. She felt conscious of him watching her, sure he was expecting there to be a horrific hot-food and broken-dish incident.

"Don't watch me, Miles. I won't drop it, you know."

"Glad to hear it. And I wasn't actually looking at you. I was wrestling with this cork. Is everyone having red? Rachel?"

"Ugh, no, thanks — got a Coke."

"I'm driving so I'm on Coke too, thanks," Marco said, clinking glasses with his daughter.

"Lasagne's a standby?" Naomi spluttered. "In my young day it would have counted as fancy foreign food."

"British cooking at its best can't be beaten," Miles said, sounding rather disapproving.

"Here we go," Kate chimed in. "If it hasn't got potatoes and gravy it's Not Proper Food. You want to get out there and live a bit, Miles, before it's too late."

"Nobody said it's not proper food, Kate." Rob was sitting at the table, already a long way down his third glass of champagne. Maybe, Viola thought, he'd decided tonight was the ideal opportunity to announce his departure from the family. Talk about a conversation-stopper. On the other hand, it would at least distract everyone from so carefully Not Mentioning Rhys. His non-presence was lingering in the room like the vanilla scent that her tenant had so loved. She could swear there were still traces of that too, struggling to make itself known over the clean smell of new paint. She would invest in some of the richest scented candles from Santa Maria Novella when she got her next pay cheque, and make sure she always blew them out before leaving the room.

"I'm only saying it's different from the old days," Naomi told them. "I didn't say I wanted to go back to them. I was a war child, remember. Powdered egg and Woolton Pie. When I moved south and discovered Italian food in Soho it was like . . . wonderland. Talk about exotic. Until then I'd thought spaghetti only came in tins."

"What's Woolton Pie?" Rachel asked, looking horrified. "Is it sheep — you know, as in, like, *wool*?"

"You're not the only one who doesn't know that," Marco told her.

"It's sort of vegetable crumble. Must have been perfect if you had a father who grew prize-winning vegetables," Miles reminded Rachel. "I bet they had to put a security fence round, back then."

"Don't be so daft, Miles," Naomi scolded him. "Nobody *stole*. You didn't. You trusted your neighbours."

"Are you going to grow vegetables here?" Rob asked Viola. "That's quite a long garden you've got. You could put a lovely little potager down at the end. Some raised beds maybe, or divide sections up with fancy brickwork. I have a . . . er . . . friend who's done that."

"Oh, yes. He certainly has," Kate hissed across the table in Viola's general direction. "He absolutely has got a *friend* with a very swish whopping great garden. You wouldn't run short of rations *there*, that's for sure. Of any sort."

"Ooh, am I missing something here?" Marco asked, eyebrows raised.

Viola gave him a warning look.

"*Okaay!*" he said. "Please would someone pass the Parmesan? Lovely supper, Vee. To think when I met you we only ate chips. But hey, that's love for you."

"Oh yuck, Dad, *perlease*." Rachel shuddered.

"Marco still does eat chips, any chance he gets," James told them.

"I'll probably grow some easy stuff," Viola said, wondering, as Rob topped up his glass, if he and Kate were going to drink enough to end up with their marriage problems spilled all over the table. "Tomatoes in pots, a few sugar snaps, that kind of thing." And cucumbers, perhaps. She'd put one of Greg's into tonight's salad. It may have been her imagination, but she was sure it had more flavour than any she'd tasted. She'd even found herself feeling surprised none of the others had commented, till she told herself not to be so silly — it was *just a cucumber.*

"You should get that gardening man friend of yours to help," Naomi suggested. "The scruffy-looking one who was always hanging around. That garden's going to need a lot of work."

"What man?" Miles said, looking alarmed. "Don't tell me you've got another . . ."

"Why shouldn't she?" Marco challenged. "You surely don't expect Viola to shut down on a sex life at her age?"

"Bleurgh! Dad, that's even worse! That's, like, *Mum* you're talking about?"

"No, really, I haven't got anyone!" Viola felt she was being cross-examined. For a few seconds she allowed the mud-streaked image of Greg and his mad, broad, wolfy smile to settle in her head, as if she'd pressed the pause button on an Internet slide show. Then she clicked the image forward to him softly stroking his finger down her face when they planted the tulips. And then kissing him. *Goodbye,* she told the pictures, feeling a deep punch of pain in her chest. Heartburn, she decided, preferring to think she'd eaten the lasagne too hot to the knowledge that she'd very much miss him.

"The one from that night, you mean," Kate said, "with the filthy green Land Rover. Greg someone?" She was slurring now, heading towards danger mode. Kate could say anything, Viola realized. It would be an absolute miracle if she remembered that the night at the police station was to be kept firmly between the two of them.

"*What* night?" Rob smirked. "Have you been out on the tiles, Vee?"

"Gregory Fabian. And no tiles, Rob," she said quietly, then made a desperate bid to change the subject. "So — Ireland. Have you checked the weather forecast, Marco?"

"*Fabian*? No! Really? *Fabian*? That's amazing!" Kate wasn't to be distracted.

"Sun and showers. The usual for August. And *definitely* usual for Ireland. James bought six umbrellas in Poundland, just in case."

"Well, you need to be prepared. You'll thank me for them, you know."

"That man who was in the flat a bit too early in the morning and smells of putty?" Naomi asked.

"*Six*? Why so many?" Viola asked.

"In case of gales and resulting brolly destruction," James told her.

"Early in the morning, was he? Interesting . . ." Miles gave her a hard stare.

"No, Miles, it's not 'interesting'." Viola gave up on the Ireland and umbrellas question. "So you can put your eyebrows back down. But what's the big deal, Kate? You don't know him, do you?" Well, of course she did, if only briefly. Viola wished they'd talk about anything but this. Any second now and the whole night in the police cells thing would be out in the open, and they'd be forcing her to pack a bag and move back to the family version of house arrest. Not a chance.

"Fabian. That name is on the family tree. Let me see . . ." Kate screwed up her face, closed her eyes, concentrating. "Dad's side. He had a sister, maybe just a half-one actually, I'd have to check. Anyway, an aunt we never met; she married a Fabian. The family lived in a huge old house by the river with what used to be a market garden. The house got knocked down in the early sixties before anyone thought of listing these places, but the old walled garden's still in one piece, I think." Kate rattled it off as if she was reciting quotes she'd had to learn for homework. "See? The things you find out when you start delving into this family history lark. That Greg, he'll be our long-lost cousin, I bet you anything. So there you are then — think of it as me doing you a favour. I've saved you from a spot of incest."

"Strictly speaking it wouldn't be incest — a bit too remote," Miles told her, looking serious. "But it would hardly be ideal."

"Oh, Miles, don't be so boring. And it would be quite all right. But Viola's not likely to want to get involved with someone at the moment, now is she?" Naomi said. "Not after everything."

"It isn't even remotely on the cards," Viola insisted, starting to clear the empty plates. "He's — was — just someone I met. A nice man. Kind." She felt very flat as she shoved cutlery too haphazardly into the dishwasher. Forks fell to the bottom and she stabbed her hand on a knife when reaching over it to retrieve them. There was blood, but not much, and she quickly rinsed her finger under the tap and wrapped a piece of kitchen paper round it. This was supposed to be such a happy evening, this new start in her own home, but it was all turning argumentative and uncomfortable. Nothing that pudding couldn't fix, she resolved, taking the lemon tart and bowl of raspberries out of the fridge.

"I don't really mind if Mum meets someone," Rachel said. "I don't want her to be all lonely and thinking only about me all the time."

"No, of course you don't," Marco teased. "That way you'd never get away with teenage naughtiness. You'd be *being watched*. Nothing worse when you're at that essential breakout stage."

Rachel blushed and started concentrating on rolling her napkin into a sausage shape.

"We should all get to know him," Kate suggested. "Invite him over and see if there are other cousins and stuff. A whole new family. Vee? Do you think he'd be up for that?"

"Er . . . well, who can say? Really, I hardly know him. And also, I mean, would you want to hook up with a whole bunch of people who claimed they were your relatives, if it was a different way round?"

"Hmm . . . I see what you mean. Could be a bit weird."

"Most of us have trouble coping with the families we've already got," Rob said, glancing sideways at Kate.

"Don't we just," she snapped back.

"Tensions there," Marco whispered to Viola.

"Oh, there so are," she murmured back.

"Excellent pud, Viola, lovely tart," Rob interrupted, giving Marco a suspicious look.

"Yes, Rob likes a *lovely tart*," Kate snarled.

"Kate!" Naomi snapped, putting her spoon down noisily. "If you've got something on your mind, damn well come out with it. The way you're being tonight there'll be blood on the carpet before the end of it."

"Well, you like a murder to solve, don't you?" Marco grinned at her, and Viola blew him a kiss for trying to keep the mood light.

"Look, we're supposed to be celebrating Viola's new go at life. She and Rachel being back in their house," Miles said. "Even though *some* of us think it's all a bit too . . . well, soon isn't the word."

"No, it's not. She shouldn't be here at all. It's stupid. Moving on should be exactly that." Kate was drooping miserably over her plate, all spirit vanished. Then she looked up, bright-eyed and manically animated suddenly. "I know, Viola, why don't you come out flat-hunting with me on Thursday? We could find somewhere lovely, overlooking the park, live in a gorgeous mansion block, flats adjoining. It would be *huge* fun!"

There was a pause, nobody wanting to be the first to comment.

"Sounds horrendously expensive, Kate. Besides, Rachel and I aren't moving from here, not now we've just got back in. Why would we? I'll help you look if you like, but I can't on Thursday."

"Why? Are you seeing *that man*?" Miles asked. "Maybe you should give your sister some help when she asks for it?" Then he murmured so only Viola could hear, "God knows, Vee, it sounds like she needs it, and she's given you plenty of *her* time."

"I'm not seeing *that man*. No. Actually . . . I can't because . . ." and she hadn't meant to tell anyone this, but sometimes, she decided, a bit of bravado could be just what it took to get them off her case, "I'm going to Paris."

CHAPTER
TWENTY-THREE

"Hey, I hear you're off to Paris with Lisa. Good on you!
And did you see Benedict Peabody being a drunk posh
git in the papers? I wasn't surprised." Amanda's phone
call was the most welcome of several the next morning.
Positive thinking like this was what Viola needed, not
the warnings of doom and disaster she was getting from
Miles and Kate. They had each called her before
10a.m. (and how Kate managed not to be groaning on
her bed with a throbbing headache was a miracle),
ostensibly to thank her for dinner, but neither had
resisted the opportunity to give her a lecture on
Travelling Abroad with Dangerous Strangers.

Thank goodness for Naomi the night before, who
had given her a hug as she left and whispered, "You
know what they say about Paris and lovers. Take
advantage while you still can." This had made her feel
both cheered up and also — if such a thing were
possible — cheered *down*, as it rather implied her days
of youth and lovers were numbered. She'd quite like to
think she'd got at least the illusion of being young on
her side for a few years yet, even if she didn't intend to
look for lovers. Especially not lovers who brought
trouble and complications.

"I did see him, the daft little bugger, though he's not such a bad kid really. He'll probably put the pics up on Facebook and his zillion friends will all click 'Like'. And yes, I am going with Lisa. It's only a day trip but honestly, Manda, if you could have heard my brother and sister going on at me you'd think I was making a three-month trek overland to China on a motorbike with a serial killer. They think I'm mad and that I'm certain to be captured for the slave trade, that's if there is any demand for mid-thirties singletons who tend to trip over things."

"Bloody 'ell, do they still think you should be locked away in solitary with your mum guarding your cell?"

"They do. For my own safety. I so wish I hadn't said anything, but they were getting more and more nutty over supper and I just blurted it out to stop Kate from going on about the possibility that someone I've been slightly sort of seeing might turn out to be some kind of cousin."

"Oo er, how very . . . um . . . rural — or even royal, come to think of it. Don't they all marry cousins? But, seriously, does it matter? I mean, unless he's, like, an actual *first* cousin, if you didn't already know him before then he must be pretty remote, cousin-wise, so it wouldn't be like you were brought up together, playing in the same sandpit and doing the family Christmas thing."

"Well, no, it's not that, exactly. It's a bit more complicated, I think. Anyway, it's not that important because I don't think I'll be seeing him again."

It almost made her cry to say that aloud. It actually physically hurt. But whenever she recalled how lovely kissing Greg had been on that night together, she also got the accompanying mental picture of him tenderly nuzzling the head of the tiny sleeping baby and gently placing it in Mickey Fabian's car.

"Oh, that's a shame, but, well, it wasn't as if you'd got *really* involved yet, was it?" Amanda said. "Think of it as a trial run. And who knows, Mr Off-to-Paris might turn out to be Mr Perfect. Or Monsieur Parfait. Just don't get carried away and decide to stay there too long — it's A-level-results day next week. We've got to be on duty at Med and Gib for our poor students, God bless the sweet young things. I hope we get to do more celebrating than consoling."

"How was the family supper?" Greg's call straight after Amanda's wasn't from his mobile number, so it took Viola by surprise, and the sound of his voice made her heart pound.

"Um — it was OK, thanks. You know, *familyish*."

"As much fun as being out with me?" His voice had its usual teasing edge, which always made her smile. Viola felt bad about not being very communicative, but she was putting off the moment when she would have to tell him she knew about the baby and give him her decision about not seeing him again. It wasn't something she felt should be done over the phone, and yet how else to do it? Deciding to be sensible was a complete pain, but the ditzy airhead she now knew she'd been, marrying Rhys only eight weeks after

269

meeting him, had vanished over the past year, leaving a far more thoughtful and wary woman in her place.

"A grown-up" was what she now realized she was, and about time too, even though so far it wasn't proving to be a whole lot of laughs. She knew she was deliberately denying herself many a lovely moment, all the silly fun that had become such a part of being anywhere with Greg, but it had to be done. She wondered if he might think — when it came to her saying she'd seen him with the baby — that she'd been tracking down either him or Mickey, checking on them. Stalking, even — oh, the irony. Given her own experiences of being harassed by weird strangers after Rhys's death, she could almost laugh. But only *almost*.

"I've got five hundred crocus bulbs that would enjoy the company of your dibber, if you fancy it," he told her, evidently having given up waiting for her reply.

"Um . . . Well, it's a bit difficult at the moment. I wanted to talk to you about . . ."

"Ugh. Sounds serious. Don't. Hey, though," he went on, all enthusiasm, "did you ever hear that story about the German prisoner of war who was taken out to help plant a load of cheer-up bulbs on a grassy bank in Torquay, I think it was?"

"No, what happened?" She should finish this call but he was laughing now, and she hadn't the heart just to cut him off coldly. Oh, how she'd miss him. Funny how someone so recently arrived in her life had become so essential. But then, she reminded herself, that had been how it had all started with Rhys.

270

"Everyone said how hard he worked and how careful and trustworthy he was, but when spring came the crocuses spelled out Heil Hitler all along the seafront! We should think of some words to plant. Not that message, obviously."

"No, definitely not that." She felt, and knew she sounded, flat and miserable, but she was completely incapable of shattering his mood.

"So — when would be good for you? Thursday?"

"Ah — no, sorry, Thursday I can't do. Going on a day trip to Paris."

"Oh. With friends?"

"One friend plus two we haven't met. Like a sort of . . ."

"Blind date. Right." He sounded a bit deflated and she felt bad. This really wasn't how to go about things.

"Not a real date, more just a . . . I don't know, a keeping Lisa company thing. Sort of." She was waffling now and more than slightly hating herself.

"Not that there's any reason why you shouldn't go out with anyone you like," he said. "Free agent, free spirit, all that."

"And you as well? Free, I mean. Are you really?" One last chance, she thought, bracing herself to hear him fess up.

"Completely," he replied. He suddenly sounded serious. "Er . . . what exactly are we talking about here? I was hoping to see you again, is all, and I did think we had a good time together the other night, didn't we? Was it just me? I didn't think it *was* just me at the time. But if you're already seeing someone else . . ."

"Me? No. No, it's not that."

"Or did my rogue cucumber poison you? Look, if you want to tell me to sod off, just say."

So she took a deep breath and was about to do some kind of version of "just say", when he suddenly added; "Sorry, Viola, there's a client just come in, urgent work stuff. Talk later?" And before she could reply, he'd gone.

Each of these mornings since she'd been back at Bell Cottage, she'd slightly dreaded the day's first glance out of the front window in case there was some love token to Rhys pinned to the magnolia again, or some badly handwritten poem shoved through the letter box. So how long would it take, Viola wondered later when the doorbell rang, for her stomach not to turn over apprehensively every time there was someone at the door?

Half of her hoped, in spite of everything, and in spite of there only having been a fifteen-minute gap since his call, that it would actually be Greg, who'd rushed over to see her on the spontaneous off chance. The other half dreaded a worst-case nut job manically attacking her with a knife. Thank goodness for the spyhole that Marco had insisted she have put in. There, swimmily distorted by the wide-angle lens, stood Naomi, arms folded across her front like the late Les Dawson hitching up his comedy bosoms, one hand clutching a bunch of deep purple gladioli. Viola took the security chain off and opened the door, standing well back to allow her whirlwind-mood mother and her floral burden in.

"I've had Kate on the phone this morning and she says now you've come back here and look like you're settling, she's decided she's moving into my flat. Was that your idea? Because I don't want her to." Naomi, as usual, came straight to the point. "I know you all think I need someone living in to keep an eye on me in case I fall down the stairs and end up lying there for days in a helpless heap, but I don't want Kate there. She won't keep to her own side like you and Rachel did. Oh no. She'll wander and fuss and she'll poke around the place, interfering, going through stuff. I told her, I said, why should *she* be the one to leave her house? She had said it was Rob that was going. Have you got the kettle on? No sugar for me — Monica says we've to watch for diabetes. I don't think a biscuit would hurt, though."

Naomi settled herself at the kitchen table, laid the massive heap of gladioli down in front of her and drew breath for a moment, while Viola tried to take in what she'd said.

"Are you sure it's such a bad idea?" Viola ventured. "Kate and Miles are worried about you being on your own, and if Kate's happy to . . ."

"Don't be daft! *She* says it'd only be till she finds somewhere else, but once she's in I know I'd never get her out. Before you blink, she'd have the builders in and be trying to turn it all into flats, telling me, 'It'll pay for itself.' I don't think so. Vee, I can't and won't sell it and that's that. I like it the way it is. You'll have to tell her."

"Kate doesn't listen to me. She thinks I'm not even capable enough to run my own life, let alone tell *her* what to do."

"She knows you're capable all right, but she's jealous of you, that's her trouble."

"Jealous? Wow, that's a new one! What have I got that she could be jealous of?"

"She'd think of something. She just always has been, right from when you were little. Even as a great big girl of fifteen, she eyed up your My Little Pony castle and sulked because she thought she'd never had anything as big as that. She had, as it happens, but she'd forgotten and there was no persuading her. A lot of her old toys went during the move."

Viola put mugs of tea and a plate of Jaffa cakes on the table and sat down opposite Naomi.

"So you know about her and Rob splitting up?" she said.

Naomi considered. "Well, only what I gathered from last night — talk about an atmosphere with those two — and what she said on the phone this morning about him going off with a golf woman. She hadn't said anything before. But I knew Kate wasn't settled, hasn't been for a couple of years now."

"She hinted about that — that there'd been some kind of break-up before. So Rob hasn't been quite the safely neutered Labrador I'd always taken him for."

"Not many of them are, love. But then scratch most folks and you'll find it's a case of still waters."

Viola frowned, trying to make something of her mother's muddled metaphor. "Hmm. Do you mean everyone's got their secrets?" Hadn't they just, she thought, yet again picking at the wound by bringing to life the little tableau of Greg, Mickey and the baby. If it had been anyone else she'd have felt quite sentimental in that car park, thinking, ahh, such a tender scene. She rubbed her head, quite literally trying to dislodge him from her mind.

"Oh, most people have secrets. Even you've got one or two, haven't you?" Naomi looked at Viola intently.

Viola sighed. "No. I don't think so. Nothing worth keeping secret, anyway." Then she smiled at her mother. "And what about you? How many have you got?"

To her surprise, Naomi looked wary, as if she were thinking hard. "One or two. Everyone of my age has. And if they haven't, they haven't lived. Anyway — I must go. Got a cemetery visit to make, lay a few flowers."

Well, that explained the gladioli. They'd never been something she'd thought she liked, but the purple colour of these was so deep, it was almost black. The petals had a lustrous sheen, like the gleaming pelt of a well-fed animal. "Anyone I know?"

"Oliver Stonebridge. Your old Uncle Olly. It's the twenty-fifth anniversary today."

"Oh, right — yes, of course. Paint in my hair . . ." She smiled, thinking of how she'd told Greg about this.

"He was always a good friend. The best." Naomi stood up and looked past Viola, through the open French doors. "Hell's bells, the state of that garden. You'll have your work cut out there." It sounded, to

Viola, like something fairly random to say as a distraction.

"I've made a start, weeded up the first half of the left bed. But, look, would you like me to come to the cemetery with you?" she asked.

Naomi was fiddling with her handbag now, looking for car keys. "No, love, not today. Maybe another time. You've had enough of dealing with the dead."

"Don't forget your flowers, Mum," Viola said, gathering up the exuberant gladioli as Naomi was now halfway to the door, leaving them on the table.

"Oh, those aren't mine. I've got roses from the garden for Oliver out in the car. No, I found these leaning against your door. No note that I could see, so it can't be a welcome back from the neighbours. I reckon you've got a secret admirer. It'll be that man you don't talk about. The one who isn't your cousin. Don't listen to Kate, she wants to leave well alone, that one."

Viola felt cold inside. No card, no note. The Rhys factor again, it had to be. Just when she was beginning to feel safe. The possibility, no, *probability,* hit her like the sudden realization that you're about to be felled by serious flu. Was this gesture, along with the cards, from the woman who'd been with Rhys when he crashed the car? For the first time since she'd made the decision to move back home, she really wondered if she'd done the right thing. As soon as Naomi's Fiat had gone from the driveway, she crammed the gladioli, lovely as they were, into a bin bag and took them straight outside. If whoever had brought them happened to be passing before the rubbish collection the next morning, they'd see those lustrous purple flowers sticking out of the top of the bag and be sure to get the message.

It was only a few times a year that she'd visit Oliver's grave. Although it felt fine to chat to him now and then, Naomi wasn't under any illusions that she was talking to a spirit that could hear her. She didn't really believe in the fetishization of the dead, and usually kept out of the cemetery unless she had a friend to bury and had to stand around a freezing graveside wishing she'd worn her furry boots. And in this huge municipal death stadium she didn't like the rows of graves, all lined up too close together so you couldn't help thinking you were treading on actual people. Feeling the lumpy ground beneath her feet always made her want to apologize to the occupant.

Oliver would hate it here. He'd wanted, he'd once told her when he first got ill and the end stage still seemed an unfathomable distance away, to be cremated and scattered over the Vale of the White Horse, but he couldn't have told his wife (or if he had, she didn't take any notice), because once Monica knew it was going to be terminal she'd started shopping for fancy granite as if she were looking for a new kitchen worktop. Naomi knew the sparkly black stuff and the gold lettering wasn't at all what he'd have picked for himself. If he *had* to have a headstone, he'd certainly have preferred a lump of unpolished Dartmoor granite with some simple words incised: Oliver Stonebridge Smith, artist, and the relevant dates. He never liked a fuss.

Someone had got there first. Monica, certainly. Last year had been awkward, as Monica's own car had been out of action and she'd asked Naomi to drive her. Which of course she had. She could have wriggled out of it somehow, but a promise is a promise and Oliver had trusted her to keep an eye. But she hadn't felt able to share the grave-time: some things just couldn't be done. She had made some excuse about awkward parking arrangements and stayed with the car, half listening to Radio Four's afternoon play, while Monica arranged her carnations in the flower holder on the grey granite chippings. Naomi had gone back alone later, after the two of them had had tea and scones in John Lewis and Monica had returned to her flat happy enough with a new petit-point kit. Naomi had sat on the cold granite for so long that early evening, just talking about the summer and how much she still missed and loved him, that she became chilled and stiff and she'd had to haul herself up on the arm of the next grave's stone angel. Oliver would have quite liked an angel, she thought now, as she walked along the cemetery path with her white roses. A magnificent, muscular angel with vast wings and a beautiful, sad-boy face.

Naomi stopped at the graveside, nodded a polite hello to the next-door angel and sat down with her roses. She never put them in a vase, didn't arrange them among Monica's carnations. Instead she scattered them loosely across the granite chippings. They wouldn't last long, but that was the way with so much that was perfect. It didn't matter. All that mattered was the memory and the love that had outlived Oliver.

CHAPTER
TWENTY-FOUR

The day was going to be a hot one, and it would be roasting in Paris. At an hour that had even seasoned commuters yawning in their tube seats, Lisa and Viola headed for St Pancras to meet their dates. Viola felt quite excited — if a bit nervous — about the day. It would be so good to get away and think of nothing but enjoying herself, taking in the sights of the city and giving what she was supposed to be doing — working on the War Poets selection for the new term's A-level intake — a complete miss. Also, she wouldn't be there when the bin men took the gladioli away. She'd almost shuddered as she passed them that morning when she left, seeing their beautiful, soft purple blooms sticking out of the bag on the pavement.

Greg hadn't texted or called her again, and she felt bad about putting off the moment when she had to have the this-can't-happen conversation with him. At least for this one, carefree day she had a good excuse not to think about what to say, how to say it, why it had to be done. Not that she should have to say much, not once she'd made it clear she knew about the baby.

"I should have gone for flats like you have," Lisa said on the tube, looking at Viola's shoes. "These aren't that high, but if we do a lot of walking I'm going to regret every millimetre of heel by the time the day's half over."

"It's Paris — you could buy some others?" Viola suggested, feeling quite joyfully frivolous.

"In August?"

"What's wrong with August?"

"Paris is pretty much closed in August, or so I heard."

"Not shops? You're kidding me."

"Dunno. Something I read. Everyone Parisian goes away till autumn."

"Oh, they can't, not all of them. I don't believe it. The place will be packed with trippers. So if it's shut, why are we going then?" Viola began to wonder if this was a good idea. Lisa couldn't be serious. Nobody closed down an entire city just because the residents liked a holiday.

"Toby said it's the cheap season. He sounded as if that was a top plus." Lisa wrinkled her nose and grinned. "Doesn't sound promising, does it? I was hoping for a Eurostar champagne breakfast. I'm thinking we'll buy our own."

"So Toby is . . . yours? What's mine called?"

"Oh he's Ed, a mate of Toby's — I think he said they work together, something to do with marketing. I wish I knew more about him than that. Sorry, Vee. I don't know anything about Toby either, though I've seen a photo and read his version of what he's like, but you can usually take that as a piece of fiction. I think on the

DateMate site the only thing we had in common was being Pisces. If yours is a total dog you can . . ."

"What? Back out?" Viola interrupted. "No, I wouldn't do that to you. I mean, what would you do with the two of them?"

"Um . . ." Lisa smirked. "Well, it'd be a first. And now that the divorce is final I did promise myself I'd try pretty much anything, tee hee. I'm a new woman, me."

Ed and Toby were there to meet Lisa and Viola as arranged at the top of the tube escalator at St Pancras, and Viola immediately wondered why they were dressed as if they were heading for the seaside, each of them wearing baggy cut-off combats, polo shirts and trainers. Ed's shins were so white they reminded her of the stems of leeks. Viola could just imagine Naomi's face, all pursed up, cat's-bum style, in disapproval of the overcasual take on what to wear to one of the world's most elegant capitals. Viola and Lisa were both in dresses, Lisa's a caramel and white shift, Viola's a blue flowered Jigsaw tea dress, both of which would be more than up to lunch in the swishest of Paris's restaurant selection. The men were a few years younger than Viola, late twenties like Lisa, she'd guess — maybe that would do to excuse the sartorial lapse. Ed's right forearm had a tattoo of a running tiger that looked as if it had been drawn by someone who was only at the apprentice stage of the craft. The inside of his other wrist had a heart with an unreadable name in it. Could be worse, she decided charitably, it could have been a swastika.

"Hello, *laydeez*!" Toby greeted them, arms up as if to hug them both at once and waving a clanking Tesco bag. "Are we in for a top day out!"

You couldn't, Viola reasoned, *not* be excited about getting on a train in one country to go to another. As their party boarded and found their seats she felt quite zingy about the day, in spite of the not-so-lovely appearance of Ed and Toby and the fact that they were in the cheapest seats. That didn't matter at all — it wasn't as if it was a long trip. The main thing, she told herself, was simply to get there and then enjoy the city and forget about family, stalkers, Greg (ouch) and *everything*. Also she must — she decided — try to get past her first impressions of Ed and Toby: there was a lot more to people than their dress sense — she mustn't be snobby about it, even if Ed's shirt did have a Tottenham Hotspur badge where classier versions might have a little polo player or a crocodile.

"So much for champagne," Lisa murmured to Viola as Toby unloaded cans of lager from the Tesco bag and spread them out across the table. "They don't serve it in Standard class."

"Here's breakfast!" Toby said, pulling packs of Scotch eggs out of the bag. "Sorry, girls, these are as close as I could get to a proper fry-up. Neat thinking, huh? That's what you get in marketing. It's all about solutions." An elderly couple across the aisle were dealing with a flask of coffee and steaming croissants from the station coffee shop and gave them a disapproving look. Viola sympathized.

By lunchtime, Viola had concluded that you could see a lot of Paris from the open top of a bus but you didn't get to see inside any of the museums, or the galleries; nor did you get to sit in the Jardin du Luxembourg with fancy ice cream, or stroll along the Left Bank thinking about the poetry of Baudelaire and the theatre life of Colette.

"The best bargain, this, don't you agree, laydeez?" Ed said. "All of Paris spread out below us, and chauffeur-driven too." Toby and Ed sprawled across the seats, faces up to the hot sun and turning redder by the minute. By the Eiffel Tower the two of them had downed the last of the lager, and by the time the bus stopped at the Louvre they'd taken their shirts off and their pale chests were getting as blotchy as their faces.

"Let's go and sit down the front," Viola whispered to Lisa as a party of Americans got up and left the bus. She and Lisa went and sat in front of a group of German trippers, telling the men they thought the view would be better and that not to bother to move, they were OK.

"Any view would be better than Toby's naked torso," Lisa said as they settled on the front seats. "God, this was *such* a mistake. I'm so sorry, you must hate me for this!"

"Hey, it's only a day out of our lives, what can it hurt? And it's quite fun really — a kind of see-it-all view of the city for the horribly lazy. We could just abandon them both, I suppose, but they've got all the travel arrangements and ticket things. I'm fine with sticking it out — after all, there might be another hundred facts about marketing that Toby can tell us. Lunch soon anyway, surely. It's getting pretty late and I'm starving. Any idea where they've booked? Or even if?"

Lisa giggled. "Probably McDonald's!"

"Wouldn't surprise me. No, really, we're going to get off this bus at the next stop if we have to drag them; we'll get into a cab and go up to Montmartre. It'll be touristy enough for the blokes but pretty enough for us, and there are loads of restaurants. OK with you?"

Lisa looked back to their half-naked escorts. "Oh yes. Anything's fine by me, just so long as they put some clothes back on. I am *so* complaining to DateMates about this. I didn't think I'd need to specify that I'd quite like someone who knew about keeping his top on in public. Jeez."

More lager. Where did they put it? At the kerbside restaurant under a shady awning, Viola ate her steak frites and salad and drank red wine and wondered if men's bladders were actually four times the size of women's, given the amount of liquid they could put away. She also thought how lovely it would be to be doing this day trip with someone to whom she felt a tingling attraction. She'd guess Greg wouldn't be guzzling beer by the gallon and complaining about the waitress not speaking English, although he might be eyeing up the neat grass by the funicular and considering how much better it would look as a wild-flower meadow. She watched Toby trying to get the attention of a living statue, a girl entirely in white, dressed Marie Antoinette-style and perched as still as a pillar up on a plinth, occasionally winking at any man who took her fancy. She didn't wink at either Toby or Ed, though on the plus side they did at least have their shirts back on.

"I could do with a sleep," Toby said as the waitress took their plates away. He then took hold of Lisa's hand from the table and moved it down to rest on his thigh. "Or at least a lie-down." He smirked at her. Viola watched Lisa wriggle her fingers free and pick up her wine glass.

"We could go to Sacré-Cœur. If you're tired you could sit down in there while we look around," she told him.

"Nah, you're all right. Course, we should have booked a two-dayer, then we'd have a hotel to go back to. If I'd known we'd get on this well . . . you know?"

Lisa smiled politely. Ed moved his chair closer to Viola's but it got stuck in a grating on the pavement and he lurched across the table, sending lager bottles crashing to the ground.

"Shit, sorry!" he said. "This chair's fault — it's wonky tat." Waiters appeared with dustpans and brushes and Viola was relieved that Toby agreed it was time to pay and go. "Been here too long anyway," he said, collecting up their credit cards to divvy up the bill. "It isn't a late train. That would have cost another ton. You don't want to spend a bomb on date one, do you? Just in case . . ." He winked at the living statue and she made a hissing noise at him.

"I've pulled!" he said, punching the air.

"I don't think so, love," Lisa told him.

"Oh, sorry, darling," he apologized, giving her a clumsy hug, "that was wrong of me. I'm already with a beautiful woman, couldn't want another."

"Not one all painted in matt emulsion anyway," Ed agreed as they headed down to the funicular. "Things would get very messy. She'd get stuff all over your Mr Man."

"Just the way I like it," Toby chortled. *Mr Man?* Viola caught Lisa's eye and they burst into unstoppable giggles. Toby took this as encouragement and put his arm round Lisa, who wriggled free on the pretext of adjusting her shoe strap.

After an afternoon of lazing along the banks of the Seine and managing not to see a single famous painting, any couture shops or the inside of any glorious church, Lisa whispered a heartfelt "Nearly over," as they climbed on to the train for the journey home. Ed and Toby had sorted the seating as they boarded, so Viola and Lisa were ushered into seats opposite each other by the window and the men sat beside them. Viola felt a bit trapped. On the plus side, Ed hadn't so much as tried to hold her hand, and in spite of the shirtlessness and the industrial volumes of beer he'd been reasonably polite. She was glad all expenses had been evenly split and even if the day wasn't to be one of her life's travel highlights exactly, it was different and fun and had given her a very sharp reminder of the sort of man she wasn't going to be looking for. If she ever was, that is.

"Work tomorrow." Ed sighed, watching the edges of Paris slide past. "Early meeting about feasibility and management indices."

"He means how many phones their branch has sold this month," Toby said, rather sneerily.

"I don't flog phones, knobhead," Ed snapped, then turned to Viola. "Sorry, long day. How was it for you?"

"Interesting," she said, opting for honesty. "Excellent lunch." Well, it had been.

Opposite, Lisa had closed her eyes. Viola watched as Toby took the chance to have a good stare at Lisa's breasts. His hand was under the table, aiming for Lisa's thigh, and Viola wondered if she should give her a gentle kick, wake her up so she could deal with him in whichever way she chose.

"Sweet, aren't they?" Ed's mouth was too close to her ear and she shifted sideways a bit, but almost hit her head against the window. "All paired off now. Neat," he murmured at her. "You're one hot lady, you know."

If I'm hot, she thought, it's only due to the weather.

"You like me. I can tell," he persisted. Across the table, Lisa slept on, Toby's eyes following the rise and fall of her chest. Viola said nothing, concentrating on the fact that it was now less than half an hour to St Pancras, and then she could escape.

"I know you do, don't deny it. I'm making you gooey in your wee-wee, aren't I?" He was almost slathering in her ear now and was reaching for her hand.

"*What?* Er, no, you're absolutely not!"

288

Lisa woke up with a jump. "All right, Vee? Are we nearly there yet?"

"Not long now. I . . . er . . . I think I'll just go to the loo. Won't be long." She picked up her bag and pushed past Ed.

"Don't keep me waiting," he said, smirking.

"I'll come too," Lisa said.

"You'll have to climb across me." Toby spread his legs out and leaned back.

"No, I won't; you'll get up and let me out, like a gentleman," she told him.

"Oh, I love a strict woman." He grinned, complying, but stroking her bum as she passed.

"Oh God, you won't believe this." Viola managed to keep her laughter in till they were out of range and she could tell Lisa what Ed had said.

"*No!* Eugh!" Lisa giggled. "How are we going to lose them at St Pancras? They seem to think we're gagging for it. Any idiot can see we're so not."

"Too right. I don't want to be introduced to Ed's *Mr Man*."

"Aaagh, don't!" Lisa laughed.

The train was slowing now. "Where are we? It didn't stop at Ashford, so . . ."

"Ah, Ebbsfleet." Lisa peered out of the window as they pulled into a station. "Are you thinking what I am?"

"Yep. Definitely. Come on." Viola and Lisa raced along inside the train till they were a couple of carriages further away from their dates, and when the train stopped they opened the door and jumped out, dashing for the shelter of the exit and hiding behind a drinks machine till the train pulled out again without them, and without leaving two bewildered men looking up and down the platform.

"Did it!" The two of them high-fived each other and then looked around.

"And now," Viola said, "the bit we didn't think of. How the hell do we get home from here?"

CHAPTER
TWENTY-FIVE

"You *hitch-hiked*? Honestly, Vee, you have *no* sense at all, have you?" Viola really shouldn't have told Kate, because she knew quite well what her reaction would be, but when Kate turned up a couple of days later with swatches of curtain fabric plus a heap of estate-agent details and a request for an opinion about flats, it was somehow irresistible.

"Hey lighten up, Kate, I wasn't on my own. I was with Lisa and we were fine. We got a lift in a truck full of music equipment all the way to the O2. Lisa's seeing the driver for a drink tonight *and* he can get her tickets to shows."

"Oh well, she landed on her feet there then, getting off with some random roadie." Kate pulled a disapproving face.

"Compared with the semi-formed Neanderthals we'd been with in Paris, I'd say yes she did, actually. I loved the hitching bit. I felt like a teenager again. I've been a parent since I was twenty so I think I'm owed a bit of reckless fun."

"God, Viola, don't you think you've had enough of reckless for a lifetime? You know what your luck's like. Fate-tempting really isn't a hobby option for you. And I don't know how you can live in this hexed house. Sell it. Come and get a nice flat near me, then I can keep an eye on you."

"An eye? No chance! And you can't blame the house, Kate. It's not the tiniest bit hexed. And just because I made one stupid mistake with my life doesn't mean I have to spend the rest of it being too timid to breathe. You're looking good, by the way. I like your hair shorter, it suits you." She'd had the colour done as well, Viola noticed. No trace of those greying roots, just some subtle shadings of dark blonde and copper. Way to go, she thought. "Is it about getting Rob back? Let him see what he's missing and then he'll be begging you to take him back again?"

"No, it's not! It's about new beginnings, all that. Moving on, as they say, in fact as *you* say." Kate smiled — a beaming sort of smile that looked as if she absolutely couldn't prevent it. If this hadn't been her habitually pessimistic sister with a divorce on the cards, Viola would have thought she was up to something. It was good to be able to change the subject. Another moment or two and Kate would be sure to mention Rhys. She always seemed to. If she were really keen on the moving-on thing, she'd do better to stop referring back to him.

"*And* you've got make-up on. In the morning. That's so not you. Come on, what's happened? Have you been out somewhere? *Are* you seeing someone?"

"Of course I'm not!" Kate blushed, looking suddenly girlish. "And the only place I've been to is a wedding, while you were swanning about in Paris. One of the

292

golf-club fogeys married a Lady Player. It was quite a sweet event, even considering how off weddings I'm feeling. And you had to laugh: there was this guard of honour of oldies with niblicks or wedges or whatever the fattest sticks are called. They're off to live in a bungalow in Lytham St Annes, so at least that's two less people breaking my windows — or what *used to be* my windows. I only went so I could watch Rob making cow eyes at *her* across the room. You should see her, Vee. She's got candyfloss hair like Margaret Thatcher's in the nineties and no beam end at all. Just flat down from neck to feet. He used to like my curvy bum."

"Perhaps she's got . . ."

"Ugh, no, whatever it is, don't say it!" Kate put her hands over her ears. "I *really* don't want to think of them *in that way*."

Viola laughed. "I was only going to say, maybe she's got an enviable handicap, golf-wise, I mean."

"Well, in a way she has got a golf handicap. She's got Rob. Wait till she finds him standing by her dishwasher clutching a plate and looking puzzled, like there should be some magic code to make the door open. By the way, did you talk to that Greg bloke about us all being distant cousins? Tracing Dad's side of the family back is fascinating stuff. Mum's will be all cotton workers and mill girls, I expect. I'll do them next."

"Er . . . no. I haven't actually seen him. I've been going over next term's courses, trying to work out if I can persuade the new bunch that they'll love *Northanger Abbey* if they just think of it as part of the connection from *Dracula* to the *Twilight* books. Kind of Jane Austen lite."

"If you don't want to tell him, maybe I will," Kate said, laying out the fabric swatches on the kitchen table all across Viola's books and notes.

"No! No, don't, Kate. Just leave it, will you?"

"You've had a row, haven't you?" Kate gave her a beady look. "See, you're learning at last. If it starts going bad, just walk away."

"Not a row. I don't know him well enough even to have a row."

"I'll admit he seemed nice."

"Too nice, maybe."

"Too nice, yes, not that trustable. Anyway don't lose touch, I've got questions for the family-tree thing."

"Oh, Kate, can't you just leave it? Please?"

Viola started looking through the fabrics, avoiding Kate's probing. Vertical stripes would be good for Roman blinds, she thought, trying to summon up interest. She didn't want to talk about Greg, especially to Kate. When she got back from Paris she'd immediately checked the house phone in case he'd called. Nothing. He must have taken her wariness as a sign to get right out of her life. His abrupt end to that last call did make her wonder if it was Mickey who'd strolled into the office, not a client. Good, she told herself. Excellent. Problem solved, without her having to listen to him admitting his interest in her was just a cheery on-the-side dalliance. Pity it didn't make her feel as truly relieved and content as she should be. Dangerous stuff, all this: to be avoided.

"OK, I won't contact him then, but you really should talk to him, you know," Kate said, holding up a piece of pale linen patterned with big blue tulips. "At least if he knows we're slightly related it might put him off chasing you. Because obviously you don't want that."

That was another ouch moment. Viola let it pass. Kate went blithely on, "He's been here, though, hasn't he? Since our dinner here the other night?"

"No, he hasn't. Why do you say that?"

"Just the roses at the front, looking all glossy and tidy and no old dead petals. Or have you got yourself a real gardener? No — you couldn't afford one. You didn't deadhead them yourself, did you? I hope you didn't go up a ladder. Miles would have a fit if he knew. So would Mum."

Viola felt cold. Why would Greg come and do her gardening? After her negative attitude on the phone, he certainly wasn't likely to come round and trim her roses. Kate couldn't be right, surely; the dead petals must simply have fallen off.

"No, it wasn't me. I hadn't noticed. Like I said, I've been up to here in books for next term while Rachel's away, sorting lesson plans for the new intake and the new syllabus. I don't think I'd have noticed if someone had taken the roof off the place. But hey, I'm going to look."

She went to the front door, followed by Kate, and opened it warily, as if Greg (or whoever the phantom rose-tidier was) might be waiting in the porch to pounce. It could be the gladioli-sender. Who might also be the person who sent the horrible anonymous cards.

If so (though why they'd want to take on garden chores was a mystery), it could all add up to another dose of full-scale stalking. Worst of all, how terrifying if it were the woman Rhys *had* gone off with, coming back, haunting, blaming, hating her. This was far more disturbing than back at the beginning, when Rhys first died. At least then it hadn't been just one lunatic obsessive, but several hysterically silly overreacting fans. How could she ever, back then, have known she'd feel safer with the numbers? Too late now, though — no way was she going to move out of her home and hide away again. This *had* to pass.

Kate's dog Beano was in the porch pawing at something behind the big stone pig that Marco had given her years ago as a birthday present.

"What's he got?" Viola said as Beano dragged what looked like muddy paper out from behind the statue.

"Looks like something the postman dropped, I think," Kate said, pulling him away. "Here, some sort of card by the looks of it. Maybe a welcome-back one from a neighbour. Did you get any of those? Anyone send you anything?"

Viola shook her head. "No. Next door came round with an apple pie and to tell me she hoped there wouldn't be any more of 'that nonsense like before' but that's all."

"Oh. Nice and sympathetic then." Kate sounded despondent.

Viola took the envelope from Kate, her hand trembling. It had been hand-delivered and her name on the front was not — she was glad to see — in the same tremulous capitals as the kitten card had had. But that didn't necessarily mean anything. She'd look at it later, when Kate had gone, but not now in case it was vile and frightening. It would be hard to hide a reaction to that, which would result in Kate talking to Miles and them ganging up on her in an onslaught of I-told-you-so.

She stepped further out into the garden and looked up at the roses. "Oh, wow, how could I have not noticed? They look amazing!" The flowers were luxuriantly thriving, but with all the tatty, browned blooms cut off. With treatment like that, they'd probably still be flowering at Christmas. "It must have involved a ladder but I haven't got one, so you don't need to worry about it being me up there, Kate."

Aaagh — another lurch of the stomach. Whoever it was had taken the trouble to do even the highest ones, up by her bedroom window. Which meant someone had been up at looking-into-the-room level. This was beyond creepy. And yet, if it *was* Greg, what was there to mind? If things had worked out he'd have seen the inside of the room soon enough. This could only have happened when she and Lisa were having their Paris day.

"Well, it looks pretty damn professional," Viola said, going to sniff one of the lower blooms and trying to sound a lot more upbeat than she felt. "And if they'd like to come back and tackle the jungle in the back garden they'd be very welcome."

"Aren't you going to open the card?" Kate asked, as they went back into the house.

"Oh, no, it's OK, it can wait till later. Let's look at the material and then at your flats. I'll make some coffee." She tucked the card away in the cutlery drawer. An hour later would be more than soon enough.

Monica wasn't herself. Naomi realized this as soon as she arrived at the flat (where she was let into the main building by a conveniently outgoing resident) and saw the empty plastic milk bottles lined up on the corridor carpet outside her front door, as if they were to be collected on a regular milk round. Monica always bought her milk from the corner shop up the road because she liked the small anarchy of the owner breaking up the four-packs of baked beans and putting them for sale on the shelves, disregarding the signs on the cans saying "Not to be sold separately". She probably hadn't seen a milk roundsman in all the years she'd lived here. She might be perfectly all right, of course, just a bit scattier than usual, or she might have gone seriously loopy overnight. You heard of that happening. The trick was to work out whether it was a sign of swiftly advancing dementia or just down to some fixable infection, where the brain would sort itself out after a good dosing with antibiotics.

"Monica? It's me, Naomi." She knocked on the door and waited, feeling nervous about what she'd find.

"Come in; mind you don't let the cat out," Monica said, as she opened the door.

"You haven't got a cat." Monica's old Siamese, Bertie, was long gone, and pets weren't allowed in the flats.

"Oh, haven't I? No, I expect you're right. I've been wondering where he was. So it means that if Bertie's not here, I haven't got him any more, yes?"

At least she remembered the cat's name. Was that a good sign? Naomi hoped so.

"Something like that, love. Are you feeling all right?" Naomi could see Monica was looking gaunt, suddenly quite a lot older, although she'd seen her only a week ago. It was as if five years had somehow lurched by in that time. She hadn't brushed her hair and the back of it stuck up like sheep's wool in a hedge. That wasn't like her. Monica was always very meticulous about appearance. And about appearances. She'd never have divorced Oliver, not a chance: it would have looked slovenly and careless, losing her husband to another woman. No point dwelling on it all these years on, Naomi told herself. It was down to her to be the friend to Monica that she'd promised the slowly dying Oliver she would be. As it turned out, that hadn't been at all difficult. Monica was the talker and do-er, Naomi the listener and thinker in their set-up. It was an ideal combination for easy companionship. And it meant Monica never asked her any questions about Oliver, because she'd never been curious or imaginative enough to want to know why Naomi quietly mourned him just as much as she did. In fact, even that was something she'd probably not noticed.

"Coffee first, or shall we get going?" Naomi went into Monica's kitchen and had a quick look round, hoping she wouldn't find unwashed dishes stuffed into the oven or potatoes in the cutlery drawer. All seemed well, though she still felt uneasy.

"Going? Where are we going?"

Naomi saw Monica catch sight of herself in the hall mirror and frown, as if this was a face she didn't quite recognize. Perhaps she too had glimpsed the newly lost years. Monica put a hand up to her untidy hair and squinted at her reflection, puzzled.

"We're going to the library, Mon, do you remember? I'm after another Lesley Cookman murder story and you said you wanted to give Maigret a go."

"Maigret. French, smokes. Yes, I like him. Fine, I'm ready." Monica turned and stood looking at Naomi, as expectant as a child.

"You might want to run a comb through your hair first, pet," Naomi suggested, getting Monica's jacket down for her from the peg on the back of the door. Monica obediently went into her bedroom while Naomi waited, holding the well-worn garment close to her body. This was going to be someone else to miss, and possibly not too far ahead now, because Monica would be absent for a long time before she actually went. Naomi made a decision, a tough one she knew instinctively was right. She just hoped her family wouldn't try to oppose it. And if they did, well, it would be time to tell them why they couldn't.

CHAPTER
TWENTY-SIX

Of course she should have checked on the day they appeared. It was entirely her own fault and she shouldn't have just taken her mother's word that there was no card; she should have looked. If the envelope had fallen down behind the stone pig, how could Naomi have thought to look there for anything? Viola sat at the kitchen table in front of her computer and read the words on the card again. It was a website link and just "Greg". The link was about gladioli, specifically the meaning of the name and including: "*The flower of infatuation, a bouquet signifying that the spear has pierced the giver's heart with passion*".

She almost laughed — the lines were what Greg would surely have declared "totally vomit-inducing", and she could tell he'd chosen them on purpose to make her giggle. But all the same, it was a bold declaration to go with those flowers. And there had been so many of them. Not wrapped or ribboned, just loose. Viola-coloured too, the shade of the darkest pansies: not a random colour choice but thought right through, just for her. Overwhelmed with regret and guilt, Viola relived the moment she'd angrily stuffed the lot of them into a bin bag and dropped them next to the household garbage on the pavement ready for the rubbish collection. The stalks and blooms had spiked through the plastic as she'd rammed them in, protesting at their treatment, struggling to get out. Petals had scattered across the pavement.

"Oh God, I'm such a stupid, stupid idiot," she told herself. And yet, there was still the scene with Mickey and the baby. If Greg was the baby's father, he had no business sending her romantic floral messages, however completely, utterly delightful.

She picked up her phone and clicked on his number and went outside to sit on the sunny terrace while it rang and rang. She was just about to give up when a woman answered.

"Greg Fabian's phone." This was a harassed and impatient voice. Viola was thrown for a moment, realizing that the sharp tone was definitely Mickey's. Her instinct was to hang up immediately but she'd been in the same position herself, back in the days when Rhys had been as free with his phone number as he had been with his cock. Not a lot hurt more than silence down the phone from a surprised mistress.

"Oh — hi. Is Greg there?" she asked, hearing herself sound overbright.

"No, Viola," Mickey snapped. "And I'm assuming you are Viola because that's the name that's come up here; no, he's not. He's gone off to a shoot near Oxford with a truckload of cycads and left his bloody phone here in the office because at the moment he is being a totally useless pillock. If you want him, he'll be back about four. I'll tell him you called." And she was gone.

"It was, like, so brilliant! We had to feed the horse and do all the tacking-up and stuff. They teach you all that. And then at night we'd stop by some, like, little pub or wha'ever where you can get showers and food and that, and there's always music. I wonder if it's like that all the year round over there or just for tourists? Ireland is just so cool. And we kept meeting up with the same people, so funny, like families on the same trail?"

Rachel had barely stopped talking to breathe since Marco brought her back. She looked slightly different, Viola thought as she watched her whizzing round the kitchen, all skinny limbs and swooshing hair; maybe taller, maybe that noticeable bit older. The child in her was slowly receding and the beautiful young woman she was becoming was breaking through. Only a few more short years and she'd be leaving home. Had Naomi felt these punches of impending loss with her own children? If so, she hadn't shown it. Maybe that was something you did as a parent, keep the pain of separation to yourself. Or maybe when the day came it just felt natural. She certainly hoped so.

Naomi had once said that when your children want to leave home and get on with their own lives it shows you've brought them up properly, because turning them into fully functioning grown-ups was the whole point. If only Kate and Miles thought the same about *her*. Miles had called that very morning to ask her if she was feeling guilty yet about leaving Naomi in the house by herself. "She must be missing having you and

303

Rachel around," he'd said, pushing the message as hard as he could.

Given the muddle she'd got herself into so far since she'd been back at home, Viola was (almost) on the point of wondering if he was right. All she could do was take each day at a time, like a recovering drunk, and right now she was baking a cake for the book-group meeting that night. Here, for the first time, on her own premises. It wasn't a big deal but it felt like an achievement, somehow.

"Birthday on Thursday!" Rachel squeaked now as she opened the fridge and started foraging. "What have you got me?"

"I'm not telling you! What would you like to do on the day? Go out somewhere? We could take some of your friends for dinner somewhere or you could invite them here and I could cook?" Even as she said it, she realized that having your mum around along with your friends wasn't likely to be a welcome idea on a fifteenth birthday. If she cooked for them here, she'd end up feeling she should banish herself to her room for the evening. If they went out . . . well, surely her only role would be to provide the taxi service and a credit card and then disappear.

Rachel emerged from the fridge, clutching a yoghourt and a carton of apple juice. "Um . . . Mum? Do you mind if I just go over to Emmy's for the evening? It's just, I know it's my birthday and everything, but she says she's got something planned for me."

"Oh. Well, yes, I suppose so. Yes, OK, why not?" That had actually given Viola a bit of a jolt. It was as if Rachel was ahead of her in the thoughts of independence. When she'd been little, Marco had always come over to join in her birthday celebrations. Parties with classic old-school jellies and games when she was small, then taking friends to a film and for a burger later. The year Rachel was ten, Viola, Marco and James had taken her to Disneyland Paris. But now she'd be fifteen — it was her choice.

"So what's she got lined up? A pampering session? Film and a sleepover?"

Rachel gave her a look. "We're not, like, *twelve*! I don't know — she just said it's a surprise. So is it all right? You don't mind?"

"No, I don't mind." Viola forced a smile. "It's your day, your choice. So long as you're careful. No alcohol."

"*Mum*. Leave it, I'll be fine."

"I know — but I don't want you to do anything silly." Oh Lordy, how like her own mother she sounded. She had to stop worrying so much. Rachel wasn't *her* — she must stop expecting disaster to strike any second. Being accident-prone surely couldn't *actually* be a gene. Could it? "Sorry — but you can't blame me for worrying. It comes with the mother territory. I won't be able to hang out with you for long during your birthday morning — I have to be at Med and Gib. Results day. I suppose some of them will get theirs online but a lot of the students will want to call in, get together with each other for a bit of support."

"And to get lashed in the park after." Rachel peeled the lid off the yoghourt and licked it.

"Yes, probably. A tradition. Maybe we could have lunch?"

"Yeah, maybe. Wha'evs." Rachel was now battling with opening the apple juice, all interest in her birthday apparently gone. Then, as she was pouring the drink into a glass, she looked up and gave her a dazzling smile. "Love ya, Mumsy!"

"So . . . Paris." Charlotte sounded as if she were about to open the case for the prosecution. The evening was a wonderfully hot one and they were all outside on Viola's terrace, facing the tangled wreck of overgrown foliage that was her garden. She'd done quite a bit of weeding, but everything seemed to be growing faster than she could control it. And as for the lawn, it was more of a hayfield. A dozen hollyhocks in shades of apricot and yellow and cream stood high and triumphant way above the weeds, leaning against each other like drunk girls in cocktail frocks, and there was a coffee and walnut cake on the table and a couple of bottles of chilled Sauvignon Blanc. For the moment, with friends around to divert her, so long as Viola kept thoughts of Greg — and the fact that he hadn't returned her call — out of her head, she actually felt close to contentment.

"Paris." Lisa grinned. "Honestly, Charlotte, you'd have *so* loved it. The men were wonderful, fabulous manners, absolute gentlemen and they knew the city *so* well. All the sights, up the Eiffel Tower and through the best parts of the Louvre, Notre-Dame — couldn't have been better."

"Yes, and a lingering lunch at the Café de Flore, where we talked of Beauvoir and Jean-Paul Sartre . . ." Viola backed her up.

"Oh, *amazing*! Just *perfect*!" Charlotte was delighted, and looked as if she intended to claim the success was all down to her.

"No, Charlotte. Not." Viola couldn't keep it up and broke into giggles. "In fact so bad that we abandoned ship — or rather train — on the way back and hitched home."

"Oh, that's so sad!" Jessica sighed. "I was hoping for a happy ending."

Lisa spluttered into her wine. "So were the boys!" she said with a deeply filthy laugh. "*Not* a chance. Though I am seeing the driver of the lorry we hitched a ride in. He was a lovely souvenir of the trip."

"Ooh, so not entirely a wasted day then. You see, something good often comes out of a right old mess," Amanda declared.

"Yes, but it's Viola we're supposed to be fixing up, Amanda, not Lisa," Charlotte said. "The ink's barely dry on her divorce. Still . . ." And she looked sharply at Viola. "There is *some* success in that department in your family, isn't there?"

"Is there?" Viola asked.

"Was it you who told her about him?"

"Told who what? About who? I'm all confused here, Charlotte. Enlighten us, please."

"Oh, come on, she must have told you by now. Your sister! Kate! Now she's single again . . ."

"Kate? Why, what's she done?" Mists were slightly clearing as she spoke. Kate and her new haircut, the thing she'd said about new beginnings.

"Your *sister* met that *Daniel* man." Charlotte paused for a suitably dramatic few moments. "At a wedding. Well, obviously a wedding, because that's what he does. *And* they're seeing each other. A *lot* of each other, if you get my drift. He called and told me, sounded keen."

"Yes. Yes, I think we all get it, Char, no need to spell it out," Amanda said.

"And she hasn't told you?" Jessica asked. "I thought you and she were really close. She was always around such a lot when — you know — when, your husband . . ."

"Died," Viola said, fleetingly half expecting to see Rhys rising up from the overgrown grass protesting that of course he wasn't really dead, cariads, it was called *acting*. "Yes, she was. But she . . . well, she doesn't say a lot about herself. Never has. Hey, though, if she's met someone, that's great. That Daniel was lovely."

"Rather too old for you of course, sweetie," Charlotte pronounced. "But an acceptable Older Man for Kate. A bit of immediate-rebound attention after a split is such a boost to the old confidence. I just hope she'll be gentle with him, because I happen to know he's looking for something that is more than a fling."

"Oh, I'm sure she will be, and good luck to her," Viola said. "And are we going to choose a book for

September while we're here? *The Pursuit of Love* seems a bit of an inspired choice, doesn't it? In the circs . . ."

Rachel hadn't expected to feel this bad. It was only a *party*, she kept telling herself. And if she'd been organized enough and thought the whole thing through and talked to her mum, she could probably have sorted staying over at her dad's and gone to Ned's party with total permission. Or she could maybe have got Gemma onside and been allowed to go back to hers after and sleep on her velvety patchwork sofa with the scent of patchouli wafting about and the constant noise of the buses whizzing up Kensington Church Street. Then the next day she could have gone straight to Portobello Market with her to help on the stall, which was what she most wanted to do. Instead, she was stuck in a big old bunch of lies and she hated herself for it.

"I'll be grounded for ever if it all goes wrong," she confided to Emmy as they ate ice creams on the swings in the park, getting grumpy glares from the mummies of toddlers.

"We'll be fine. It's not like you won't actually be coming back to mine after, is it? So saying you're staying over with me is true. And you haven't said what you're doing, only that it's a surprise."

"But we'll have to get the night bus back. I'm quite scared about that. Everyone says it's all drunks and fighty people. I heard someone at school saying her boyfriend got stabbed."

"He was just being dramatic. He cut his hand on a glass he broke in the pub and wanted a better story. Come on, don't be so snobby, Rache! Where did you get that from? Half the people on that bus are like *olds* with bus passes who've been to . . . oh, y'know, opera and stuff. Don't get so antsy about it. And anyway, if you do get caught, what can they do? It's, like, your *birthday*. You're entitled to break out a bit. We can always say it was a last-minute thing, not planned."

"It's only that Mum's big on trust. She's been so let down before — it's like she needs me to . . ."

"You can't be responsible for your mum's hang-ups," Emmy pointed out. "That way you'll make a whole bunch of your own. So are we on for Thursday night or not? Please say we are; I really liked that Jaz. Or was it Baz? And I can't go without you because you're the one with the invite."

"All about you, is it? I mustn't be responsible for my mum but I've got to put you first?" Rachel still had doubts, but was feeling the beginnings of the thrill of adventure. And Ned was being persuasive too, texting her all the time when she was in Ireland, telling her he missed her and was wanting to see her again. "Yeah, OK, we're on."

CHAPTER
TWENTY-SEVEN

"Yay! Topshop VIP shopping experience! That is *to'ally* sick. Thanks so much, Mum." Rachel flung herself on Viola and hugged her hard.

"So you like it then? It includes a personal shopper, nails and so on and £100 of clothes vouchers. And it says you can take a friend along too."

"Like it? Love it. Ace happy. And thanks for bringing me the coffee and the choccy croissants, completely yummy. Gran would say you were spoiling me."

"She'd be right. But it *is* your birthday, so it's allowed. And feel free to return the favour when it's mine, won't you?"

"Yeah. I will."

Viola sat on the edge of Rachel's bed and felt hugely relieved — trying to find a present that a fifteen-year-old girl wouldn't pick over in barely disguised scorn wasn't that easy. "I can't hang about, I'm afraid. I have to be at the college by nine so that I can see what they all got and arrange my face the right way for each of them."

"Hope they've all passed," Rachel said, through a crumby mouthful of croissant. "Cos it must be so mizz if you don't. All those years of school and then you leave with nothing. Hope that won't happen to me."

"Oh, most of them will be fine, and so will you when it's your turn. There'll be a few who don't make their uni grades, but something else will work out for this lot." She thought of the idle, affluent Benedict Peabody, his secure bank job awaiting him after a long luxury-travel break — if any job could be said to be secure. But he was one lucky sort. She knew he'd even make that press photo of him partying into a sort of badge of honour. In fact, there wasn't one among her last intake who couldn't have afforded to do a couple of years' work experience for nothing. What would happen when it was Rachel's turn? Marco — who would do anything to help her if he could — said the advertising business was full to capacity with unpaid workies and interns bodging away at tasks no one could any longer afford competent professionals to do. The fashion business — which Rachel was so keen on — would surely be the same. Helping on Gemma's stall was definitely to be encouraged.

"So, lunch with Marco and me later? He's going to drop by with your present and wait here till I get back from the college," Viola said as she got up to leave for Medway and Gibson.

"Er . . ." Rachel frowned. "Um, well, that would be cool but I thought you said it was OK to go over to Emmy's? I mean, not that I wouldn't love to, but, you know, you said it would be all right and it's . . ."

"Oh — I thought that was just for the evening?"

312

"Well, not really, it's more of an all day *and* evening thing. Please?" Rachel looked as woefully plaintive as only a negotiating teenage girl could.

"All right, no worries. But stay here till your dad's been round, won't you? He'd be pretty hurt if he turned up with your present and you hadn't waited to see him."

"Course I will! And anyway, I want to see what he's got me. I hinted massively when we were in Ireland, so he really can't get it wrong."

She was slipping away from them fast now, Viola thought as she started up the Polo. Fifteen. Naomi had once said that was very much the Little Cow stage with daughters. Rachel wasn't at all a little cow, but she was pretty determined. She had a knack of asking for what she wanted with the reasons why she should have it all stacked up neatly in case of argument. The next couple of years were going to be tricky.

Greg hadn't called back, which ironically told her a whole lot. As Viola drove through the early commuter traffic she wondered about calling him again to explain the mix-up over the gladioli, but his silence indicated that her suspicions had probably been right. If Mickey hadn't told him about the call then it was probably for a very good reason. And if she had and he chose not to do anything about it, well, OK, maybe it was best to leave it. On the plus side, she supposed she should give herself some credit for getting out before any real damage was caused. That was a bit of a first; maybe she really was growing up and putting the hex days behind her at last. Pity the thought of that didn't, in this case, make her feel a lot like celebrating.

As she turned in through the Med and Gib gates, past a few photographers waiting to get shots of the more gorgeous exam celebrants jumping up and down, shrieking and hugging, she felt another tweak of sadness when she saw the line of espaliered fruit trees which were flourishing beautifully. When challenged about those while they were out planting the tulips, Greg had neither confirmed nor denied that they were his work, but had muttered something about an old song about apples and teachers. "Teacher's pet," she'd then teased him, and he'd replied with the wolfy grin and a naughty sparkle, "Oh, do they? Excellent." Oh, if only, she thought, giving in for a moment to how she'd really feel if things were different.

Sandra Partridge, formal as ever in a dark suit, high heels and shiny tan tights in spite of the roasting temperature outside, was already in the college hall with three computers, several staff members and a heap of papers and brown envelopes, somehow making the place look like a polling station on election night. Viola, walking in and taking in the scene, felt nervous for her students, especially the ones who'd previously had a tough time at regular schools and had seen the tutorial college as a quiet refuge from bullying. Also, there were one or two who had fallen behind at previous schools due to problems such as glandular fever or ME — here they'd been given flexible time and calm space to work their way through slow recoveries as well as the A-level courses. She crossed her fingers for them all, even the wilder ones like Benedict.

"Good morning, Viola." Sandra's face gave nothing away about the results. "Good holiday so far?"

"Yes, fine, thanks, Sandra. I've been moving back into my own home and am up to here in sorting. How about you?"

"Oh, you know, the usual. Too much to catch up on and never enough time." She turned back to the computer, clearly not intending to elaborate, and leaving Viola to speculate whether she meant that it was family, house renovation, celebrity gossip or serious reading that she'd failed to catch up on. There wasn't much point asking: Sandra liked a lot of executive distance. She thought of asking her if she'd seen Benedict on the front page of the *Mail*, but decided it would be too much of a tease on today of all days. Tempting, though.

"Hey, Vee — how have we done? Do we know yet?" Amanda bounced into the hall, wearing jeans, flip-flops and a flowery top.

"Mrs Breville — this is a work environment," Sandra Partridge tutted at her, looking her up and down.

"But it's still the holidays for another few weeks, Sandra," Amanda said, pulling a face at Viola while Sandra was studying the computer.

All Viola's students had passed. Even Benedict Peabody had managed a C in English, which was about right, by Viola's reckoning. If he'd got an A she'd have had to suspect he and his über-rich family had nobbled the markers. His pair of girl admirers had each scored an A grade, also unsurprisingly, and one of them had secured a place at Cambridge.

"Hey, mine have done pretty well." Amanda looked up from the lists, delighted. "No disasters at all! I was half expecting a tearful bunch demanding remarking, but it looks like they won't need it. How about yours?"

"Really good. Though Benedict might wonder why he didn't get more than a C and ask for a recount. If he does, I'll remind him he mostly smoked his brain away over the last three terms and he's done pretty well considering. Aha — talk of the devil, here they all come."

"'Lo, Vo!" A hyper-bronzed and sun-blonded Benedict strolled into the hall with a cohort of slouching mates. Sandra handed their envelopes over and told Benedict and his girls that they were to open them outside, near the gates. "You must have noticed the press out there," she said, looking at the girls, who immediately started fluffing up their hair and unfastening a couple of top buttons.

"Hello, Benedict — good summer?" Viola asked, grinning at him.

He gave her a sharp look. "I had you down as a *Guardian* reader," he said.

"And you're right. But sometimes I walk past news-stands and catch a glimpse of headlines. Looked like you were having fun, anyway, which can't be bad."

"Was ex-cell-ent! Polzeath with the olds. They're still down there so it's, like, party at mine tonight, celebrate this. Or not," he replied, waving his envelope at her.

"Don't worry," she said, giving him a smile. "Come back in when you've had a look at the results."

She didn't really expect him to. Outside, little groups of students squealed and bounced and the photographers snapped away at the most photogenic. Benedict's girls pouted and giggled and flirted with the cameras. Sandra Partridge watched from the window and smiled contentedly. Some of those girls were close to model standard — this lot could make several front pages, which would mean hugely useful free advertising for the college.

"Thank you! You were fuckin' ace!" To Viola's surprise, Benedict rushed back in and gave her an enormous hug. "Like, *really* happy! Thank you!"

"Ah, bless the boy," Amanda said as Benedict and an ever-growing collection of friends left the hall to go out and celebrate. "Sometimes it's all worth it, isn't it?"

"Yes. Sometimes it just is," Viola agreed. "Always feels strange though: they get quite close and you know them pretty well and then, suddenly, you know you'll probably never see them again." Ridiculously, she felt a bit like crying. Who would ever have thought she'd react like that to the absence from her life of Benedict Peabody?

"Just you and me for lunch then. I've brought food, in case you'd rather stay here? I'll make us a salad, if you like." Marco was waiting at the cottage for Viola, stretched out on a lounger on the terrace with a mug of tea, the *Guardian* crossword and a view of the crazily overgrown lawn.

"A salad would be perfect, thanks, Marco. I feel like I've been awake half the night thinking about the results and now it's all over and done I'm knackered." Viola flopped on to a lounger alongside him and kicked her shoes off.

"I'll get us a little glass of something," he said, getting up and giving her a quick kiss. "I put a bottle in your fridge to chill. Rachel's gone over to Emmy's and said she'll see you in the morning. She was a bit mysterious about it; almost devious, I'd say. Ah, teenagers, don't you remember it well? I was *baaad!*"

"I think she was only like that because Emmy's planned a surprise, so she doesn't know exactly what she's going to. Did she like her present?"

"She did. Which isn't *remotely* surprising, because there can't be anything she didn't tell me and James in Ireland about the various hair straighteners and volumizers and the benefits of every single one. Even I couldn't get it wrong. I slipped her a few quid as an extra as well. Oh, and while you were out Kate called and said she'll be round with a present. How were your students? Did they do well?"

"They did, actually. Some of them better than I'd expected, none of them worse. Perfect, really. Even Sandra managed to crack a smile. I thought her face would shatter."

Marco went into the house and came out with two glasses of wine. "So why don't you *sound* like it's perfect? Are you all right?"

Viola thought for a moment. "I'm all right and I'm not." She got up and went into the kitchen and pulled

318

the pair of cards out of the dresser drawer, then took them back outside. "I had these — well, you saw the first one, but I had another — just before I moved in. It's kind of given me the creeps a bit. And then . . ."

"And then?" Marco came and sat beside her and put an arm round her. "There was more? Because this one with the kittens is horrible. Who'd send it? One of those nutters from after Rhys died?"

"Well, who else? Though I thought they'd long moved on. And nobody outside the family knew I was coming back here."

"Must have been someone *inside* the family then." He almost laughed, but seemed to think better of it.

"*What?* Are you serious? Which one? No, they wouldn't."

"No, look, sorry, I didn't mean it, I was just being flippant. Ignore me, darling. And ignore this. If there's been nothing since, then it's gone away. Destroy. Destroy and forget."

"Do you think Miles, possibly? He didn't want me to come back here, not *at all*. And Kate didn't either. But they wouldn't stoop to *this*. Would they?"

Marco said nothing. They both sat in thoughtful silence for a moment, then the doorbell rang. Viola went to answer it, her heart beating fast, hopelessly thinking it just *might* be Greg. A single Greg with no baby and no commitments. Just him with a lovely bag of bulbs to plant in the middle of the night and a kiss to die for. *Stop it*, she told herself, as she opened the door to her sister.

"Hello! I've brought a present for the gorgeous Rachel and something for you as well." Kate handed over a gold-wrapped parcel and a large white envelope. "I'll just leave them and run, too much to do, people to see! Open that envelope though, it's full of family-tree info — you'll be interested." And she was off, racing back to her car in what looked like a new pair of madly high scarlet shoes, a sure sign that Kate was at last really enjoying life. She'd been depressed and a bit dowdy for way too long. All that had gone wrong with her and Rob had certainly taken its toll, but it looked like she was moving on. Good luck to her, Viola thought.

Marco was in the kitchen, assembling a salad of figs, cheese and prosciutto. There was a big crunchy rustic-style loaf on the board beside him.

"This is so sweet of you, Marco. I don't deserve it."

"Of course you do, darling. And it's our daughter's birthday — even if she's run off with her shrieky-teen mates, it doesn't mean we can't celebrate. Now — tell me some more about this man with the nursery that Kate was dropping such subtle — not — hints about recently."

The two of them carried the salad, plates and bread outside and arranged them on the table under the sunshade.

"I've heard of him," Marco said, after Viola had explained about Greg. "The Fabian plant-rental set-up is the biggest in the ad business, but I don't know him personally. Is he devastatingly gorgeous? Have you . . .?"

"No. I wish I had but I haven't. And I don't think it's likely now. I've goofed again, Marco. Goofed yet again and so, so stupidly, whichever way the truth turns out." And the tears that had been threatening all morning found their way from her eyes.

"Hey, don't cry! That cheese is already over-salty and you'll make it worse, dripping on it. Come on, tell Marco *all* about it and we'll see what can be salvaged."

So she did. And the worst bit was telling him what she'd done to the flowers. "They were so beautiful and it was such a beautiful thing of him to do but before I found out they were from Greg, what was I supposed to think, after getting those cards? I was so scared it was the mad person, persecuting me. And I couldn't tell anyone, because I want to stay here. I can't uproot Rachel all over again."

"A mess, yes, agreed. But if he really is with someone else . . ."

"I don't suppose I'll ever know now. I called, left a message with the Mickey woman but he didn't call back. Says it all. And we were going out to plant crocuses." She sobbed but giggled through it, realizing how ridiculous that sounded. "Oh, I wish I'd gone — those bits of fun with him were pretty damn innocent, and he was lovely just to hang out with."

Marco frowned. "Yes, but hanging out with someone who's attached to someone else, that's dangerous stuff, Vee. Best out of it, do we think? Long run? There'll be . . ."

"Someone else. No. I don't think there will be. I really *do* give up. First Rhys, then this. Still, at least this time nobody died. Comes to something when that's the only plus, doesn't it?"

CHAPTER
TWENTY-EIGHT

Rachel felt way out of her depth on just about every level. This was one seriously palatial house with huge creamy rooms and enormous abstract paintings everywhere. Ned had let her and Emmy in, hugged her, pointed them towards a massive basement kitchen, saying to help themselves to drinks, and then vanished. Emmy poured herself some wine but Rachel, still preferring sweet drinks and secretly wishing there was some 7-Up among the many bottles and cans on the worktop, scooped up a tumblerful of a drink full of fruit that had been mixed in a big bowl. Pimm's, she heard one of the other girls say. She tasted it warily and was relieved it seemed to be mostly lemonade. She stuck close to Emmy, wondering how she could give the impression that she wasn't totally out of place, knowing nobody and feeling awkward.

There were so many people who all seemed to be each other's best friends, and every one of them looked like they were way older than her and Emmy. It was a hot night and most of the partygoers were draped over each other out in the garden, lolling on the terrace steps, smoking and drinking, giggling and chatting. Flicky-haired, skinny-legged confident girls were squealing at each other as if they'd never heard anything so hilarious *ever,* and most of what she overheard was about A-level results, which uni and which flights to Costa Rica.

"I want to go home," Rachel murmured to Emmy. "I'm feeling, like, about *twelve?*"

"Don't be ridic. This is, like, *so* lush."

"*Ridic?* We've been here five minutes and already you sound like *them.* You'll be all ya ya ya by the time we leave."

"No, really, give it a chance. Let's check out the garden, come on. Those Jaz and Baz blokes must be somewhere."

Rachel quickly gulped down half her drink, a passing boy in a torn dinner jacket topped it up from a jug he was carrying, saying to her, "You'll love this. Really retro gear," which she didn't at all understand, and she followed Emmy out through the huge, folded-back glass doors into the garden where more and more people were collecting. Jaz and Baz appeared and suddenly Emmy had vanished with them, whirled away to join a group of smokers sitting on a blanket under an apple tree. Rachel felt abandoned and a bit lost and thought about finding a sofa inside the house where she could just curl up and read a book till Emmy was ready to go home. This was *not* how it was supposed to be.

"Hey, schoolgirl. Did you miss me when you were away in your gypsy van?" Ned was beside her suddenly, pulling her in close to him. She had some more of her drink and giggled as he nuzzled her neck.

"I did. You know I did — I texted you. Are you going to uni soon? Or gap year?" He'd be doing one or the other, she thought, leaving her too soon after they'd met.

"Like, no? Some time away then I'll be an intern for a bit, you know?" he said, plaiting his fingers through hers and leading her back towards the house. She could sense all the girls on the way turning to look at her. A pouty girl with blue pussy-cat whiskers drawn on her face actually hissed as she passed. She could feel them appraising her clothes, her hair, her body, and wondering where the hell she'd come from that she could actually pull the host, but she no longer cared. The evening had turned right around. She was *with* Ned and they *weren't*. This huge, gorgeous place was *his* and *he* was *her* boyfriend. It felt good. She quickly drank some more of the punch because that made her feel good too.

"Let's get you a better drink. That cheap stuff's shite and you don't know what's in it." Ned pushed through the crowd in the kitchen and opened the vast fridge, pulling out a bottle of champagne. "We'll take it somewhere we can talk and I can give you your birthday present. This lot's so fucking rowdy."

"You got me a present? You remembered!"

"Course I did. Come with me, I'll show you."

Rachel followed him up the basement stairs, through the hallway to the next staircase and then hesitated, nervous, wondering quite what Ned had in mind. Part of her was excited and curious and eager. She decided not to listen to the other, boringly sensible part that was suggesting she tell Ned that today was only her fifteenth birthday. Two girls were sitting smoking on the stairs. They looked up at her with glittery hard eyes and smirked at Ned. "Starting early, babes?" one of them commented, shifting aside to let the two of them pass.

"Just getting a bit of peace and quiet," he told the girl as he led Rachel past them. "You can't have a conversation out there."

"Conversation. Yeah, right," said the other girl sniggering. Jealous, Rachel thought, trying to concentrate on keeping her balance on the stairs. They seemed to undulate beneath her, uncomfortable and slightly scary. How was she supposed to get down them again if they kept wobbling about?

From Ned's bedroom window Rachel could see right across the private garden square to the building where her dad lived, though she couldn't tell how far away it was exactly because it kept moving nearer, so it felt right in front of her, then retreating, like it was a hundred miles away. Days later, she remembered she'd been telling Ned this and he'd laughed; she remembered the bang of the champagne cork popping but then everything else was blank till the bit in the hospital where the lights were hideously white and she was throwing up into a cardboard bowl and wondering why her mum was crying and shouting down the phone, calling her aunt Kate an evil, scheming bitch.

It was much later that evening when Viola, fresh from a soothing bath (with no hazardous candles) to ease the aches from spending the last daylit hours digging dandelions and sorrel and loosestrife from the flower beds, remembered the envelope that Kate had left for her. She wrapped herself in her white waffle robe, made a cup of tea, then flopped on the sofa and opened it. Inside was a big sheet of paper with a roughly scribbled family tree, in Kate's handwriting.

"Told you we were all related, even if it's a bit distant!" was written on a yellow Post-it note. Viola's first thought was to bin the whole lot, but she absolutely couldn't resist a really good look through the names. Whether engaging in a genuine hobby or through sheer cussed control-freak nosiness, Kate had certainly been thorough, and the names went back a few generations. Viola found their great-great half-aunt who had married a Fabian and who turned out to be really very distant, relatively speaking, from Greg. Though less distant, she realized, moving to her desk and switching on a lamp for a better look, from Mickey Fabian. For there she was, on the tree further up than Greg and connected by a series of second and third marriages: only a few years older than he was and yet aunt to him, just as he'd said. And in turn, ah, there was Mickey's baby, one George Fabian, six-month-old cousin to Greg. "Oh God, how fucking typical," she breathed. "I am *so* stupid."

She reached immediately for her phone and clicked on Greg's number before she could dither about and think of how she was to explain how she came to be studying his family tree in such fine detail, or at all, because what kind of sane person would, frankly?

"Viola. This is a surprise." It didn't sound like it was such a good one and Viola almost hung up.

"I just wanted to apologize."

"You're not keen on gladioli, then," he said, laughing, but sounding as if that were just a nervous reaction.

"I'm so sorry. I had no idea they were from you. I only found the card a few days later. I'm so, so sorry. I'm a total idiot but I can explain about it all and I'd like to. I did call and left a message with Mickey, but you didn't call back. So I assumed . . ." She was rambling now, sounding a bit desperate.

"Did you? I didn't know. If it was the day I forgot my phone, then Mickey wasn't exactly on speaking terms with me. And I'm a bigger idiot. I walked past a bin bag overflowing with my totally wrecked flowers and still pruned your sodding roses. I don't think I twigged, if you'll forgive the pun. It didn't cross my mind that you could be so brutal to them or to me, not after we . . . And then I thought about it, and your trip to Paris. Well, you know, I can just about put two and two together, even though I'm a mere man."

She hated how sad he sounded. She hated how untrusting she'd been.

"Greg, believe me, I had plenty of reason to assume they were from someone else. To say it's been . . . well, difficult over the past year or so doesn't really begin to cover it."

"You kept it very much to yourself. You could have said."

"I know. Well, no, I couldn't really. It's not something I talk about. But I will, if you still want to hear."

"OK. I do. So come and tell me."

"What, now?" Viola glanced at the clock. It was close to midnight. What had she been thinking of, calling him at that time? *Herself*, Miles would probably have said. He wouldn't be wrong there.

"Yes, why not? Can you?"

"Rachel's out tonight so . . . well, I suppose I could. Where are you?"

"On the big sloping grassy bit by the railway embankment, just over that roundabout where I planted the quince. The crocuses, remember?" He sounded warmer now.

"Shall I bring a dibber?"

"You must never leave home without one," he said. "Don't be long."

"OK. This is completely mad but, yes, I'll come."

Viola was halfway down the stairs, hurriedly dressed in jeans and a dark top and feeling an excited anticipation that she'd thought was no longer part of her life, when the house phone rang. It was nearly 12.30 a.m. She picked up the phone, her hand trembling and excitement leaking away fast, leaving only fear, because a call after midnight, when your daughter is out somewhere, is never going to be good news.

CHAPTER
TWENTY-NINE

Oh God, oh God, please let Rachel be all right. Viola almost flung herself at the Accident and Emergency desk, just willing the girl behind it to tell her it was all a mistake, that Rachel was fine, all a fuss about nothing. A splinter, a tiny cut, a sprained ankle, something trivial, fixable, anything they could laugh about one day soon when the cold terror of the moment had long gone. It must have been like this for Naomi, back in Viola's childhood when it seemed she was forever falling over something, losing possessions, breaking the odd bone. Could it run in families? Awful to think so — Viola wouldn't wish her own unlucky track record on anyone, least of all her own daughter.

Viola had been to this hospital only once before. *This* was where she'd had to come on the terrible night of Rhys's crash. Only minutes passing through A & E that time though, on the way to the mortuary to identify him. Miles had been with her, efficiently and briskly steering her through the corridors, offering to do the identification for her, saying she wouldn't want to see Rhys all mashed up, but she'd insisted, and besides she was his next of kin, and in fact he'd looked surprisingly peaceful. The injuries that killed him had left his face still beautiful. She remembered thinking how pleased he'd be about that; such a horrible irony. Right now, she just prayed hard that she wasn't going to have to go through anything like that tonight.

"Mrs Hendricks . . . er, yes, I've got your daughter's notes here." The girl at the desk was taking it slowly, managing to look as if finding patients' records was not something she had to do every day, and her brow was furrowed with concentration. Viola could see a half-eaten sandwich on the desk, a smear of mayonnaise on a booklet about bereavement.

"She has notes?" Rachel had surely only been in the building less than an hour: what was to write up?

"On the computer here." The girl still seemed confused, and kept tapping the side of her head with her pen.

"Vo?" Benedict Peabody suddenly appeared next to her, looking pale and scared.

"Benedict, hello! What are you doing here? Are you all right?"

"Friend. Girl." He looked hunched and worried, his Cornwall-surfer-tan grey under the harsh hospital lights. "Are *you* ill?" he asked.

"No, no, it's Rachel, my daughter. I had a call . . ." She gabbled the words as she looked past him, frantic and frightened, hoping to see Rachel come bouncing through the double doors beyond the department. Drunks were slumped in chairs, a mother and child were both crying quietly in a corner and several other patients sat staring blankly, waiting to be called.

"Oh Jeez. What? *Rachel*? No shit." He was looking at the floor.

"Sorry, Benedict. I need to find her, can't talk. I do hope your friend is OK."

She turned back to the dithering receptionist. "Sorry, but where can I find her? Have you got her name right? Rachel Hendricks?"

"She's through there with her mate." Benedict pointed to a pair of swing doors as the receptionist carried on clicking the computer and tapping her head. "They wouldn't let me in. I didn't know . . . I mean, I had no clue, honestly. I just, like, met her, you know, down Portobello."

"You know Rachel? My *daughter* Rachel? Are you sure?"

"I didn't know her surname. Didn't connect her with you, not once, no way." He was defensive now, clearly waiting to be told off. "I didn't give her anything. But . . ."

"*Give* her anything? Give in what sense? Tell me what you know, Benedict: what *the hell* is wrong with her? Has there been an accident?"

"No, not an accident. Or, well, yeah, in a way. Her drink got spiked at my party. She'd had quite a lot of drink as well and she went all weird and collapsed so we got an ambulance. I didn't know she was only fifteen." He kicked out at a pillar. "Fuck, why didn't she *say*?"

Viola could almost have let herself smile at that. Why on earth would any just-fifteen-year-old girl tell a boy she fancied that she was way too young for him? "And

I didn't know she'd be at your party! I had no idea you even knew her. She never said," she snapped at him. Poor boy, she then thought, it was hardly his fault. "So what the hell did this 'someone' give her?"

"Not sure." He shrugged. "OK, it was ketamine. Soz."

"Jesus, what completely *stupid* idiots your so-called friends must be!"

"Sorry. I didn't know. I wouldn't have let them."

"Mrs Hendricks?" The tapping receptionist looked as if she'd had a breakthrough. "Your daughter's been a patient here before, hasn't she?"

"No. No, she hasn't. Look, I do want to see her, please. Have you got it right? Rachel Hendricks."

"Oh!" The mists cleared from the receptionist's face suddenly. "My mistake! I've got her down as *Katherine* Hendricks — to be called Kate, it says here."

"Kate is her middle name; now can I please . . ."

"Oh, well, that explains it! Silly me. See, I thought she was the same as this other one, but the age doesn't tally. I had her down for a head injury, about a year and a half ago. Right, I'll book her in again then." She started pecking at the keyboard with her long blue nails.

Something shifted in Viola's brain, something about as seismic as it could get. "What date, the head injury?" she asked, hardly more than whispering, already knowing exactly what she was going to hear.

"I can't tell you that, sorry. Patient confi —"

"February 24th?" Viola interrupted.

332

"How did you know?" Viola was looking at a big smile and wide blue eyes as astonished as if she'd accomplished an especially amazing trick.

"Lucky guess," she said. *Lucky.* Hardly. The photograph she'd found in Kate's bedroom of Kate, Rhys and herself at her wedding came to mind. Rhys and Kate, looking at each other and laughing. Had it been going on even *then*?

"Your daughter's through there." The receptionist pointed. "Cubicle three."

Viola pushed past Benedict and was through the doors before the girl had finished her sentence. Rachel was lying on a trolley with a blanket over her, looking pale and sickly. Emmy was beside her and a nurse was checking Rachel's blood pressure.

The nurse looked up, smiled and said, "She's going to be all right, don't worry. Teenagers — we get this."

"I'm sorry, Viola," Emmy muttered, her eyes filling with tears. "It was, like, so someone else's fault, not ours."

"It doesn't matter, Em. Nobody's died. It doesn't matter." Viola took her daughter's hand and squeezed it gently. Rachel opened her eyes and squinted at her mother. "'m OK, Mum. Please don't fuss about it, will you?"

"No. I won't fuss. Not right now, anyway."

Rachel looked a lot younger than fifteen, more like a small, ill child. Would police be involved? If so, that was probably going to be more Benedict's department, poor lad.

"She'll be fine," the nurse said. "Vital signs are all normal and she's thrown up all the alcohol as well, so that'll help. I just need her to stay for an hour or so to be on the safe side, then the doctor will sign her off and you can take her home. I'd get a cup of tea if I were you. You look like you could do with one. Machine's in the corridor, in reception."

"I will, then I'll come straight back and wait with Rachel. Emmy, tea?"

"Yes, please. Two sugars?" Emmy's voice was small and defeated-sounding.

Viola leaned forward and gave her a hug. "It'll be OK. You did the right thing, bringing her here and calling me. Give me a minute, I'll be right back with the tea."

Viola went out of the building and moved a little way apart from the small collection of nervy smokers exiled from the department. The night was soft, still warm and heavy-aired as if a thunderstorm wasn't far away. She pulled her phone from her bag and scrolled down to Kate's number, feeling anger and hurt deeper than any she'd ever, ever, experienced before. Oh yes, bad news definitely came in the middle of the night: Kate was about to get some *right now*.

"Waited till 2, planted and left. Take it you changed mind." Oh God, Greg! At nine in the morning, Viola emerged from nowhere near enough sleep and found his message on her phone when she went down to the kitchen to make tea. The night before, all thoughts of hanging out in the dark and planting a load of bulbs

334

had gone from her head the moment she'd had the call from Emmy. He'd understand, wouldn't he? She hoped so, but for now, with all that was on her mind, it was a little as if she wanted to put him in a cupboard and bring him out later after she'd dealt with Kate, wherever she was. She hadn't been at home — at 1.30 in the morning. To Viola's furious frustration, nobody had answered either Kate's home phone or her mobile, and she'd shouted impotently into the cold void of voicemail.

She quickly texted Greg: "So sorry — was a daughter emergency. Talk later?"

Viola took tea upstairs to Rachel, but she was fast asleep still. For about the fourth time since they'd got home, Viola gently felt her forehead for signs of fever, but her skin was cool and soft. The poor girl was going to have one hell of a hangover when she did wake, so Viola left her to sleep and went and had a shower. Marco, who she'd called as soon as she woke, was on his way over. Kate she would see later that morning, and then . . . oh God, what actually to say?

After she'd been unable to contact her sister, the momentum of the spontaneous fury that would have given her the immediate words she needed had died down, and she had spent the whole restless night rehearsing all kinds of speeches, every sort of confrontation. If only this didn't have to happen at all, but it was going to be today, and it looked like it was going to be more public than she'd anticipated. Naomi had phoned, rounding all three of her children up for a family conflab later that morning, and making it sound important and serious enough for there to be no excuses for backing out. There would be no chance to get Kate alone before then, so it would have to *be* then.

"Oh my goodness, look at the state of *you!*" Marco, clutching tissue-wrapped flowers, came out to the garden with Viola to where Rachel was lying on a lounger in the sun with sunglasses on, and an expression of ongoing agony. "Do we feel sorry for ourselves or what?"

"I so do," she agreed. "Never, ever, going out again. Not that Mum will let me, anyway, I'm certain sure."

"Oh, you'll be over it soon. Here, a nice little posy of get-well sweet peas for you."

"Oh, gorgeous, thanks!" she said, inhaling their scent. "But can't you just be cross with me? Mum is."

"Too right I am!" Viola told her, smiling at Marco.

"She's cross with you for lying and being sly, and so am I, don't even *think* of doubting it. But we're far more relieved that you're not in intensive care. What were you doing, being just up the road from me and not even calling in? I call that rude."

"Sorry, Dad." A big tear trickled down Rachel's cheek.

"Hey, don't cry. You can't be a teenager and not make mistakes. It goes with the territory."

"It's not just teenagers," Viola said wryly. "There are plenty of grown-ups who still make them."

Of all the places to have it out with Kate, Viola wouldn't have chosen the front path at her mother's house. Viola pulled up in the Polo just as Kate was getting Beano out from the back of her own car. Miles climbed out of the passenger seat, looking, Viola thought, even plumper and more lumbering than usual.

"Any idea what this is all about?" Kate asked. "A three-line-whip kind of summons from Mum? Perhaps she's going to announce she's flogging off the homestead after all."

"You two wouldn't be keen on that, would you?" Viola said.

"Well, we have always said it wouldn't be sensible. You know my ideas on the perfect solution. Perhaps she's going to ask you to move back in." Miles looked pleased with himself at the prospect of being right.

"You haven't returned my calls, Kate," Viola told her. "Are you avoiding me?"

"What calls? Sorry, I must remember to check my voicemails. And no, of course I'm not avoiding you. Why would I?" She locked her car and bent to put Beano on his lead, fussing with his collar.

It had to be now. Viola felt her heart rate whizz skywards.

"Kate, I know what you did. And if you'd listened to your phone you'd know exactly what I mean."

Kate, still crouching over Beano, seemed to freeze. "Did when?" she said eventually, not looking at Viola.

Viola took a step closer and Kate stood up and faced her, frowning, eyes cold and glittery. Viola was aware of the front door opening and Naomi coming out. Miles went over to Kate and took Beano's lead from her. For a moment, Viola had the impression that he must be thinking there was going to be a full-scale fight.

"I was at the hospital last night with Rachel and I found out."

"Is Rachel all right? What happened?" Miles asked.

"She's fine. But you weren't, were you, Kate? Not when *you* were there. You hurt your head in the crash. *You* were in the car with Rhys when he died. *You* were the one who called the ambulance."

Breathe, Viola told herself. In and out, stay even, stay calm. All three of them were lined up now, in front of her. Naomi standing to the side, Kate in the middle.

"And even after you'd run off with my *husband*, cheating bastard though he was, at the hospital you even nicked my bloody *name*. Why didn't you use your own? Or Rhys's, come to that?"

"I don't know." Kate sighed. "I panicked. I just *panicked.* I was hurt, just . . ."

"*Hurt? You* were hurt? Rhys was *dead!*"

"Fucking hell, Viola!" Kate screamed at her. "Do you think I didn't know that? I had to climb over his *body* to get out of that car and then sit next to it in the fucking *ambulance* and then later say *nothing* and keep it all bottled up while everyone felt sorry for *you* and you were the big victim at the funeral! Mum and Miles wouldn't even let me grieve properly just so *you* wouldn't get upset! It's all about bloody *you*! All about protecting precious little accident-prone, unlucky baby *you*!" She unlocked her car and opened the door to climb back inside, then looked back at the others, furious and tearful. "So you see? Now she knows and we can all stop playing bloody charades!"

"You knew?" Viola accused the other two, feeling faint. Neither of them spoke, which told her everything. Kate waited by her open car door, looking unsure.

"You sent those cards," Viola suddenly realized, feeling chilled. "Even now, you wanted me out of my own *house*."

"Every time I went there, it reminded me of being with him. And of seeing *you* playing happy families with him. How do you think that felt? I'm so sorry, Vee." Kate was crying now. "But you know, you hadn't a clue about Rhys. You never loved him, not really, and he didn't love you — I was just too married to Rob at the time we got together and I hadn't the guts to leave till it was all way, way too late. Rhys was *everything* to me." She leaned against the car and sobbed. Miles went and put his arm round her, looking like a big awkward boy.

Viola felt sick. "Oh God, that's exactly what Rhys said about you," she said, her voice quiet and empty.

"Come into the house *now*, all of you," Naomi commanded, "You'll have old Joe next door coming out with his video camera. Come on, I'll put the kettle on. Or maybe I should just open the gin."

"I don't want to," Viola said, backing away. "I just want to go home, back to Rachel. Marco's with her."

"No, you *have* to come in. I've got things *I* want to say. I've made a decision and you all need to hear about it."

Viola felt exhausted. All her fury with Kate had melted away at that one poignant sentence: "*Rhys was everything to me*". How much more Kate must have lost than she had when Rhys died. And she'd carried that loss and that love in silence all these long, sad months.

Miles led the still sobbing Kate into the house behind Naomi, and Viola trailed in after them.

"Straight through to the back garden, I think. Fresh, reviving air." Naomi ushered them outside and went back into the kitchen and switched on the kettle. Viola, reluctant to join the other two, hung about in the kitchen, taking the old Jubilee biscuit tin out of the larder and piling up Jaffa cakes on a plate.

"What's the decision? Can you tell me now, then I can go? I don't want to stay here with Kate." Viola could hear her own voice sounding sulky, like a bad child.

"You're staying. Just hear me out. This isn't any easier for me than what you've just put Kate through." Naomi made the tea.

"What I've put *Kate* through? All this time, you've all known she'd been going behind my back with my *husband* and you can say that?"

"Sometimes keeping quiet is the best thing all round," Naomi said as she followed Viola, who had arranged a tray and was carrying it out to the terrace table. "You might learn that one day when you're older, but I sincerely hope you never have to."

"So *are* you selling up?" Miles asked Naomi, smiling in an anxious sort of way as Viola poured the tea.

"No. I can't sell up. But I'll have the company in the house that you seem to think I need. I'm moving Monica in here. She's going downhill and I can see she's going to need looking after. I'm selling a couple of paintings which will give me enough to do up the flat a bit for her, for when she gets frail. We'll muddle through her illness together, and it'll be a long one, I'm thinking."

Kate stopped sniffing into a tissue and looked at her mother, puzzled. "But why do you have to take care of her?"

"Because I owe her. That's why," Naomi said bluntly.

"Why do you owe her? Do you mean money?" Miles asked.

"No. I owe her something far more precious than that. Loyalty," Naomi murmured.

"Then why not sell this place and move to the flats where she lives?" Viola asked. It seemed a reasonable idea.

"Ah." Naomi smiled at her. "Well, I can't. The thing is . . ." And she waited for a moment, considering, avoiding looking at any of them. "The house isn't actually mine to sell."

"Jesus, whose is it then? Did you remortgage?" Miles looked worried. Viola could almost have laughed.

"It's mine for my lifetime, that's all. You remember Oliver Stonebridge, all of you? Well, of course you do, especially you, Vee, because you saw more of him. Well, he bought it for me. After I die it goes to his daughter. So you see, I can't sell it."

"So . . ." Kate seemed to be thinking aloud. "What was Oliver to you . . . Was he . . . um . . . ?"

"Yes, he was," Naomi said quietly. "He was, as you'd put it, Kate, *everything* to me. And Monica — well, she was the wife he'd planned to leave. But then he got cancer and there didn't seem much point causing more hurt than his death was going to, so we just continued as before, until . . . until he died." Bizarrely, she then chuckled. "As Rachel would probably say, Viola, 'end of'."

"So Monica's *daughter* gets this house after you've gone? After you've looked after her mother for her and done the flat up at your *own* expense?" Miles looked as if he wanted to punch someone.

"Ah well, not exactly, Miles. You see, that's the thing. He and Monica had a son and he lives abroad. But . . . and I know this is going to be a shock, Oliver and I *did* have a daughter. It's Viola who will inherit the house."

CHAPTER
THIRTY

I am only a half-sister, Viola thought later as she drove home, not a whole one. She tried saying out loud, "Viola Stonebridge Smith". It had quite a ring to it but it wasn't *her*. She'd been Hendricks since she and Marco had married and she'd happily stick with that. Half-sister to Miles and Kate. Poor Kate, what she must have gone through. And her mother, with her many years as the secret mistress of a man who couldn't bring himself to leave his wife. She didn't know whether to love him for that or hate him. No point in either, she knew. Nothing was to be gained from blaming the dead. She could at least give her mother a choice about the house, though. If it was possible to sell up with her consent, and if Naomi wanted that option so as to move to Monica rather than the other way round, then she'd do her best to make it happen.

To her surprise and delight, as she drove through the Bell Cottage gates she saw Greg's Land Rover parked beside her front door and Greg inside it, reading *The Guardian* with his feet on the dashboard.

"Hello, you," he said, climbing out and hugging her as soon as she was out of her car. "I can't seem to pin you down to a meet-up, so I thought I'd just come here and get you and shout at you for standing me up last night. You are an elusive beast, you know."

"I'm so sorry. And I'm so sorry about last night. It's been a traumatic time all round. So, so sorry. I'll tell you all about it when I've had a moment to catch my breath."

"It's OK, please stop apologizing," he said, stroking her hair, soothing her. "I've got part of the gist. Your ex was here and told me about your daughter and the hospital. He's taken her out for a late fry-up lunch and said he'll take her to a film as well, so not to expect them back till much later. He did say I could wait for you in the house, but I thought it would look presumptuous."

"Oh, it would have been fine. But anyway, come on in now, please. I need to feel, I don't know, *grounded*. I've just found out things about me that I probably should have known for, oh, most of my life. Takes it out of you."

"He's not so bad, your ex," Greg said as they went inside. "I thought I'd want to punch his lights out when I rocked up and there he was, like he belonged here. I mean, I didn't know, did I? I suddenly thought, hey, you're not as single as I'd assumed."

"I'd thought the same about you."

"I know. Maybe that blank-page thing wasn't such a good idea. But there's time. And your ex, well, he likes a beer and doesn't support Manchester United, so I reckoned he's not all bad." He looked serious for a moment. "You and he, you seem to have a friendly thing going. Reconciliation ahead? Because if there's a chance that'll happen, then perhaps I should start on the 'Maybe we can still be friends' speech."

"Greg!" She laughed. "Marco is as gay as Brighton Pier and lives with a lovely man called James. So, no, I don't think there's a chance we'll be getting back together, much as we're fond of each other!"

"Phew, so I'm in with a shout then?"

"Oh yes. Yes, you are." And, as it turns out, as a wonderful bonus you're not even remotely related to me, she thought a few minutes later when she surfaced for a moment from kissing him. Oh the irony, that she had Kate to thank for that family tree and the discovery that the baby was his tiny cousin. How tenderly he'd held that baby, she remembered. Who couldn't love a man like that?

"Excellent," Greg said. "Which means we have to go and deal with those crocuses one night soon, before they start sprouting."

"We do? Why? Are they in the wrong place?"

He laughed. "In a manner of speaking. When you didn't show up in the night I planted the whole lot in a complete pissed-off fury. They spell out, very large and very clearly, a *very* rude word. I think in the interest of not upsetting the faint-hearted who happen to be passing on a bus next spring, they really need rearranging."

Viola giggled. "Oh no! All my fault, I'm so sorry! I'll certainly come out with you and help."

"You can. But right now I want to show you my latest soppy gesture, even worse than the gladioli, but you must promise not to laugh or we're so, as the kids would say, *like, over*."

"What gesture? I'm so sorry about those other flowers," she said, snuggling close.

"That was then — and it's nothing to do with those. It's this one." He led her out through the kitchen doors and on to the terrace. "I did it as soon as your ex and daughter were out of the door. Nearly did myself an injury climbing over your back fence."

It took Viola a few moments to take in what he'd done. The side borders looked just as she'd left them. It was the lawn that was different, so ridiculously different. The edges had been mown so there was a neat, curved border, but the middle had been left long and the grass and rampant buttercups were interspersed with cornflowers, poppies and ox-eye daisies, like a gorgeous, wild and wonderful little meadow.

"Oh, you've made it heart-shaped!" she gasped. "It's fantastic! You are totally mad, you know? This is *so* stunning!" She hugged him.

"The plants are still only in pots at the moment. Even I couldn't get them in that fast. Of course, from down here it's not the best view." He looked at her, sparkly-eyed, and pulled her close.

"Ah, no, you're right," she said, catching what he meant and feeling instantly thrilled. "It would be much better seen from an upstairs window." She took his hand and smiled at him. "Come with me?"